CINDERS LIKE GLASS

Victorian Retellings

CLARISSA KAE

CARPE VITAM
PRESS LLC

Copyright © 2021 by Clarissa Kae

Cover Design © 2021 Sweetly Us Book Services

Photo Credit "Beautiful woman in a ball gown" (c) grape_vein via Adobe Stock All rights reserved.

No part of this book may be reproduced in any form or by any electronic or mechanical means, including information storage and retrieval systems, without written permission from the author, except for the use of brief quotations in a book review.

To my family, both by blood and by bond

ACKNOWLEDGMENTS

As a young child, my daughter suffered from a debilitating stutter—but her utter determination coupled with the consistent kindness of a speech therapist, she overcame her disfluency. Only when she is beyond stressed, does the stutter return.

Like Lady Ada's own disfluency, this book had its share of challenges and it would have been shelved several times over if not for the herculean efforts of my community.

To Damon, who shouldered the family load while I recovered from my concussion and to the girls, who circled the wagons—first to help me heal, and then to support their sister while we search for answers.

Esther Hatch who is the greatest author wife a girl could ask for, from scrambling to read through my novel to offering fabulous criticism. Jolene Perry, Melanie Jacobson, Kaylee Baldwin, Jenny Moore and Raneé Clark—thank you for letting me cry and vent and cry some more. When motherhood felt too daunting, you reminded me of the good—and that writers are human too.

Raneé and Kaylee, yes, you both need a second shout out. Not once have you made me feel guilty for missing deadlines. Your kindness is unforgettable.

And my lovely Sarah Reynolds and Loretta Porter for never backing down from a challenge, you both deserve medals.

There are many other authors, fans and neighbors who've come out of the woodwork to take care of our little family. I cannot thank you enough.

—Clarissa

I

Lady Ada Whitworth

Ada Whitworth shivered in the early morning light of her room. The fireplace was empty and would remain so. Her growing income would never be large enough for wanton luxury. A morning fire was for the upper echelon, not the lower rungs of nobility. Her maid had grown feverish yesterday, and Ada had insisted on her room being heated. The usual panic began once more. Ada had plenty of funds in her secret account to warrant such an expense, but with her birthday still a month away, her life was not yet hers to captain.

The busy hum of the servants echoed below. Wrapping the quilt around her shoulders, she tiptoed over the cold floor to the window. The Whitworth household was not posh enough for rugs. Outside, the morning London bustle was beginning to stretch and awaken. Their cozy townhome was smack in the center of the country's elite, a complete opposite to their financial situation. Ada was well aware of her place in life, her gratitude a warmth in her isolated world.

She placed a hand to the cool glass. She was rather foolish. With her hand on the window, she wished for her childhood home on the Welsh border as if she'd left a dreamy existence for a dark future. Her past was far from idyllic. Her adopted father was the only bright spot among murky memories.

Ada stepped back from the window. She had once dreamed of leaving England, mailing letters of her adventures to her adopted father. Now he was in the London cemetery with the rest of his ancestors, and Ada wouldn't leave the willowing Lady Rochelle to her grief. His passing had changed Lady Rochelle, gutting her entirely. Her once sharp tongue had become silenced. The wit and temper were snuffed out. She now unwittingly depended on Ada for everything but the roof over her head.

In a simple day dress, Ada crept down the hall to her maid's room. Opening the door, Ada winced at the hinge's squawk, nervous she'd woken her feverish maid. The fire was small but crackling with hope. Ada crept to the open window, careful to keep the cool, fresh air circulating throughout the night—doctor's orders. There was a growing fear of carbonic acid building inside the rooms from fireplaces and lamps. Ada would do what was required. She couldn't afford to hire a second maid. Ada had too many secrets to keep. Two maids would be too high a risk.

The maid's face was still flushed and her breathing shallow. Ada felt a quiver of worry once more. London had felt the boom in both illness and babies in the last decade. Mother Nature seemed to be trying desperately to keep everything in balance. Ada would know; her real parents were gone before her first birthday.

Above the maid's bed was a painting Ada had created during her last winter up north. The scene made Ada pause, wondering if the clean, country air would bring healing to her servant. Ada swallowed hard. In truth, her adopted father had died in his ancestral home with fields and fresh winds surrounding them. Perhaps mortality came when it pleased, regardless of location.

Ada stoked the fire, feeling rather helpless. Her adopted father had welcomed her as a babe, claiming Ada as his own. He wasn't too far off —Ada was his niece, her real father the younger brother. The late earl had insisted everyone address her as *Lady* Ada. Everyone but Nikolas, the rightful child, obeyed the kind man. The late earl had doted on her and so did the servants, but Lady Rochelle and Nikolas would have preferred she disappear.

Her adopted father had refused to be called *adopted* by the time Ada turned four, and when her talent of drawing blossomed, he spared no expense. The portrait on the wall was evidence of her education. She kept the geode her father had found in her own room. His friendship with the curious Sir Charles Lyell had grown into a partnership, the earl funding the expeditions.

Ada was dragged—quite happily—to several lectures, her father asking her to draw Lyell's collection of rocks and artifacts. Her father couldn't have known her talent would be her saving grace. Ada was the anonymous artist behind the famed *Thames Tales* gossip cartoon, a secret that kept their stomachs full and the main fire lit.

She descended the creaky stairs, trading the warmth of her servant's room for the drafty main floor. Dressed in yesterday's clothes, Lady Rochelle sat perched on the bay window, her face stoic and vacant. She had not slept again. A kerchief tucked in her hand, the countess mirrored a marble statue, her pale skin alarming in the early morning hour. When her husband was alive, she'd wait by the front window of his old ancestral home. She had a wicked temper but held an abiding love for him. She'd tried for years to give him a daughter. Ada was an eternal reminder of the slight.

"Lady Rochelle?" Ada whispered.

The countess didn't glance her way. Her hand didn't move. Nor did she appear to be breathing. Years before, Lady Rochelle would pretend to not hear Ada. At the memory, a sliver of hurt pierced Ada. The countess could very well be returning to her former self.

Quietly, Ada stepped closer, following Lady Rochelle's gaze. The knocker-upper ambled down the street, his lamp in one hand and cane in the other, tapping the window panes of the working-class—raising those without watches and clocks, costing a penny per month. Windows flickered to life with shadows and light. Street lamps were snuffed out like candles in the wind. Early-rising servants marched up and down St. James's Square. Purple streams of a summer sunrise began filling the dull, gray London streets while Lady Rochelle stared at the mundane.

Ada reached for the countess's shoulder just as a carriage moved, revealing a large wagon. Across the wagon's canvas was an advertisement for the queen's upcoming exhibit. News of the exhibition had been emblazoned on every paper for months. The queen and her husband built the ridiculous glass castle. Ada had made a mint poking fun at the building in her gossip cartoon. In the top left of the canvas was *Lyell Artifacts*. Ada inhaled sharply. The late earl had helped fund Sir Charles Lyell's adventures. But there was no recognition on the wagon. Sir Lyell's sketched profile was just below the wording—the same profile Ada had drawn years before. She'd given the drawing to the Scottish geologist before the earl died. The betrayal stung. Sir Lyell had erased her father from his history.

"Lady Rochelle?" Ada gently laid a hand on the countess's shoulder. The poor woman had been up all night again. "It's time for bed."

At the touch, the countess turned, blinking as if just waking from a stupor. "Ada?"

Pulling Lady Rochelle to her feet, Ada forced a smile. "You need to rest."

The woman's lip tightened into a hard line, her hand clenching the kerchief, knuckles white.

Ada stiffened. She'd waited for cold affection from the countess to reappear. It'd been years of quiet acceptance from Lady Rochelle, not quite affection but warmer than the continual rejection from Ada's childhood.

Lady Rochelle shook her head. "No."

"No?" Ada echoed. She rocked on her heels, unsure of what to do next. She had an appointment with her solicitor later and would need to sneak out of the house without her maid. Ada would not be able to take her adopted mother—heavens, no. Ada was hiding her income from both Lady Rochelle and Nikolas. Ada managed the household and hired servants only because the countess was grappling with grief. Lady Rochelle kept up on her mountain of letters delivered daily but nothing else. Ada waited; if Lady Rochelle were finally able to stand on her own two feet, Ada's world would soon be caged. She had a month until she came of age and could be her own woman. Freedom was close enough to taste.

"No ..." Lady Rochelle sighed, her shoulders hunching forward. Her voice was small, delicate—a ghost of a whisper. "I don't want to go upstairs and pretend to sleep."

Ada kneeled next to the countess, catching the dark circles under the woman's eyes and the hollowing of her cheeks. The countess wasn't just skipping sleep. She was avoiding meals as well. Ada reached for the woman's hand, wishing there were words of comfort. But grief wasn't a destination to leave behind. It lounged on Ada's shoulders and lay with her at night, surprising her in the middle of a drawing. She didn't know how to ease the pain of a spouse. Ada only knew the loss of a loving parent—and at that, she'd not allowed herself to fall apart.

"Shall I give you a tonic?" Ada whispered.

Lady Rochelle turned, her eyes flicking to Ada's neck. Ada reached for the necklace she'd worn every day since her sixteenth birthday, a single, misshapen pearl on a simple gold strand. The late earl believed that beauty came from discomfort, the sand became a pearl, the cinder flakes of charcoal became drawings, and orphans became daughters.

"No." Lady Rochelle dropped her hand. With a subtle shake of her head, she sighed. "I believe it is time we spoke with your brother."

Your brother. The words echoed in Ada's mind.

Lady Rochelle—a woman who insisted on being called Ada's *adopted* mother—left the room. At nearly twenty-one years of age, Ada had never, not once, heard Lady Rochelle refer to Nikolas as *your brother.* The late earl was the only family member who refused to think of Ada as anything other than his rightful offspring. Outsiders referred to Nikolas as her brother but only because of the late earl's insistence. Lady Rochelle, never. Not once—until now—uttered those words.

Ada had lived in fear of the cold, distant return of Lady Rochelle, never daring to imagine the woman becoming softer, closer. She touched the pearl on her neck, the moment fleeting. Whatever warmth Lady Rochelle had begun to feel would soon be squashed. Nikolas did not hold Ada in the same regard. And Nikolas's opinions were gospel to the countess.

A shiver crept up her neck, fear tying her tongue. Nikolas was not here. Ada was in no danger of being humiliated. Just the mere mention of him had stolen her words.

A carriage traveled down the street, pulling her focus back to the wagon advertising the exhibition. *Lyell Artifacts*. Nowhere was her father's name, the man who'd funded every adventure. Lady Rochelle had spent the night and early morning hours staring at the complete erasure of her husband's endeavors. The cold pearl grew warm in Ada's hand. She alone was the last of the late earl's projects. And she would not abandon him now.

2

Edwin Harrison, Duke of Girard

THE GRAND HALLS OF THE ROYAL COMMITTEE CHAMBER WERE FILLED with gold filigree, marble columns, and hours of excrement that fell from peerage lips. Without a sound, Edwin turned his back on the latest—and most worthless—Earl of Rochelle. The blockhead pontificated on the evils of society while completely ignoring his own part in the French scheme. A bloody spy had infiltrated English nobility to plot the queen's assassination at the upcoming Great Exhibition. Lord Rochelle—along with other gentry—had been named in a damning letter. But the earl seemed oblivious to his doom. Rochelle had not bothered to confess why he tried to steal the royal locksmith's daughter. The woman was now married to a brute of a baron.

Edwin steered clear of romantic whims. He'd been promised to a family friend since he was a toddler. She'd come from an impeccable family, not a stain or rumor in sight.

Groans and earnest eyes from the committee begged Edwin to silence Rochelle, the greatest man England had ever born—if you asked him. Edwin wouldn't ask him. Edwin didn't give a fig about Lord Rochelle or his morality. Edwin Harrison was tasked with securing the crown and catching the elusive French spy, known only as *le Tailleur* or, more simply, the Tailor. The sooner Rochelle spilled a secret, the faster Edwin could escort him off the property in chains.

"Lord Rochelle ..." A committee member sighed in exhaustion. "You've not answered a single question regarding your part in the assassination plot."

Edwin smirked, turning his profile to catch Rochelle's reaction. Edwin could feel the committee's gaze and unasked questions, but he'd earned his nickname as the Dark Duke and, in all sincerity, secretly loved it. His hunt for traitors among the *ton* had added fire to his reputation. It kept his peers at bay. Talking had never been his forte, and patience was a trait he'd gone without. Truth be told, speaking with people or even being around the lot of humanity exhausted him.

"Assassination plot?" Rochelle's mouth fell open, a hand on his chest.

Tension fell heavy in the room. Revolution was a new cancer, spreading into the desperate alleys of a starving country. Edwin abhorred chaos. England had grown too fast, too quickly. The younger generation romanticized the possibility of war while the older generation clutched their pearls in fear. England needed order—and to be rid of a certain spy. The east end of London had fallen into heavy poverty. The middle class dubbed the area the Abyss, where only sins and thieves thrived.

"You think I, Lord Rochelle—" Rochelle shook his head and spun in a dramatic circle. "Have you forgotten that Queen Victoria appointed my father—"

"It was a clear enough question." Edwin's voice cut through.

The room fell still, all eyes turned to the Duke of Girard. The air grew warm, the walls heavy. Edwin felt the weight of their silence. He'd long ago learned the intimidation of a quiet tongue and gray-eyed stare. Edwin clasped his hands behind his back, arching an eyebrow. "Did you assist *le Tailleur* in any capacity?"

"That's a rather broad question, Your Grace." A glint of mischief sparkled in Rochelle's eyes. "What if I'm not aware of helping him?"

"How often are you unaware?" Edwin's voice was low. The committee seemed to lean forward. He took one more step closer. "Are you in need of assistance?" He waved a hand. "We have many capable doctors to help you return your grasp on reality."

Rochelle's face fell, realization hardening his boyish face. If the earl was unaware of how he'd helped, Edwin was threatening him with torture. That, or an extended stay in an insane asylum. Edwin didn't care which choice Rochelle believed. The queen's safety was what mattered to the duke, not a selfish earl.

"I do not know who *le Tailleur* is." Rochelle's bravado disappeared. "I am a man who bargained with a locksmith for a bride." He held out his hands. "My heart is broken as she was given to another man."

Edwin fought the groan. The earl reminded him of another nobleman that tried to coerce his way to the crown. The Earl of Rochelle was more cunning than Edwin had given him credit for. The confiscated letters spoke of Lord Rochelle and a woman he would steal. The woman could have been the queen or the locksmith's daughter—someone gifted at picking locks. Edwin doubted Rochelle was a man mourning unrequited love. The Earl of Rochelle was far too infatuated with the sound of his own voice to care about another creature.

Edwin ignored the earl's pleas of innocence and leaned into the window facing the courtyard of Buckingham Palace. Lord Rochelle's performance had ebbed and flowed for hours, revealing nothing. Edwin knew the man was guilty. If the earl's father had not already passed, this scandal would have surely finished him off. The late Lord Rochelle was proper, kind, and above all else, honest. A virtue his son, the current Earl of Rochelle, had never mastered. Blast it all, Rochelle had never even *tried* to be honest, never mind mastering morality.

The surrounding committee was tiring of Lord Rochelle's petitions. The tension crackled in the stifling room. Edwin hadn't wanted the plonker to speak today. He'd thought it best to question him with concise parameters and have him respond in writing, not let Lord Rochelle give a dissertation on his own righteousness. But the committee rebuffed Edwin, citing his younger years. He'd only just nipped past his thirtieth year while the rest of his grey-haired companions—aside from Rochelle—were nearing their sixtieth, or more.

Below in the courtyard, a couple walked slowly from the queen's private quarters, gazing rather stupidly into each other's eyes. The man was enormous—Lord Pichon, the baron who Rochelle had just complained of. Lord Pichon had recently married the tiny woman at his side. She might have been a beauty, but her father was a confessed thief. Only Lord Pichon would be daft enough to enter matrimony with a criminal family.

Lord Pichon whispered something into his wife's ear. She glanced up, allowing her face to be in full view. Her eyes were wide—open and loving. Edwin backed away from the window. The look of adoration was too intimate for him to watch. He pulled at his cravat, feeling both warm and foolish. It was just a look between spouses. And yet, a strange feeling of loneliness crept in.

Rochelle cleared his throat, gathering strength for another round of proclamations. The queen had gifted his father with a title and earldom because of the man's character—that, and his dedication to science. The late earl was a dear friend and mentor to the queen's husband. Both men were hoping to welcome foreign nations to the Great Exhibition—a completely foolish idea. The monarch was letting her sensibilities get in the way. Inviting the nation's enemies into her bosom was not the way to show the world Britain's strength. Edwin would never understand the queen's desire—or for that matter, her husband. Both wanted to show Britain's superiority in the arts, in technology, and of course, science. They'd constructed a glass monstrosity that was going to be a beast to secure. But the queen had entrusted Edwin to keep the country safe. She supported him when the committee was offended at his words. He would be loyal to her until the bitter end. Or better yet, he'd avoid a bitter end altogether.

The prime minister left his seat, quietly making his way toward Edwin's perch at the window.

"Make it stop," the prime minister grumbled next to Edwin. "You're the bloody Duke of Girard. Do something."

Edwin scoffed. The committee was only ready to do things his way now that their ears were bleeding from Lord Rochelle's ridiculous assault. "This could have been avoided."

"How were we to know he'd go on like this? It's been hours. *Hours*." The poor man shook his head. "The bloody twit doesn't shut up."

Edwin stifled a smirk. If he was a smiling man, he'd be grinning like a school boy. Lord Rochelle was well received when he'd first opened his mouth but with the afternoon sun cooling, and lunch missed completely, the goodwill had dimmed.

"Rochelle." Edwin kept his voice low. Like his father, the lower he spoke, the more people leaned in.

"Your Grace." Lord Rochelle held out his arm. "Let me offer—"

"Stop," Edwin barked. He straightened his stance, feeling the tension crack like a whip. With one word, Edwin had silenced the plonker. He'd also offended a handful of gentlemen, their eyebrows raised in horror.

Lord Rochelle bowed with a flourish. "Of course."

"Your testimony is received." Edwin nodded to the secretary. "Because of your penchant for over speaking, if we have need of clarification, we will communicate—"

Lord Rochelle opened his mouth.

"—through letters." Edwin stifled his smirk as Lord Rochelle snapped his mouth shut. "We are adjourned." Without another word, Edwin marched toward the door.

Lord Rochelle was quick on his feet, at Edwin's side in a moment. "Your Grace."

He offered a letter—and a grin far too mischievous to be innocent.

Edwin stepped back. "What is this?"

"Surely, the great Duke of Girard has received a letter before?" The words were light, feigning innocence.

Edwin whispered, "And yet a letter is the reason you are here."

Lord Rochelle's eyes widened slightly. He quickly recovered, a smile growing on his lips. "I hear congratulations are in order."

Edwin didn't reach for the letter. He wouldn't be tempted by a twit. "And for what reason am I to be congratulated?"

Lord Rochelle opened the envelope with a flourish. Gads, the man was insufferable. With his pinky extended, he pulled the letter out, the envelope settling on the marble floor. "Lady Catherine is engaged, Your Grace."

Edwin stared at the earl. "Lady Catherine?" He blinked. Lady Catherine—the woman he was informally promised to—was *engaged?* He couldn't remember the color of her hair or even how old she was.

Lord Rochelle placed a hand on his shoulder. "We're one in the same."

Edwin brushed off the earl's hand, growling. "What are you playing at?"

"We both know the loss of love." Lord Rochelle backed away, his hands up in surrender. "You must truly hate the man who stole her away."

"You are on the verge of losing your title and status. And now, you'd go to such great lengths to tarnish another woman? Was Lord Pichon's wife not enough?" Edwin kept his voice even.

A crowd of gentlemen began to gather, fanning Edwin's temper. The committee was supposed to be interrogating Rochelle not leaning in for gossip.

Lord Rochelle's smile grew with each added nobleman. He glanced at his nails as if he was bored. "I had the father's permission. As did you. I had the certificate, which is more than what you had. I, at least, pretended to court the woman. You haven't spoken to Lady Catherine or her family in months." He whistled to himself. "Or is it years?"

"What is your point?" Edwin's mind raced. The earl was far more cunning than Edwin had thought. Only his family—and Lady Catherine's—knew of their betrothal, informal as it was. He wasn't lovesick. She'd chosen another, or so the letter said. Edwin had a sneaky suspicion Lord Rochelle was at the center of her sudden engagement.

The earl held up the letter, making a show of the announcement. "And to a Frenchman, no less."

The committee whispered amongst themselves, eyes wide and ears leaned in.

Edwin cleared his throat, his eyes boring into Lord Rochelle's. "I shall send my utmost congratulations." Without another word, Edwin spun on his heels and quit the marbled room.

3

L ady Ada Whitworth

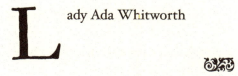

ADA TUCKED HER PACKAGES UNDER HER SEAT IN THE FOYER, HER weekly trip to *Petticoat Lane* a fruitful venture. The secondhand shop was beginning to carry higher-end clothes, and Ada was more than grateful. For a fraction of the cost, she could look every inch the lady her late father had intended. The blue silk dress she wore was not only exquisite, but inexpensive.

She avoided her reflection in the window. This was her first visit to her solicitor's office without her maid. And she'd already had to redo her hair twice without a servant's help. Her hair was wild and unruly. Only the late earl and her maid loved the golden curls. Ada swallowed the impending grief. Her maid's health was deteriorating. Ada might be forced to hire another. She straightened her shoulders. Her father had taught her to think practically. Logically, Ada hadn't planned on the added expense.

Nikolas would soon come sniffing around, wondering why Ada and Lady Rochelle had not begged him for more money. Council taxes were due last month. Ada had paid them without so much as a word to her brother.

Birds chirped and dozens of carriages rolled by the busy London window. The world, as it were, seemed very intent on passing Ada by as she sat waiting for Mr. Thomas's long-winded client to leave. She felt comfortable coming late in the day when no one of substance would be conducting business, herself included. She was not a true lady. Nor would she ever become one. She was simply a woman still in need of legal guidance. Now more than ever.

The low rumble of Mr. Thomas's voice carried into the entryway. With the slow turn of the afternoon, Ada feared she would have several birthdays before she'd see her solicitor. As if summoned by her thoughts, Mr. Thomas appeared at the door, ushering out an older gentleman. Her solicitor winked at her, having been a longtime friend of the late earl.

Mr. Thomas shut the door behind his client and beamed at Ada. "Come in, my darling."

Stepping into the small office, Ada waited for the click of the door shutting. Once Mr. Thomas sat, she pulled her package from her bag. Her visits were as consistent as they were private. No one needed to know she was the artist behind London's notorious gossip cartoon.

"How are you, Lady Ada?" Mr. Thomas sat opposite her, his smile still wide. He'd always regarded her with the same deference of the late earl's.

Ada slid the package over the desk to Mr. Thomas. The man's eyes crinkled as he took her hidden drawings. He pushed his glasses up his nose like he'd done every other week for nearly two years. When Ada was a small child, and Mr. Thomas had considerably more hair and fewer wrinkles, she'd accompany her father. Even after the late earl was granted a title by the queen, he refused to trade Mr. Thomas for a more prestigious solicitor.

"How are you faring, Lady Ada?" He reached across his desk and squeezed her hand affectionately.

"I am well." For the first time in years, Ada wasn't lying to dear Mr. Thomas. There was something hopeful about her brisk walk to St. James's Square. The wagon advertising Sir Lyell's exhibit had sparked an idea. She'd come up with a plan to reignite her father's scientific legacy. She just hoped Mr. Thomas would agree with her plan.

With each passing month, Ada felt more secure in her skill as an artist. And more confident in her earning potential. She could see a future, perhaps too modest for what the *ton* would expect but hopeful enough for Ada. Their quaint townhome just a few streets over had been a wedding gift to her adopted mother. The late earl had been keen enough to keep the property out of the estate. It was the only property Nikolas couldn't touch—yet. If Lady Rochelle passed away, the property would go to Nikolas. She shivered at the memory of his last taunting.

"Are you cold, my dear?"

"No," Ada blurted. When Mr. Thomas sat back, his brow furrowing, Ada added, "Truly. I'm fine."

He seemed to consider her with searching eyes. "If something is bothering you, know your secrets are safe in here, my dear. Mark my words."

Heat crept up Ada's neck and through her cheeks. *Your secrets are safe in here.* She was sure her face was turning a deep crimson. A proper lady wouldn't have secrets, but Ada couldn't afford to wait for luck to strike.

Ada had relished the relative freedom of the past few years. Her brother was gallivanting across the country, devouring women and cards like a drowning man coming up for air. His visits had thankfully become sparse. Her father was in the ground only a month before Nikolas had packed up Ada and Lady Rochelle, shipping them to London. Nikolas cried that money was tight and he couldn't afford their lavish lifestyle. Lavish was as foreign to Ada as French. No one had ever assigned *lavish* to Ada. She lived as frugal as she could.

Until two years ago.

Gently setting aside Ada's package, Mr. Thomas pulled an envelope from the locked drawer of his desk—just like he'd done every month. He slid the envelope across the table and paused. He opened his mouth only to close it. Warmth fled the room. "Lady Ada ..."

The hope Ada had begun to feel dimmed. "Is there something the matter?"

He didn't move his finger from the paper. "The royalty checks have been deposited and here is the accounting." He cleared his throat, his eyes downcast.

"Mr. Thomas?" The solicitor had deposited her earnings like clockwork, routinely giving Ada an accounting receipt. There was no reason for Mr. Thomas's concern. Unless Nikolas—Ada's throat tightened, her tongue growing thick.

"Your brother ..." Mr. Thomas took off his glasses and rubbed the bridge of his nose.

"My b-b-b ..." Ada took a deep breath. Her tongue wouldn't work. She clamped down the fear. This was Mr. Thomas. He was not her brother. Just the mere mention of Nikolas had her pulse racing. She clenched her hands into tight fists, her nails biting into her palms. Nikolas was not here, only Mr. Thomas. She forced her hands to relax.

Mr. Thomas sighed, pity in his eyes. He'd known Ada far too long. The poor man had witnessed her stuttering as a child, brought on by her brother's relentless teasing. Nikolas could charm the devil. He was able to convince his parents he'd done nothing wrong. Ada wondered if his charms would still work on Lady Rochelle. The countess was a shell of her former self. Unlike the *ton,* she had married for love. With a front row seat to the woman's grief, Ada witnessed the inescapable loss of stalwart devotion.

The solicitor searched her face. Softly, he said, "Your brother has landed himself in a bit of trouble."

Ada's tongue still felt thick. "He is always in trouble." She spoke slowly. Deliberately.

If she could keep *brother* or *Nikolas* out of her mouth, she just might keep her pride intact. Mr. Thomas had always been kind, but Ada didn't want—nor could she afford—a return to her stumbling tongue. She could not care for Lady Rochelle and command the household staff if she couldn't speak. Word traveled fast, and she knew all too well how people treated those with disabilities. *Dullard. Moron.* It'd been so long since she'd been insulted, but the words still stung. Her brother had once threatened to send her to an asylum, believing her inability to speak properly was evidence of an unsound mind.

"Lady Ada?" Mr. Thomas reached for her hand, softening the

abrupt turn of their conversation. Nikolas was not a common discussion between them. A loyal sister would be filled with concern. All Ada wanted to do was steer the conversation to safer waters.

"I need your assistance." She sat up straight when he arched an eyebrow. "Sir Lyell is featured at the Grand Exhibition. Or rather, his scientific discoveries."

"You mean Sir Lyell's *and* your father's discoveries?"

"Correct." She swallowed hard. She needed to keep her voice steady. Her father had been gone for years. The lump in her throat was overwrought. And yet her fingers trembled.

Mr. Thomas's gaze flicked from her face to her hands. "Lady Ada, how can I help?"

"I would like to draw the exhibit."

He leaned forward. "You would have to meet with Sir Lyell."

"Sir Lyell knows I draw." With a shake of her head, she shrugged away the solicitor's concern. "The profile on the advertisement was my creation. Granted, several years ago but mine nonetheless." She remembered gingerly offering the sketch to the slender baron. He took the paper with gusto, asking for more drawings. She was far too shy to answer. Ada wondered how differently her career would have been if she'd loosened her tongue that day.

"Does he know of *Thames Tales?*" Mr. Thomas sat back. Ada shook her head. He cleared his throat, an old habit. "We have something else to consider before we try our hand at the exhibit. The Duke of Girard visited earlier today."

4

Edwin Harrison, Duke of Girard

On the edge of respectability, where old reputations and new money faded into each other, Edwin sat in his carriage, his focus on the solicitor's office. A wagon advertising the queen's Great Exhibition was across the street. Edwin stretched, wondering what secrets Mr. Thomas held. A few hours earlier, Edwin had questioned the solicitor. The older man had clearly been hiding something. Edwin could sense the deceit in every word Thomas had spoken.

Edwin would ferret out the man's secrets if it was the last thing he did. The shiny new Earl of Rochelle was a thorn in Edwin's side. It wasn't enough that the plonker had become entangled in a dangerous French scheme, but he'd gone ahead and tried to humiliate Edwin.

The announcement lay on the seat next to him. Lady Catherine was to be married. To a French dignitary of all people. Edwin should be furious or at least annoyed. And yet, he couldn't remember the color of her eyes. Or the sound of her laughter. He'd accepted his fate to marry the family friend and hadn't questioned his future. He was neither sad nor angry. If he was being honest, he felt a mixture of relief with a sprinkle of loneliness. He'd never courted another woman. He winced. He'd never courted *any* woman, not even Lady Catherine, his informal betrothed. He grimaced. His *former* betrothed. He had left his university days, trading hours of studying law for hunting criminals. Lady Catherine had fallen in love with a Frenchman while Edwin had fallen in love with hunting one, the obnoxious French spy, *le Tailleur*.

The hunt had brought him here. Edwin folded his arms and lay back against the carriage. There'd only been one elder gentleman entering Mr. Thomas's office followed by a glorious, golden-haired woman. Until she'd walked across the garden, the solicitor appeared to be aging at the same rate as his clients. Edwin wondered who would expire first. If Mr. Thomas had not been so nervous earlier, Edwin would have left the man alone. His office neighbors were as boring as him. Even Mr. Thomas's personal affairs were as sterile as the man's reputation. But one mention of Lord Rochelle had the solicitor avoiding Edwin's gaze.

Edwin had come for one thing, information on Rochelle's financials. Mr. Thomas was the late earl's solicitor—it only made sense that Rochelle would keep the same man.

And yet, his focus was no longer on Rochelle or Mr. Thomas. He'd been consumed by a blasted woman.

A flicker of blue had caught Edwin's eye. A woman, her bodice and skirt the deep blue of sapphire, had briskly marched up the walk toward Mr. Thomas's office. The skirt had tiered flounces, the silk material accentuating the feminine sway of her gait. Perhaps it was a blessing Lady Catherine had found someone else to wed. Edwin would rather rot than pay for a dress made in silk. The wide, circular skirt was rather vast, underlining the fact she walked alone. Not a maid or companion in sight.

Whoever designed the latest fashion was in league with the silk trades. It should be a crime to force men to pay for outlandish, ridiculous fashions. Edwin would know. He was fastidious in his accounting, much to the annoyance of his steward. Edwin would rather hire another of his countrymen to work for him than commission a cashmere shawl—which the lady had appeared to be wearing. She, of course, *had* to be a lady. The quality of her boots peeking out from under her skirt announced her status if her silk dress hadn't already.

The lady had glanced over her shoulder at Edwin's carriage. He sank back despite knowing she couldn't see him. He'd designed the windows with increased flux, darkening the view for outsiders. The lady's golden hair—so coveted in the current fashion—was parted in the center, brushed down, and arranged heavily on the side, hiding her ears. Her bonnet was simple, a blue silk ribbon tied under her chin and the brim shortened away from her delicate face. Her eyes were hidden in the shadows of the bonnet.

If Edwin was a betting man—he was not—he'd guess her golden hair and pale complexion would give the lady blue eyes. Green at the very least. He paused, realizing he was again leaning toward the glass instead of hiding in the shadows.

She had turned from the carriage—several golden strands fell from the bonnet. Her shoulders hunched, the bag clutched in her hands tumbling to the ground. Using her reflection in the office window, she had pulled her bonnet off. A tumble of thick golden curls crashed around her. She had made quick work, her fingers fast and effective. In less than a minute, her bonnet was back on her head, the hair tamed once more.

Without a second glance to the carriage, the lady had slipped inside. Edwin fought the temptation to follow. He'd stalked dozens of men, predators of the highest order, and yet one little miss had held his attention long after she'd disappeared.

He grunted. He was not a fool. His interest was in the solicitor, not the customers. Or rather, one customer in particular. The Earl of Rochelle. An earl, not a lady.

He sank back. A knock sounded on the window. He groaned at the sound. A familiar, spindly man opened the door, shoving his arm into the carriage, the sleeve filleted open. The blood red tattoo of the Welsh dragon stared back at Edwin. He never knew the Welshman's given name—nor would he be granted the privilege. Edwin had secretly called him Gray Knight, in part because of the bushy gray hair adorning nearly all of his face—the other part, because of the aura of authority the man possessed.

Edwin nodded to him. "How many more men can you spare?"

The soldier climbed into the carriage, sitting opposite Edwin. He lifted his chin. "Dozen or so."

Edwin had sent the messengers, calling for the Welsh soldiers to come together. Finding an English earl at the center of an assassination plot had Edwin suspicious of English nobility. His dukedom was on the border of both countries, Wales and England. If he had to choose, he'd trust a sheep farmer to an English dandy any day of the week. "Do they know who I am?"

"Aye." Gray Knight dipped his head. Smirking, he winked at Edwin. "No offense, Your Grace, but we always knew you preferred the Welsh. If we were itching for a new queen, we'd have done it ourselves. No need for dancing with the French."

"I sent a list—"

"Aye. Thomas is a tricky fish." The soldier pulled an envelope from his vest pocket. "He's a bit high and mighty, but you're wasting your time, Your Grace." Gray Knight nodded to the office. "The young Lord Rochelle doesn't use Mr. Thomas. I can assure you."

Edwin sat back, his mind filtering the facts like a card player. The Earl of Rochelle had a fortune at his disposal—despite being on the verge of bankruptcy just a few short months earlier. He was a horrendous gambler and a notorious rake. He was everything society abhorred. And yet, he could charm a snake into submission.

The soldier fidgeted. "You're unhappy, Your Grace?"

Edwin tried to smooth his face. He'd been accused all too often of the seriousness in his stare. "I need him followed. I need to know why he's flush and how he suddenly became so."

Gray Knight folded his hands and arched his eyebrow. "You don't want anything to happen to him?"

"No," Edwin said with a sigh. Queen Victoria would have his head. She knew him too well and had forced him to promise the earl's safety. "The Ninny is protected by the queen."

"He what?" The man's mouth fell open. "He's trying to kill her."

Edwin shrugged. "Until we can prove it, she wants him unharmed." He waved at the office. "She gave his father the title."

"Good fathers don't make good sons. And good sons don't always come from good fathers." The man *tsk*ed, one hand clenching into a tight fist, the red Welsh dragon dancing along the forearm.

"How many are there?" Edwin motioned to the man's forearm.

"More of us have sworn allegiance to our native country than have sworn allegiance to the Tailor." He smiled, two of his cracked teeth winking at the duke.

Edwin ran a hand over his face, exhaustion settling in. "I have a duty. I'm sworn to protect the queen."

"Aye."

Edwin's hand fell. "I need it to be known ..." The soldier leaned forward. Edwin lowered his voice. "If you discover the earl to be—without a doubt—a threat to the queen, take him. Bind him. Preferably his mouth as well. I want to speak to him before he can poison any other nobleman. I need information from him ..." Edwin let the sentence hang between them.

Gray Knight's face grew somber. Slowly, he nodded. "It will be done."

"Without a doubt." If Edwin was paving his way to hell, he wanted it to be worth it. Edwin would sacrifice his own salvation to save his queen, Lord Rochelle be damned.

5

Lady Ada Whitworth

The solicitor's office was cold, just a few degrees warmer than outside. But that was not what made Ada pause.

"Duke of Girard?" She sat back, her hand gripping the blue silk of her skirt. "The Duke of Girard came here?"

The name was more than familiar. Well, sort of. The only time she'd been introduced to nobility was when her father was bestowed an earldom. Although she *had* drawn a lovely caricature of Girard for seven weeks straight. The duke was tasked with gathering evidence of a French plot against the queen. It didn't help that Nikolas was implicated—if one believed rumors. As the only gossip artist for the *Thames Tales*, Ada had an affinity for rumors.

"You've never met him?" Mr. Thomas pushed his glasses up his nose and frowned. "I'm sure you've crossed paths ..." He let the rest of the sentence hang between them.

Ada might not have met the duke in person, but she'd drawn him to perfection, according to her readership. The duke had a bully reputation. Girard was the queen's guard dog and never took no for an answer. He could cow a dragon. *A dragon.* What a lovely cartoon that would make. It would be glorious, the great Duke of Girard spanking a French dragon on the bottom. Oh, or perhaps a French dog. Ada couldn't help smiling. She loved teasing the *ton.* Ada had even begun attending a few operas. Not for the music, of course. Sitting in the back with her shy maid, Ada would spy on the unsuspecting noble class.

Most women her age were paraded about by mothers eager for a match, but Ada would never have a season. The late earl provided a stipend for his wife, but the cost of readying for a season was more than their meager living could afford. Even now, when her sketches had tripled their income, Ada preferred to hire servants—not an expensive season. She was without true rank and dowry. Her future was made by her own two hands, thank you very much.

"No, I believe I've never met him," she said quietly. She knew her solicitor was well aware of her sketches.

"He asked about your brother." Mr. Thomas shifted uncomfortably in the seat. "And his assets."

"Assets," Ada repeated dumbly. As the only male in the family, Nikolas was her guardian until she became of age next month. He could siphon her accounts without any recourse. "Does he know?"

"By *he* do you mean the duke or Lord Rochelle?" Mr. Thomas arched an eyebrow. His face, his posture, and even his hands stiffened at the question. "I take my vow of secrecy quite seriously. No one knows who you are."

Ada's drawings were once relegated to the last page, the forgotten space. The paper now charged a premium to hopeful advertisements wanting to be placed near her sketches. She'd climbed the ranks from nobody to somebody—well, sort of a somebody. No one actually knew who the artist was. Except for saintly Mr. Thomas.

"Thank you." Ada would never understand the solicitor's loyalty. She was grateful all the same.

Mr. Thomas frowned once more. "The duke was more interested in your brother than you."

Ada leaned forward, her hands grasping the chair's armrest. All of

London was watching the duke's every move. Bets were being made on who was involved in the scheme. Just last week, Ada had drawn a very confused sketch of Girard chasing his own tail—a rather curly, pig-like tail. "What did he want?"

"Girard wanted to know if I had any information on hidden assets." His gaze flicked to the envelope.

"No, please tell me, no." Ada groaned, burying her head in her hands. Her income was her future, her only hope of freedom. This couldn't be happening. She'd worked too hard for too long. "If Nikolas finds out, every last farthing will be gone." As would any future royalties from past sketches.

"I don't think you understand." Mr. Thomas tapped the envelope. "Girard made some shocking accusations, my dear."

Her head shot up. "So he does know?"

His brow furrowed with confusion. A look of realization crossed his features. "Oh, you mean about the *Thames*—no. The cartoon was never brought up. Not that it would be. There are far too many layers to link back to me, let alone you. No, my dear, the duke believes your brother is guilty of treason."

"Oh, good." She sighed in relief—then froze. "That sounded better in my head."

Mr. Thomas gave a wry smile. "I was careful in my answers, but you should know the duke was rather forceful."

"What do you mean?" Ada felt a twinge of shame. If her brother was guilty of treason, he couldn't have access to her accounts. There was a growing possibility she could be free of him. Forever.

His grin widened. "I told him I've not been trusted with Lord Rochelle's assets in years and that your brother does not shadow my door."

"Oh, thank you." The words came out like a sigh. Ada had not realized she was holding her breath until that moment. Nikolas had taunted her through childhood, allowing her to breathe easy once he'd left the family home. But since the earl had passed on, Nikolas's role as guardian was a constant shadow. He, alone, could dictate Ada's future.

"Lady Ada?" Mr. Thomas's face grew somber. "The duke means to freeze all of Lord Rochelle's accounts."

"Did he say why?" Dread grew in the pit of Ada's stomach, her throat tightening once more.

"Your brother was specifically named in a letter." He swallowed hard, his Adam's apple bobbing. "And he might have tried to steal Lord Pichon's fiancé."

"The queen's cousin?" Ada groaned. Nikolas couldn't have been this foolish. "Lord Pichon and Girard?" Of all the men to trifle with, Nikolas had to choose the most potent.

"Lord Rochelle is currently in custody." Mr. Thomas waved his hand.

"Oh." She shouldn't have sounded so relieved.

"Hence the reason for Girard's visit. He aims to freeze every penny to prevent your brother from leaving the country."

"Oh." This was a decidedly different *oh*. She leaned forward. "If he *did* leave the country, he'd never be able to return. Correct?"

Mr. Thomas arched his eyebrow. "If you help him evade the law, you will be liable."

"Drat," she murmured.

"Ada Whitworth." His voice had become firm. "Helping your brother out of the country will not improve your situation."

"I beg to differ."

His gaze flicked to the envelope. "He could still control your finances from France."

"Are you sure?" Ada swallowed the rising panic. Her brother was rather convincing—except the duke seemed to be immune to his charms.

Mr. Thomas nodded solemnly. "Or worse. The duke could confiscate your funds *and* you'd be charged with aiding—"

"Fine." Ada waved her hand. "I surrender."

"I know you wish for freedom from him." Mr. Thomas tapped the envelope. "Would you be open to another prospect?"

Ada wasn't like her brother. She wasn't foolhardy. "There is no other prospect."

He took his glasses off, placing them gingerly on the desk in front of him. "I've known you all your life."

Ada lowered her gaze and shifted in the chair. The room was suddenly too warm.

"I promised your father, or rather, both of your fathers—"

"You've kept your word, Mr. Thomas," Ada blurted. She hated speaking of her natural father. She didn't know him. And the earl, oh that sweet man. She couldn't utter a word against him. He was worthy of all the reverence, but she didn't want to dwell on the loss. She would never be able to thank the late earl for his insight, for his gift of freedom in nurturing a talent—a rather bankable talent. But the truth of the matter was Ada simply couldn't speak of him. Her childhood stutter would creep up her throat and tie her tongue. Words failed her. Art never did.

Mr. Thomas sighed softly. "Have you considered marriage and how that would keep you from your brother's grasp?"

"I cannot afford a season, Mr. Thomas," she said flatly. It was completely true, but even if it wasn't, marriage was not something she wanted to think about. A husband would immediately own her income. Would she simply trade one tyrant for another? "And to be true, my brother would have a say in it."

Mr. Thomas tilted his head in thought. "How would he ever know? You'll be of age in a month."

Ada held up a finger. "The banns." Then two. "The gossips would—"

He circled the desk. "I don't mean to be indelicate, but do the gossips know about you?"

Ada stood there, her mouth slack. *Do the gossips know about you?* She glanced down at her hands in her lap. In truth, she was a nobody. The *ton* knew of her brother. He was an earl and a rake. But Ada Whitworth? "No, I suppose they don't. But therein lies the problem. As you said, I'll be of age in a month. Is there not more freedom in remaining single than plunging head first into a marriage?" All that she had would be her husband's. She could not simply skip from her brother's threats to the chain of matrimony.

"Your brother has a power over you, Lady Ada. He's threatened to sell his mother's house. Among other things." He hesitated, his words appearing to hurt him. "I simply wish for you to be safe. Protected."

"There are only two men I trust, Mr. Thomas." And one of them lay in a cemetery on the hill.

"Will you think on it, please?" Mr. Thomas's voice was kind, making his idea all the more painful. He placed the papers in her hand, evidence of her income should anything happen to the solicitor. The late earl would be proud of all that Mr. Thomas had done.

"Thank you," she whispered.

Ada walked in silence back to the quaint townhome in St. James's, the clouds darkening above her. She forced the pleasantries with Lady Rochelle and went to her room. At her desk, she opened the envelope. Not only had Mr. Thomas accounted for her profit, he'd added a row of names at the bottom.

A heaviness wrapped around her shoulders. He'd labeled the list *respectable misters*. And there was the slight. He'd not included a nobleman—not that Ada was foolish enough to hope for a titled husband—but the complete omission underlined her position. She refolded the envelope, placing it in the bottom of her trousseau. The only sacred place where neither man nor maid would look. Her brother had abandoned Ada and her mother, but he never tired of sending subtle threats.

Ada went to the bay window. Nearly a year ago, Nikolas had threatened to sell the roof over their heads. His eyes had been rimmed with drunken rage. He'd lost another hand. It'd been months since she'd heard from him—Ada should have known. Nikolas was never idle. She leaned against the window. When Nikolas was desperate, there was no telling what he'd do.

6

Edwin Harrison, Duke of Girard

WHITE'S MIGHT BE THE CLUB OF CHOICE FOR THE UPPER ECHELON OF society, but Edwin could light the entire building on fire and not shed a tear. Surrounded by the *ton*'s elite gentlemen, Edwin sat on the dark leather arm chair and tossed the newest issue of the *Thames Tales* to the side table with an annoyed grunt. The bloody paper was ridiculous, depicting him as a vengeful twit. Edwin didn't search for the elusive spy *le Tailleur* out of spite. He did it for God and country. There was right and wrong in the world, black and white. If people could understand that basic principle, he could spend his days in more productive pursuits. Edwin had already spent the better part of the day finding every penny the idiotic Lord Rochelle still had. *Lord.* Edwin sneered at the word and pulled the watch from his waistcoat. His informant was late. Again.

The dark paneling on the club's walls did nothing for Edwin's mood —a dozen smiles and a summer abroad couldn't brighten his day. Not that he'd been abroad in years. His life of diplomacy and foreign affairs on the continent were gone, replaced with ferreting out secrets. Every day. The same routine.

He rubbed his eyes. The predictability of his life had once thrilled him. The queen's praise of his meticulous nature was once a boon to his pride. But it'd begun to feel more like a noose around his neck.

A crowd of noblemen grew. They wouldn't approach him. Edwin could feel their gaze and unasked questions. He could almost hear *that's the Dark Duke* on their lips.

Edwin pulled at his collar. He blamed the Earl of Rochelle, the most worthless English earl, for his foul disposition. And Mr. Miller's tardiness. Logically—and Edwin prided himself on his logic—his mood and Mr. Clarence Miller's late arrival had nothing to do with Lord Rochelle.

But Rochelle was a spineless coward. That, in and of itself, made the fool a satisfying target, long before he'd ever become a traitor. And thankfully, after today, the dolt would be a *desperate* coward. Under order of the queen, Rochelle couldn't touch his ill-gotten fortune.

"Your Grace?" Mr. Miller asked with his usual measured tone. His approach was silent. His investigations even more so.

Edwin stifled his annoyance. He didn't do surprises. He rather liked hearing someone approach. Edwin motioned to the oversized chair next to him. "Sit."

"Ever the picture of hospitality." The solicitor sat with a sniff.

"Oh, blast. It's not you who's earned my ire."

"Your apologies are just as astounding."

Edwin fought a smile. "You must be very secure in your position as a solicitor."

"Quite."

"I could fire you." Edwin tested him—having failed to stop the smile from growing. Mr. Miller wasn't just Edwin's solicitor. He was *the* solicitor of the *ton*. Miller had been instrumental in ridding the queen of an overbearing advisor the moment she was crowned. Even the self-righteous baron, Lord Pichon, used Mr. Miller's firm—just as the previous baron had. And if the lovesick couple experienced the fruits of matrimonial bliss, the future baron would also utilize the solicitor's firm.

"Oh, but how would you fill the time?" Mr. Miller's gaze flicked to the paper on the table, amusement tugging at his lips.

Edwin followed his gaze to the *Thames*. "This country needs a new hobby."

Mr. Miller shrugged and gave another of his customary sniffs. "Or perhaps a certain duke could gain a new hobby. Or a spouse. Shall I commission an advertisement for you?"

"I'm more than happy in my solitude, Miller."

"Have you mentioned that to the scowl on your face?" The older man quirked an eyebrow. "I watched you for a good ten minutes and your solitude was anything but jolly."

Blast the man. If he wasn't the most brilliant solicitor of all time, Edwin *would* sack him. Not that Miller would care. He was the fourth son of a duke and quite literally didn't give a fig for the opinions of his father's peers. Edwin sighed. "As lovely as your company is, I do have somewhat of schedule to keep."

With that, Mr. Miller sat back and folded his long, thin fingers in his lap.

Edwin lowered his voice. "I went to the three solicitors you gave me."

His eyebrows rose as if to say, *And?*

"Most of Rochelle's fortune was with you." Edwin rubbed his eyes again. He'd spent too many nights chasing leads. Revolution was still a romantic notion to the poor, the hungry, and the angry. Like an illness, it seeped down desperate alleys.

"Most of his fortune," Mr. Miller repeated. He leaned forward with a sigh. "How much money did he have?"

"A few thousand pounds." It was quite a sum of money but not shockingly so.

Mr. Miller's eyes widened. He'd clearly expected a different answer. "Only a few thousand pounds?"

"And nothing with Thomas."

"That's impossible." The solicitor glanced about the room. When a group of young bucks moved past them, he lowered his voice. "Ada Whitworth visits Thomas every other week."

"I visited him on Thursday."

"And?"

"You are a chore," Edwin said with a groan.

"Naturally." Mr. Miller waved his hand once more. The blasted fool didn't care if Edwin wanted to throttle him. "And what did the illustrious Mr. Thomas have to say about our favorite traitor?"

"That he does not manage Rochelle's money. Or any of his assets." Edwin sent a glare to an approaching butler who quickly spun on his heels. The poor man was only doing his job, but Edwin didn't come to White's for the drinks. Or the company. He came to gather information.

"Did you ask about Ada?"

Edwin frowned. "Why would I ask about his sister?"

"My dear Edwin—"

"Clarence," Edwin warned. He was a bloody duke—and more than that, he was the queen's lead advisor.

The solicitor must have caught the fading patience in Edwin's eye. Mr. Miller quickly added, "Your Grace, it would seem that Mr. Thomas was careful in his wording. If he is meeting with Ada on a regular basis, he is *not* managing the earl's assets but rather the sister's. And if it were me—" He placed a hand on his chest. "If I was the solicitor in question, I would have said exactly the same thing to protect my client."

"You would deceive me?" Edwin spoke the words slowly, his temper flaring.

Mr. Miller rolled his eyes. "Not to you, of course. But if someone came asking about your assets, I certainly wouldn't roll over and let them have their way."

"You told me Lord Rochelle abandoned his family."

Mr. Miller held up a hand. "And he has. But the gentler sex is more forgiving than us. She might still be under his thumb. Nothing is off the table with the earl."

Edwin sat back, his mind pulling the details together. The Earl of Rochelle had been on the verge of bankruptcy just last year. He was a noted gambler but had somehow accrued real estate in several counties along with a sizable savings. Clarence Miller hadn't sent his suspicions to Edwin; the queen would not have been able to freeze his assets. The earl's father was a man of character, but even his modest earldom was destitute within months of Rochelle inheriting. "We still don't know how the blasted plonker became so flush."

"We know *why* the earl became wealthy." Mr. Miller scoffed. "He was clearly paid handsomely for participating in the Tailor's scheme."

Edwin sent him a searing look. "How very astute of you."

"What we need to know is *who* lined his pockets."

"Again—"

Mr. Miller leaned forward, his eyes eager. "I've kept careful tabs on every penny that Rochelle has brought in. Each home he supposedly won in a game of cards with each victim accusing the earl of cheating."

"What are you saying?" Edwin rubbed his eyes. He needed sleep—a year's worth. The last time he'd been this exhausted, Edwin was chasing Sir Conroy, another gentleman who thought he was too clever to be caught.

"I'm saying that Rochelle was known for cheating at cards long before he ever won. He teams up with our lovely Tailor and suddenly begins winning." Miller held out his hand. "The men who signed over their homes to him believe he cheated. We have eight men eager to get their homes back. Well, they *were* eager to get their homes back. They've suddenly grown quiet."

Edwin ran a hand down his face. "Why would you play cards with a cheat?"

Miller shrugged. "If he always loses, would it matter?"

"Do you think his sister is helping him?" Edwin tried to remember if he knew her, but his mind was blank. His focus had been on the earl and Lord Pichon's hysterical mother.

Another shrug. "I'm not sure."

"So, you've given me nothing." Edwin winced at his tone. Had he always been this much of a bully? "Apologies."

"Lord Rochelle does not think well of his sister. He refuses to call her *Lady* Ada since his father passed." Mr. Miller's face softened. "He's taken great pains to make sure she—and his own mother—doesn't receive a penny from his estates." He shook his head and tucked his chin. "He did inquire at the expense of an asylum though."

"For whom?"

"A woman. I'm not sure if it was for his mother or sister."

Edwin folded his arms across his chest. "Are they insane?"

"I doubt Miss Whitworth is mad." Mr. Miller smiled wryly. "She meets with a solicitor frequently. Surely you can attest—"

"That would drive anyone mad."

A hand to his chest, the solicitor smiled. "You wound me."

"I've combed through every home Rochelle owns. I've never seen his family." Another puzzle. Edwin had never been in a mess this tangled.

"Lady Rochelle was gifted a townhome as a wedding present. Her late husband kept it separate from his estate."

"Ah." Edwin grinned. "Rochelle can't touch it."

"Not yet." Mr. Miller frowned and pulled at the edge of his sleeves. "As far as I know, he inherits the home when Lady Rochelle dies."

"And you're their solicitor?"

Mr. Miller nodded hesitantly. "Which leads me to wonder ..." Another wave of his hand.

"Why is Miss Whitworth—"

"If you want answers from Mr. Thomas, you'd best call her Lady Ada."

"Blast it all." A growl escaped. "Why is *Lady* Ada meeting with Mr. Thomas if you're the family's solicitor?" There were still missing pieces, but Edwin knew he was close. And Lady Ada was the key.

7

Lady Ada Whitworth

Approaching the florist's shop, Ada felt keenly alone. The doctor had suggested sending her maid home. Ada paid for the transport but didn't have the strength to replace a loyal employee. If Lady Rochelle were her former self, Ada would never be allowed outside without a proper companion, maid or lady. The wind nipped her ears, playfully tugging on Ada's golden curls as she pointed to the white lilies. The florist nodded his balding head, gathering the same flowers she'd picked last time. Another breeze pulled her curls over her face. She should have stopped and fixed her bonnet properly but not today. Her hair would be a mess no matter what she did—why waste the time? Even as a young girl, her hair would unwind itself from a plait by the time breakfast was over.

"Are you certain you don't want to come along, my lady?" The old florist asked—like he'd done the month before.

Ada shook her head. Buying flowers for the earl's grave was one thing, but visiting the site was something different. When her first drawing sold, Ada purchased flowers and had continued to do so on the first Monday of every month. As a girl, the first Monday was the day her father would hold her hand and take her to the shops. They would restock her paints and brushes. And when he was away, new supplies always arrived on the first Monday. Henry Whitworth—before and after becoming Lord Rochelle—brought beauty to Ada's world and now she was determined to do the same for him.

She nodded to the florist, her tongue too thick to speak. He squeezed her hand, tenderness in his eyes. Not every Monday was hard, but today seemed to be particularly gray. Her maid's departure had been horribly timed, leaving Ada alone to buy her father's flowers. Lady Rochelle would be shut in her room for the week, emerging the following Monday with a forced smile.

The sun peered through the clouds. The burst of warmth nudged Ada's mood. Perhaps today wasn't going to be quite as sullen as she'd thought. Their home—although tiny—was perfectly situated in St. James's Square. Ada's grandparents had purchased the property long before values rose. Lady Rochelle had received numerous offers to sell —much to Nikolas's annoyance—but those walls had witnessed newlywed bliss. The happy couple moved shortly after Nikolas was born, but the affection and memories of those first few years were still very much alive.

Ada steered herself toward home, hoping her delivery of pencils had arrived. She couldn't bring herself to enter the shops. Not without her father. She opted for steady deliveries after her childhood stuttering returned. That was the first episode since her father had died. Instinctively, she brought a hand to her throat. It was an awful feeling, losing control of her own body. The episodes were frightening as a child, or perhaps the fear was more from Nikolas's taunts than her lack of control.

Nikolas. The fool was thought to be a traitor. The world *had* gone mad. Nikolas was greedy and cruel but not clever. The devil inside of her desperately hoped Nikolas would be caught. It didn't matter what the crime was, she just wanted him gone. Guilt tugged at her heart. No sister should think so ill of a brother. Adopted or not.

Ada crossed the square toward her home. She'd dallied too long, and without a maid to help, she had little time to prepare for tonight's ball. Mr. Thomas—thank the heavens—had secured her an invitation to a masked ball. Granted, he thought she'd taken his advice to heart and sent along the descriptions of a handful of gentlemen. She didn't correct him. Marriage would have to wait. She had another plan in mind. One to honor her late father. Her throat tightened at the mere thought of the earl. She wanted to be a part of Sir Lyell's exhibit, or more specifically, she wanted to draw her father into more of the exhibit. He was gone, erased from her life and from history. It only seemed right and proper. He was a man of character. His legacy of science should be noted. Celebrated.

Wrangling into a gold dress, she paused in front of the mirror. The tips of her shoulders were exposed as were most of her arms. Her dress was scandalous—and perfect. No one would ever match the silken siren to the quiet, stuttering Lady Ada. She twisted her hair in a quick chignon and pulled on her overcoat, hiding nearly the entire gold dress. She peeked in the mirror. Half of her hair had already cascaded down. Her throat tightened. She would be banned at first sight if her hair was down in such a seductive way. Ada had spent enough time as a lady to know the rigors of the *ton*. With double the pins, she wrestled her hair up once more, securing an evening pillbox hat on top. She placed her brush on her small, chipped vanity, her fingers sliding over her necklace. She paused. No one would ever recognize a necklace. She slipped the delicate gold chain around her neck, her fingers playing with the single, misshapen pearl in the center.

With a black mask in her pocket, she descended the stairs, her heart in her throat. Ada hated deceiving Lady Rochelle, but the less the countess knew, the better. Ada knew good and well that Lady Rochelle's loyalty lay with her son, not her adopted daughter.

The living room was quiet, eerily so, with only the sound of Ada's dress swishing along the circular crinoline cage underneath the skirt. She carefully stepped toward the sitting room, her skirt swaying with each movement. Lady Rochelle was perched at the bay window, her dark hair obediently in place, brushed and coiffed to perfection. A stack of letters sat to her right. Her gaze was once again on the street.

"Lady Rochelle?" Ada asked quietly.

The countess glanced up, a startled look in her eyes, her mouth open in surprise. "Oh, Ada, I didn't hear you."

"Come with me." The words were out before Ada could stop them.

Lady Rochelle recoiled, her mouth falling more open.

"It's a masked ball." Ada kept her tone neutral. She needn't spill her secrets yet. "There's a new opera this weekend. It's meant to celebrate one of the performers." Her tongue began to thicken. She wasn't technically lying. Every word she spoke was true. But the real intent had nothing to do with the opera—although she attended regularly for cartoon sketch inspiration.

Lady Rochelle reached for Ada's gloved hand, her eyes taking in the gold silk. Ada winced. If the countess looked too closely, she'd see the worn edges and know of the secondhand purchase. Lady Rochelle would rather rot than wear another's clothing. The countess smiled, her eyes crinkling. The veil of grief parted for a moment, revealing a younger, brighter version of Lady Rochelle. "Go, darling girl. Masked balls are for the young and the romantic." She stood, the smile growing. "And tell me all about it tomorrow."

Ada watched the countess leave the room, the woman's shoulders upright and her chin lifted. Lady Rochelle didn't ask about the lack of companion or who was hosting the ball. No, she'd only asked for the details after the fact. This was not the woman whose shrill voice berated the earl, angry at Ada's expensive education. Tutors, paints, brushes, there was no limit to the late earl's generosity. Ada would pay him back. She would care for his legacy.

She slipped from the house into the hired carriage and pulled the mask over her face. Her reflection in the glass gave her pause. Her shoulders rose and back straightened. The mess of curls had begun to loosen, strands framing the black mask covering the top third of her face. Her eyes, the blue-green of the ocean, were striking against the shiny black fabric. She was nobody. She could be any one tonight. Once she was inside, no one would know she was once the stuttering daughter of a forgotten earl.

The carriage pulled forward. Ada's time had come. Leaving her overcoat on the bench, she held her breath while she was helped from the carriage. Her boots crunched along the drive. She lifted her skirt, careful to keep her modesty intact, and climbed the stairs to the entrance. She scanned for a side entry but stopped herself. Not tonight. She would not scurry about like a rat. She handed her invitation over to the butler. No one would be announced tonight. Masks would be donned until the last few minutes of the ball. Bets would be placed in the parlor on which gentleman wore what costume and which lady wore what mask—and Ada would be long gone by the time the results were revealed. She would be at home, hopefully with an appointment with Sir Lyell, or better yet, the name of the exhibit's director. Her letter to the baron was clutched in her hand. As an unknown woman—with a mask covering her face—Sir Lyell would never know who'd delivered the invitation for an artist. Her work would speak for itself. She'd included samples of her talent and a gesture to refuse compensation.

She entered the grand ballroom. Grecian columns and marble floors greeted her. In the very center danced a familiar man. He threw back his head and laughed. Ada's tongue doubled in size. Nikolas. Her lungs froze in terror. Her hands clenched at her sides. Her night was over before it'd begun.

8

Edwin Harrison, Duke of Girard

Edwin waited in the corner of the ballroom, his temper rising with each passing moment. Tomorrow's list of things to accomplish was growing faster than his list of suspects. A Welsh soldier had already raised several questions regarding the wagons advertising the queen's exhibition. Edwin refused to speak to the queen about the safety of marketing. She thought Edwin a touch too protective as it was.

He glared at the attendees, blaming them for the impending hours of nothing but wasted time. Flounces of silk spilled into the ballroom, and debutants pranced around, arching their necks to show off their gaudy necklaces glinting in the candlelight. The sheer volume of the crush would deter any waltzing—the one bright spot in an otherwise ridiculous evening. Edwin didn't dance. Nor would he.

But Edwin was a solid shot, a clever marksman. He glanced at Rochelle. Edwin's finger ticked as if it held the trigger of his gun. Rochelle had been released from custody, and every ounce of Edwin's body hated that fact. The queen had thought the man would unwittingly lead Edwin to the Tailor. The ball was, unfortunately, part of Rochelle's social schedule. The blockhead let off another raucous laugh, met by a silly debutante's simpering at his flirtations.

"You look as miserable as I feel." Miller stared at the cup in his hand. He eyed the duke before returning his focus to the drink. "Did you bother reading the invitation?"

Edwin sighed. He'd received the invitation, or rather, the command to attend from Queen Victoria. He'd honor the woman until the day she died, but he refused to descend to the *ton*'s idiotic entertainments. He'd rather rot with a dying pig. "I'll wear a mask when I bloody well feel like wearing a mask."

Stifling a grin, Miller held out his white mask, the ribbons dangling. "Borrow mine."

"You dare to go maskless?" Edwin sniffed at the offering. He was *not* going to wear a mask. He was the blasted Duke of Girard. His ancestors were cringing in their graves. "If you're not careful, the *Thames Tales* will make you their newest villain."

"Oh, come now." Miller chuckled, his eyes crinkling. The music and the ballroom lights softened his gray hair and typically somber expression. "Doesn't every young lad aspire to be noteworthy?"

"A cartoon is not noteworthy."

Miller shrugged. "Becoming a villain has done wonders for Rochelle. Women appear to love the idea of a traitor."

"No one would ever accuse a debutante of being bright." Edwin folded his arms and leaned into the wall. This night was destined to be a disaster.

Miller held out his cup. "Drink."

"No."

"Do something other than scowl at your fellow countrymen." He tilted his head just as Lord Rochelle pulled another young miss from her mother. "And countrywomen."

"I'm not scowling." He was indeed scowling. And he saw no end to his foul mood. Attending balls would not get him any closer to the blasted French spy. Tonight was just another waste. "What else am I supposed to do?" Edwin pointed to Rochelle donning the elaborate

CLARISSA KAE

trimmings and ostentatious padding known of William Shakespeare. At least Rochelle knew how to maintain a crowd's attention.

Miller waved his hand to the dancers. "Oh, I don't know. Dance?"

Scoffing, Edwin took one defiant step from the solicitor, his frown firmly in place. "Do you really want me to dance with *them?*" These were the sons and daughters of the *ton*, the same families who looked the other way while a newly minted earl took their homes and helped plan an assassination attempt on the queen.

Miller opened his mouth to speak but stopped, his eyes widening. Edwin followed his gaze. A woman, surrounded in gold—from her curls to her silken dress—stood at the entryway of the ballroom. Her unfortunate mask covered most of her face, leaving only a delicate mouth to view.

Edwin stepped forward, tossing back to Miller, "Who is that?"

"Do you understand the concept of a *masked* ball?" There was entirely too much humor in the solicitor's voice.

"Women come to be seen."

Miller coughed behind him. "And men come to see."

Edwin spun around. "Not all men."

"Perhaps not all women?" Miller motioned to the woman in gold. "She's covering more of her face than anyone here."

"Why come if you don't want anyone to know who you are?" Edwin was born and raised by the *ton*. He'd cut his teeth on privilege and protocol. There was a way of doing things. Edwin relished order, rules, and regulations. "Who does she think she is?"

Miller chuckled once more. "Yes, the size of her mask is evidence of her ill-breeding. What an utter disgrace, appearing at a *masked* ball with mask. The idea is quite beyond reason."

"Miller," Edwin warned.

The solicitor glanced around conspiratorially before leaning over and whispering, "Shall I quit this ball in protest?"

"You've made your point." Edwin pouted like a child. He winced and slunk back to the wall. Rubbing the bridge of his nose, he sighed, wondering when he'd regressed to the likes of a toddler.

"Have I?" Miller faced him, the mirth in his eyes replaced with concern. "Your Grace ..."

The pause forced Edwin to meet his old friend's gaze. The humor and good-natured sparring was gone from his expression. Edwin wasn't facing just a solicitor, he was facing a family friend, a university colleague of Edwin's father. "You have every right to lecture me on a poor disposition."

"When is the last time you've truly acted out of sorts?" Miller handed off his cup to a server before turning back to Edwin. "I don't think a poor disposition is the cause of your foul mood."

"I think my father would beg to differ."

Miller wiped his face and sighed. "Your father was a man of great character."

"I know." And Edwin did. He would forever strive to honor his father's legacy.

"But he was a trial of a child."

"Oh, come off it, Miller." There'd been far too little sleep for Edwin to play Miller's game.

"Edwin Harrison." Miller folded his arms, squaring his stance. "Your father was like a bloody brother to me, but he was not the saint you paint him to be. At least, not until he left university behind."

"And then he became the giant of a man." Edwin rolled his eyes. He wasn't so daft as to think his father was born perfect. The late duke was rather honest about his failings, ironically making him more saintly in Edwin's eyes.

"I meant the first time he went to university." Miller nodded to emphasize his point. "He was sent packing. Expelled. Or rather, suspended until he repented." He winced. "That, and some faculty changed. I rather think your father exhausted a few of the old establishment."

"No ..." Edwin let the word hang. He searched Miller's face for a hint of humor. Of teasing. Something.

Miller leaned against the wall and lowered his voice. "I've years' worth of tales that would shock even the most seasoned nanny. The point I'm trying to make is that you've missed that part. You've been in such a rush to put the world in careful order that you forgot to laugh. Joke." Miller threw his arms in the air and wiggled about like a child. Amusement tugged at his lips, but his eyes were still somber. He let his hands fall back to his sides. "Be silly. Be foolish." He nodded toward Rochelle dancing with another woman. "You'll never be Rochelle, but you can't exactly become your father if you've never lived."

"I've lived." Edwin wasn't lying. He'd gone through girls in university. "I've eaten and caroused my way through the continent like most young bucks."

"Right." Miller cleared his throat, a flicker of grief crossing his features. With a firm nod, he added, "I shall leave you to your thoughts then."

"Wait." Edwin placed a hand on Miller's shoulder. "I do not mean to dismiss your concern." He waited a beat before adding, "I spent my life assuming it would be a certain way. I never questioned where I would live. Who I would marry ..."

Miller stepped back. "Lady Catherine."

Edwin scratched his head, waiting for some sort of emotion. But again, there was nothing. Lady Catherine was a prepared destination, not the companion he'd hoped for. Not the intended spouse he'd taken the care to court.

"I should have known." Miller sighed, his face awash in apology.

"Don't." Edwin shrugged. "I feel nothing. I am not angry with her. I feel no betrayal, which is worse, in a way."

Miller straightened his stance, a sly grin creeping across his face. He nodded to the dance floor. Lord Rochelle was marching toward the lady in the golden dress. Miller pushed his mask into Edwin's hand. "Perhaps you should feel something tonight."

Edwin felt the pull, his feet moving faster than his thoughts. He slipped the mask over his face and cut across the marble floor. His stare—or perhaps his reputation as the Dark Duke—sent the golden woman's admirers searching for other partners.

She met his gaze, her eyes the color of a stormy sea, blue and green swirling together. She didn't wince. Nor did she look away. In a slow, breathy voice, she said, "I'll have to disappoint you."

"And why is that?" He leaned in. Tension crackled in the air. He felt it in the way her curls slowly slipped from her hat. Her every move, he was aware of.

"I cannot dance with you." Her stance was regal, her chin lifted and posture upright. She was a lady who'd chosen not to dance. The rest of the debutantes practically threw themselves at the gentry.

Edwin motioned to the rejected men leaving them. "Is there a reason you don't want to dance?"

"It has little to do with desire." A slight blush crept up her cheeks. "And more to do with education."

He held out his hand. "You've not been taught to dance?" He knew it was a lie. A lady of her status would have been lectured on the art of snagging a husband—dancing included.

"I have not." She searched his face.

"I find that hard to believe." Edwin smirked, waiting for her to storm off like the spoiled debutante she was. "Is it a game to you, rejecting these poor sops?"

She narrowed her gaze and thrust her hand on his. "You are either deaf or arrogant. I haven't decided which."

Edwin squeezed her hand, ignoring the hammering in his chest. He pulled her to the periphery and spun her to face him. Whispers grew around them. She stiffened. He drew her close. "You will be the talk of the town tomorrow."

She bent her head. "They will laugh."

He tipped her chin upward. "Can you truly not dance?"

She blinked, her eyes a dazzling mixture of blue, green, and gray. She held his gaze—and his breath. His mind blanked. An errant curl fell from her plait, caressing her cheek, breaking the spell. He inhaled slowly, unsure at what he was feeling.

"Follow my lead, and no one will know." Gently, he held a hand above her head, the other arm about her waist. The room became deucedly warm. The silk of her skirt twisted and pulled, showing her raw grace. She didn't walk on her tiptoes or bat her eyelashes. She was different, a wild rose among polished lilies. He swallowed hard, his pulse racing at the touch. "Mirror me. Place your other hand around my waist."

She did as she was told, her blush deepening to a delightful crimson. This golden goddess was not a liar.

Her pins slowly lost their grip on her hair. Her movement was graceful, but her feral hair softened her look, making her more human, more real. Edwin had spent his life thinking of his future in the abstract, a far-off destination, but this woman was living, breathing, in front of him. She was life and beauty, and for the first time, Edwin felt human—felt *alive*.

"I'm going to spin you. Then we'll dance side by side for a few steps," he whispered, aware of the prickling of her skin.

Inches from his face, she spun slowly, completely out of rhythm. Their faces were close. If he were to stop her and lean in, their lips would touch. He paused, an arm around her waist, the other above her head. Surrounding couples turned sharply out of the way, nearly colliding into Edwin and his goddess. He waited for her to squeal and simper like a practiced debutante. She did nothing but meet his gaze.

"You didn't lie," he said. Gads, his mind had become rather stupid.

"I did not." She grinned and touched her mask. "There's a certain honesty in being anonymous."

"Is there now?" Edwin's lungs filled as if he was breathing for the first time. He wanted to drink her in, every secret. Every lie. "And what would you say tonight that you could not say any other time?"

"Everything." She softened in his hands, her eyes lighting up with joy. "Absolutely everything."

Edwin would have given her the world if she'd ask for it. "Give me one thing. What is one thing you'd love to say?"

"That I'm not mad." She shrugged, breaking his contact. Her eyes flitted about as if she was embarrassed.

"I do not believe you are mad." Edwin was rather convinced he'd lost his mind, not the goddess before him.

She curtseyed, a signal that their conversation would soon be over. His heart leapt to his throat. He wasn't ready to say goodbye. He'd never danced with a woman; his sisters hardly counted. He wanted to know more. No, he wanted to know *everything* about this lady.

"Thank you for the dance lessons."

"We can hardly end them now." Edwin held out his hand once more. "Allow me one more lesson."

She tilted her head, and another strand of curls fell. "And how shall I repay you?"

"Give me a lesson on etiquette." Heaven knew he needed it.

"I apologize, but I'm at a loss there too." She covered her mouth with her gloved hand. Edwin had the insane desire to pull the glove from her hand and touch the delicate skin on her wrist. "Sir, I'm afraid all I can offer is drawing lessons."

Edwin smiled. She couldn't have become more perfect in that moment. "My father was an artist. I inherited his love for the arts but none of his skill."

Her face brightened with another delightful blush. Her gaze flicked back to his. She inhaled sharply, and her eyes widened at something behind Edwin. He turned. Lord Rochelle was behind him, a wicked grin on his face.

"Isn't this a wonderful surprise?" Anger flashed in Rochelle's eyes. He held out a hand to the lady. "You've rejected everyone else. Shall I try my hand? I'll keep it simple so you'll need not embarrass yourself."

"Rochelle," Edwin warned. He would not stand by while the worthless plonker assaulted his goddess.

"Oh, don't tell me you've a sudden soft spot for a Whitworth?" Rochelle threw back his head and laughed loudly. The woman winced at the sound. He stepped closer to her. "Why don't you tell your new admirer who you are?"

The lady opened her mouth, her lips trembling. She grabbed the skirt of her dress and spun on her heels, racing from the ballroom. Edwin ran after her, but was stopped by Rochelle's hand.

The earl circled Edwin and jutted his chin. "Never did I think I'd see the day when the Duke of Girard chased my sister."

9

Lady Ada Whitworth

Ada spent the morning waiting for Lady Rochelle to wake. The countess was asleep when Ada had come home from the ball. Ada was grateful beyond measure. She didn't want to speak of her brother or the attention she'd received. Ada lay awake all night, unable to believe she'd danced. She'd asked a servant to deliver her letter to Sir Lyell and quickly left—but not soon enough. She'd overheard Nikolas complain of the Dark Duke dancing with his sister.

She had scurried from the ballroom, her heart in her throat. Her only consolation was the Duke of Girard had no idea who she was. Ada had pushed the memory of the dance from her mind, refusing to acknowledge the hammering in her heart and the feeling of safety in his arms. She'd felt a connection with him—a horrible trick. It was one moment that would never be repeated.

She'd folded the golden dress, placing it in the hidden compartment of her closet. Nikolas would surely punish her. She didn't know the exact crime that earned his ire, but he rarely needed a reason.

There was a time, just before their father passed away, when Nikolas had begun to soften. Lady Rochelle was convinced he'd fallen in love. But then the earl died. Nothing had been the same since.

The brisk walk across St. James's Square dimmed the memory of last night. She paused in her step. If Nikolas had fallen in love, did he feel what Ada had in another's arms? Her heart fluttered at the thought. She couldn't see the duke's face last night, if indeed, he truly was the Duke of Girard. But there was a confidence in him, a feeling of protection Ada had not felt since the late earl had passed.

Ada scurried onward and went to the service station next to her solicitor's office. She filled out the needed application for a new maid, her eyes drifting to the wagon advertising the queen's Great Exhibition. She hoped Sir Lyell had received the letter. She was offering her services to draw his discoveries.

Ada slowed her pace toward home. She wasn't quite ready to face Lady Rochelle.

A carriage pulled in front of the garden, the horses large and black, the carriage new and imposing. The footman opened the door and a man descended, his countenance dark. He was tall, his shoulders and stance wide. He was neither handsome nor ugly. His hair was an indiscernible shade, not quite black or brown. Somewhere in the middle. The most remarkable feature was his stare. His gaze was steady and forceful, as if daring Ada to look away. She might have difficulty speaking, but she had pride to spare. She lifted her chin, refusing to back down.

He walked to her, his gait confident and proud. "Lady Ada."

She didn't know what to say. He'd not asked a question nor had he offered a greeting. He'd just simply noted her name.

The gentleman, the cut of his cloth and his accent marking him as a nobleman, was definitely a friend of the Whitworth family. He arched his eyebrow. "You are the sister of Lord Rochelle, are you not?"

Blast. Only a little mention of her brother, and her heart went racing. Sure enough, her tongue was thick, and Ada knew she wouldn't be able to talk. She clenched her fists at her sides. What she wouldn't give to offer a tongue lashing instead of suffering in silence. His gaze flicked to her fists. He smirked—the man *smirked* at her.

Ada narrowed her eyes and walked passed him. It was a direct cut, but she didn't care.

He circled her, his eyes wide with surprise. "Do you know who I am?"

She gave the briefest of nods and continued her march to the door. She wouldn't be cowed by a friend of Nikolas.

Once more, he circled and stood in front of her. For so large a man, he was surprisingly quick on his feet. Through clenched teeth, he said, "I am the Duke of Girard."

She froze, unwilling to back down. This was the man who'd made her feel safe. And seen. She struggled to breathe. Grief pierced her—a completely absurd emotion. She'd danced with him only once.

He waited for a beat—she assumed for a reaction. He came closer, anger flowing from him. He knew. She shivered. Girard knew it was her last night. She could feel his disdain. Her heart sank.

He searched her face. Then her clothes. He opened his mouth as if deciding on his words. He stepped back and quietly said, "I have been tasked with finding every traitor to the crown."

She forced herself to take a slow breath. She forced out a clipped, "And?"

The duke groaned. "Why is everyone so impertinent?"

At that, Ada retreated. Her tongue loosened. "I'd no idea I was everyone."

His gaze snapped to hers. "I am not a man to be trifled with."

"Then why is my b-b-b-b—" She covered her mouth in horror. She would not be reduced to a stuttering fool. Not because of Nikolas. Not for anyone. She was more than her faults. She was the blasted artist of the *Thames Tales*. Blinking back tears of frustration, she ran to the house.

The duke was hot on her heels. "If you give him so much as a penny, I will know. If you help him in any way, I will tear you to pieces."

Her butler stood frozen in shock. He appeared undecided as whether to open the front door the rest of the way or slam it in the face of the duke.

"Where were you just now?" The duke aimed a finger at her. "Your pretty face will not save you. Not when I'm done with you."

Her butler cleared his throat. "I believe I can answer where she was."

Ada sent a grateful look to him.

"I will hear it from her, thank you," Girard ground out. "And only her."

Her butler sighed. "As you know, women are often succumbed to great emotions. Especially when certain ladies have to find a new maid due to illness. Or when they have to lay flowers on a father's grave."

The duke's face fell, his mouth dropping open. Horror crossed his features. His posture straightened, his gaze flicking between the butler's and Ada's.

"Hello?" The soft voice of Lady Rochelle carried to the front door.

The countess had her dark hair swept up, and her navy dress complimented her porcelain skin. Even in grief, Lady Rochelle was a beauty. Her hair had only just begun to silver, but only Ada would know. She'd spent many nights brushing the countess's hair, soothing the sorrow from her tired soul.

"Lady Rochelle?" the duke asked, his voice several octaves higher than just a moment before.

The countess nodded. "Yes. Oh, please come in."

Girard glanced nervously to Ada. She narrowed her eyes. The man had gone from a brute to a school boy. Ada placed a hand on her hip. Something was amiss.

"Ada, darling, will you please guide our guest to the sitting room?"

Only Lady Rochelle's quiet voice could pierce Ada so quickly. "Yes." Ada curtseyed to the duke and carefully, painfully slowly, said, "Please follow me, Your Grace."

They came to the sitting room. Or rather, the *only* room they had for entertaining. Ada and the duke sat, her mother standing awkwardly by the hearth.

"May I ask who you are?" Lady Rochelle smiled prettily. She reminded Ada of a delicate butterfly. Beautiful but terribly fragile.

"Oh, yes, my lady." The duke rushed to a stand and bowed. "Your Grace." He groaned, realizing his mistake.

Ada covered her growing smile. Something had made the almighty duke terribly nervous. She knew exactly how to portray him in tomorrow's paper. The day might have started rather drab, but Ada had begun to hope for quite the adventure.

"Your Grace?" Lady Rochelle mused, a rare spark of mischief. "That name sounds familiar."

Grinning, Ada helpfully added, "He's the current Duke of Girard."

He shot her a look that was surely meant to reduce Ada to tears. The sudden change in his behavior had loosened her tongue considerably. Today was going to be rather fun.

"Oh, how lovely." The countess smiled warmly. A dazzling dimple formed on her cheek. She was the very picture of grace. "And what brings you here?"

The duke stumbled back. He'd clearly not thought of that. "I came ..."

"To speak with me." Ada grinned. "He was quite forceful at the door."

"I'm so glad you came." Lady Rochelle sat and smoothed her skirts. Awkward silence filled the room. "Oh, Ada, you never spoke of last night."

Ada turned to the duke. She would not divulge anything in front of him. "Your Grace, now that you're comfortable, what would you like to ask me?" She added a few wide-eyed blinks she'd seen debutantes sport.

He narrowed his gaze. "I was hoping to spend the evening with you, of course."

Drat. "The evening?"

"Oh!" Lady Rochelle clasped her hands together, her eyes hopeful. "How wonderful, Your Grace. Ada never entertains—"

"At night," Ada added. She didn't need her mother to confess Ada's lack of social gatherings. Nor could she risk the duke offering insights to last night's outing. "I rarely leave at night."

"Except the opera." Lady Rochelle waved her delicate hand.

The duke beamed at the countess. "Which is why I came. I'd love to accompany Lady Ada to the opera."

Ada's smile froze. The man was a cad. She attended the opera to work, not adorn a proud man's arm.

"Ada loves the opera!" Lady Rochelle clapped her hands together again. Ada hated to admit it, but the movement brought color to the widow's face. "She drags her maid to every performance." The countess paused. The maid was gone and anytime a servant left, the woman was again melancholy. All loss reverted back to her husband's passing.

Grief touched everything in this woman's life. Frustration blossomed. Ada was tired of the mourning, the constant loss.

"The opera it is." Girard arched an eyebrow, a smug look on his face.

Ada swallowed hard, words abandoning her once again. She needed to refuse, but didn't trust her tongue.

A knowing look came over Lady Rochelle. She patted Ada's shoulder. "It's okay, darling. I'm sure the duke wouldn't mind your plight."

Ada coughed into her fist, her cheeks flaming. By some merciful gift of heaven, tea arrived at that very moment. The butler whispered something to Lady Rochelle.

Girard scooted closer to Ada. She snapped to a stand and poured the tea. He followed her, leaning in. "And just what is it that I won't mind?"

Ada shivered, his breath on her neck.

"Is it your lack of dancing skill?" He was a wicked man. The duke might be chasing her brother, but they were one in the same.

She shook her head and handed him the tea. "No, your lack of etiquette."

Girard furrowed his brow and placed the tea back on the tray. In a low voice, he whispered, "I will arrive at seven." He turned to the countess. "Thank you so much for your hospitality."

"Oh, Your Grace, you're leaving so soon?" Lady Rochelle's voice rose and fell like a soft symphony. Ada felt a surge of jealousy. Her parents were able to speak freely, as well as Nikolas. If Ada could mind her tongue, her voice would never be soft. It would pummel arrogant men like the duke. And her brother.

10

Edwin Harrison, Duke of Girard

Edwin filled the carriage with curses and grunts the entire ride to Lady Ada's home. He shouldn't have accosted her in front of her home. He'd lost his head, but blast it all, he tempted the devil's sister. He blamed her for enticing him at the ball. Lord Rochelle and Lady Ada were in league with each other, they *had* to be.

Only a fool would dance with a traitor. Guilt pricked his conscience. He wasn't entirely without blame, but his ego was bruised. Edwin was the youngest advisor appointed to the queen's council. He rose early each morning to exercise both his mind and body—and never, *ever* caroused late into the night. He'd had the same bloody breakfast for the past decade. He was a man in control. Always.

Except at the masked ball. He'd confessed his lack of feelings to Miller about Lady Catherine. Like a fool, he'd marched up to Ada Whitworth of all people. He truly didn't know if Lady Ada was in league with Rochelle. She appeared to be afraid of him. Or perhaps she was just another actor like her brother.

He was bloody tired from chasing the Earl of Rochelle, the foolish earl. Lady Ada looked nothing like the earl. The resemblance to Lady Rochelle was uncanny, despite not being blood relatives. Both had thick hair—one black, the other gold—that rivaled a lion's and full lips that would tempt a saint. Edwin was no saint. That woman reeked of trouble, from her golden hair to her worn boots.

Like her brother, Lady Ada was a puzzle. Her face had fallen when Edwin mentioned Rochelle. But she'd not spoken a word against him. She met with a solicitor regularly, but her boots were several seasons worn. She was beautiful—not that Edwin cared, he didn't. He was just a man with eyes. But if he *did* care, he would be curious as to her age. She was never at the balls or other social functions. There was no reason for her to not be on the marriage market.

"Your Grace?" his footman asked, his eyes wide with concern. They'd arrived at her townhome.

"Right." Edwin climbed down from the carriage. He was still bitter. He'd felt tricked into entertaining the little minx. Guilt reappeared. He'd done the convincing, not her.

Lady Ada had to know she was a gem of the first order. She might get away with her conceited ways with most men, but Edwin would throttle her before succumbing to her feminine whims. Gads, he was in a foul mood.

The butler took his card, directing him to the sitting room. Edwin sat in a huff. Lady Ada, like most women, would make him wait. Why the gentler sex could not manage their time wisely was beyond him.

"A frown so soon?" An alluring voice called to him. "And I thought your critique would come *after* the performance. Not before."

Edwin stood, turning toward the speaker. "What in the blazes are you wearing?"

In a vision of gold and plum, Lady Ada's curls cascaded down her back in an intricate plait, both sun-drenched hair and plum fabric complimenting the other. Her dress was just out of fashion but fit her figure to perfection. She wore no shawl. The woman was asking to be tomorrow's gossip target. A delicate gold strand with a misshapen pearl in the center fell dangerously close to her décolletage. Despite his repulsion of her—and her brother—his eyes were drawn to every inch of Lady Ada Whitworth.

"Some would call this a dress." The woman lifted her chin and stared down her nose at him. A feat considering her head went to Edwin's shoulders. She was neither too tall, nor too short. Her skin—he'd initially thought was fair like her mother's, but as he stepped closer, she was neither fair nor dark. And her lips, blast it all, why did the devil's sister have to possess such full lips?

He pulled at his cravat. His heart pounded in his chest. She was unlike any other.

"That's not a dress." Edwin would know. He was a brother to four sisters. Granted, he was the baby by decades, but still—he knew what a dress was. "Your shoulders are not covered. The amount of skin you are showing tonight—"

"I am more than willing to stay, my lord." Her lips curved into a delicious smirk. "I would never want to embarrass you." She turned to leave.

"Like hell you don't," Edwin barked. "You did this on purpose."

She blinked, feigning innocence. "Did I?"

He grabbed her arm and leaned in. The smell of lavender teased him. His face was mere inches from hers. A slight smattering of freckles decorated her face. Only at this distance could he see the delicate marks. His heart calmed. Warmth settled upon his shoulders. Peace blossomed. He shook the thought. He would not be fooled by Lady Ada. "You won't make a mockery of me."

Her eyes against the purple backdrop were a piercing blue. "I would never harm a gentleman." Lady Ada looked pointedly at his hand on her arm.

Edwin stepped back as if he'd been burned. He'd behaved horribly—for the second time. He ran a hand through his hair. "Apologies."

Her eyes widened in shock, pricking Edwin's conscience. For the briefest of moments, he wondered if she'd ever been on the receiving end of an apology. Rochelle was a coward and cruel. Edwin couldn't imagine the man condescending to anyone else's comfort. He stepped closer once more and took her in—her lashes so long they dusted her skin as she blinked. She inhaled sharply as he neared. A faint blush crept up her neck.

"How old are you?" Edwin asked. The desire to know her, to help her, washed over him. He was a gentleman, and she was a lady.

She blinked. "How old are you?"

Impertinent chit. "Thirty."

"One and twenty next month."

"You're nearly of age." Edwin retreated. This woman was inching toward the shelf. She'd be a spinster soon—an impossible thought.

"I suppose I am." Lady Ada lifted her chin.

Edwin pulled at his cravat. He was a cad, asking a lady her age. Chasing her brother had thrown his mind into the madhouse. "I've not seen you."

Her lips curved to a wry grin. "And yet, I believe we spoke earlier."

Blast. "You know what I mean." He aimed a finger at her chest—her rather shapely bosom. He swallowed the rising panic. He'd lost his head. Retreating, he rubbed his eyes. "I can't say anything right."

"I know the feeling." Her voice came soft. A whisper, a breath. A caress.

His hands fell to his side. Lady Ada's profile was to him, and her shoulders were slightly hunched. Edwin stared at her. If he'd only just met her, his heart would break. She looked like an angel who'd fallen from grace, her hair a golden halo. Edwin was the cause of her pain. He was the devil, not her.

Softly, he stepped to her side, leaving his pride on the floor. There was a quality about her that left him undone, but that was not her fault. He'd behaved horribly. "Lady Ada, might we start again?"

She glanced at him warily, saying nothing. Her silence pierced him.

Edwin held out his hand. He would be better. He *was* better. "Duke of Girard."

She offered a tentative smile. After a moment, she slipped her hand in his. "Miss Whitworth, Your Grace."

"Not Lady Ada?" Her touch made his pulse hum. The feeling of peace was back.

She smiled softly. "Only to the late earl."

"You look ... beautiful." His voice caught. He shouldn't have been that honest. The woman had surely been told of her appearance a thousand times.

She peered up at him, seeming to gauge his sincerity. "Thank you, I think."

Edwin cleared his throat. He felt rather vulnerable under her gaze. And despite his better judgment, he offered, "Shall we have a truce?"

"A truce?" She arched an eyebrow.

"For tonight, we lay down our weapons." Edwin shouldn't be offering anything other than a prison sentence to this woman. And yet his traitorous heart had other ideas. By jove, he was losing his grip on reality. His hand itched to twirl a curl around a finger. He found himself leaning in. "We enjoy the music."

A delightful smirk appeared on her lips. "And pick up our weapons on the morrow?"

He squeezed her hand. "But of course."

She waited a moment. Her eyes searched him. He was exposed under her scrutiny, both a fear and a thrill. In what felt like a lifetime, she said, "I'll hold you to it."

"I have little doubt." He guided her out to the carriage. Instead of facing her on the opposite bench, he slid next to her, Miller's words from the night of the ball in his mind, *Be foolish*. Edwin wanted to feel alive. He wanted to breathe deeply.

Ada leaned away from him. "Did you put down weapons and etiquette?"

Edwin smiled then coughed into his hand. There was something enticing about riling her nerves. He should be inquiring about her brother, not causing her to blush. When had he turned into a bloody plonker? "Oh, but teasing isn't a weapon, now is it?"

Lady Ada inched toward the window. "I thought we had a truce. Making me uncomfortable is not a truce."

Edwin shrugged and breathed deeply. He was alive. Only at her side, but still, he felt invigorated. The tension fell from his shoulders. A weight he'd not realized he was carrying lifted from his chest. A smile—not forced or beguiling—formed on his lips. Perhaps Miller was right. Edwin needed to feel. "But your blush is most becoming."

She swatted his shoulder, her eyes still wary.

He laughed, the sound foreign. When had he last teased or joked? Had his humor been so long abandoned? "Weapons, my lady."

Lady Ada held out her gloved hand. "No one would ever believe you."

"It's a weapon."

"I believe that's what we call teasing." She tilted her head and leaned into him, a soft chuckle escaping her lips.

Edwin's heart lifted. Tomorrow he would pummel her with questions about her brother, but tonight—no, tonight he would let this woman be the sun and invite her light into his world.

Lady Ada's posture straightened and several strands fell from her complicated plait. She frowned, her fingers making quick work, only to fail.

"You've quite the army of curls."

She blew a strand that'd fallen down the middle of her face. "Unfortunately."

Edwin reached over and pulled a few pins. A flood of gold fell down. "Oh, I was hoping—"

"Hope and hair never go hand in hand." She groaned. "At least, not for me."

"It can't be *that* hard," he murmured. Everything could be tamed, including people. He scooted closer and roughly wrapped the hair back up.

"Ow." She winced.

"Oh." He paused. "Sorry, I was trying to help."

"And you thought *my* hand was a weapon?" She swatted his hands away. She looked eerily like his sister at the moment. "I'm going to hold up a strand. You're going to gently—and I mean *gently*—pin the hair." She laid a strand on the plait with one hand, offering up a pin with the other. "Now pin it."

He took off his gloves and leaned over, her lavender scent filling him. He took the pin from her gloved hand, his pulse racing. She did not resemble his sister at the moment. He gently needled the pin, threading her golden strand of hair back into submission.

Scooting closer, she offered another strand. "See if you can tie this one in as well."

Her hair, so soft, so silky, tempted him. Like a drowned plant, she was the sun he very much needed. Her arm and shoulder were flush against his chest, her skirt against his trousers. He was aware of her every move. Every breath.

With eyes softened by the carriage's lamp, Lady Ada turned her face to him, whispering, "How does it look?"

Edwin had one hand on her head, the other touching hers. He swallowed hard. The delicate arch of her neck. He pulled his hand from hers and cradled her jaw. He'd not been this close to a lady. Her maid should have accompanied them, or rather, her mother. He should recoil at the temptation. He was the bloody Duke of Girard—a man of reason, of conduct.

"Your Grace?" Her brow furrowed. The spell was breaking.

Grief filled him. She leaned forward, concern in her eyes.

Miller's words echoed in his mind again, *Be foolish*. "Blast," he whispered.

Her eyes widened.

Blast it all. He leaned in and brushed his lips against hers. A jolt ran through him at the touch. His mind screamed at him, yelling for him to stop. She placed a hand on his chest. He froze as the carriage came to a halt.

11

L ady Ada Whitworth

The duke's arms were around her, steady and strong. And the blasted carriage stopped.

A crash of shame and disappointment fell on her. One moment alone with a gentleman, and she was kissed. She was a fallen woman. Lady Rochelle had cried off, not able to accompany Ada. A new maid was not yet hired.

And yet, she didn't move. Neither did the duke.

Nikolas would cherish this humiliation. He could toss her out of the house. He could do what he wanted. Ada's reputation would be destroyed.

Girard's face was next to hers. The glint of gold in his green eyes winked at her. If she leaned forward just an inch, they would be kissing once more. His gaze flicked to her lips. The thought must have crossed his mind as well.

"That was unexpected," Girard whispered, his breath on her lips. With a wicked smile, he leaned in.

The carriage door opened. He shot up, reaching for the handle. His footman bowed. "We've arrived, Your Grace."

Edwin out let a slew of curses. Ada hid a smile and forced her pulse to calm down. She'd thought the duke was a dragon, but perhaps she was wrong. Or maybe she'd not been thinking at all. He sent a pleading look to her, appearing the boy instead of a duke. "Do we really have to go in?"

"I think for both our sakes, we must." The shame was still there, but Ada felt a bit of hope. She prayed he'd stay playful instead of hard. The duke from this morning tangled her tongue.

With steady arms, he helped her down. Her pulse hummed. For a brief moment, safety enveloped her like an old blanket. He kept his hands on her waist for a moment too long, his eyes boring into hers. Something more than a kiss had passed between them in the carriage. This was more than a truce.

As if from a dream, they entered the theatre. A chorus of whispers immediately surrounded them. Girard's arm tightened. His jaw clenched. The hardened duke had returned. Ada's heart fell. She was a fool. It was only a kiss and, at that, it was the briefest of touches. She was the sister of a traitor, and the man charged with bringing Nikolas down was delivering her to the wolves.

The night had taken a suspicious turn. This was her penance for going to the masked ball. Like last night, she would enter with hope and leave with shame.

Dozens of eyes stared at her, their tongues all but wagging. An older couple, both with silver streaks in their hair, walked directly in front of Girard. The man sniffed at Lady Ada, disdain in his eyes. "And who might this be?"

"My guest." Girard's tone was clipped. He stepped in front of her, ushering her behind him.

Ada felt the shame again. He wouldn't admit her name. He was hiding her. This was all a game, an elaborate ruse. The duke had meant to torture her—that was clear from his morning visit. She swallowed regret and held her head high. She would not be cowed.

The crowd surrounding them grew. Giggles and whispers tripled.

Ada's neck and cheeks went hot. She was more than likely raspberry red. Or crimson.

A man scoffed. "And does she have a name?"

Girard pulled Ada closer, a smile tugging his lips. The duke must be enjoying her humiliation. "May I present Lady Ada Whitworth?" He didn't wait for a response but guided—or rather tugged—Ada forward.

For once, she wanted to speak her mind, to keep her pride intact.

Up the stairs to a private box they went, whispers brushing them with every step. Girard helped Ada to her seat, his jaw tight once more. He sat next to her. His anger ebbed and flowed around him.

With his profile to Ada, her tongue loosened. "They will crucify you now." *And me.*

He smirked. "Nothing they say will be worse than the papers."

Her conscience pricked her. She should perhaps take a break from sketching Girard. "You've never been seen with the traitor's family."

He met her gaze. She looked away. She wouldn't be able to speak if he looked at her. The theatre darkened, saving her. He inched closer. "What would they say if I kissed the sister of a traitor, right here, right now, in full view of the *ton?*"

Breathe. "You wouldn't be that cruel."

He straightened. She felt the draft from his movement. "No, I suppose I wouldn't."

"I'd be fallen twice over. Once by you and once by my b-b-b—" Ada shook her head. *Drat.*

"Your brother?" He sighed but didn't move away. "Did I truly injure you tonight?"

She opened her mouth to answer. Her tongue wouldn't move.

Again, his steady gaze. He reached for her hand. The balcony was high enough that no one would see. He threaded his fingers through hers. "Lady Ada, you have my word. If I've destroyed your reputation, I will make it right."

Her heart raced. It was difficult to believe his words with his hand in hers. She broke the contact, her hands back in the safety of her lap.

"I do not know what came over me in the carriage. It will not happen again, I can assure you. But it was not meant to be cruel."

His promise to not kiss her again was a splash of cold water. She'd lost her mind. She should be rejoicing in that knowledge. Ada opened her mouth. *It was just a kiss.* No words came. Groaning, she cradled her head in her hand.

"If you're not careful, I'm going to have to repin your hair." His voice was a caress. "And then I'll be tempted all over again."

"And then history will repeat itself." She sat up straight. She'd said the words. Her tongue had obeyed. Hope blossomed in her chest.

Girard chuckled next to her.

"Well, isn't this adorable?" A familiar voice entered the box. *Nikolas.*

Ada didn't turn around. She didn't look at Girard. Her lungs seized. Nikolas would destroy her. The final blow would happen at the opera, a fitting end for her dramatic brother. This wasn't happening. Why was Nikolas here, in the duke's theatre box? With just his voice, she was reduced to a sniveling young girl unable to speak.

Girard leaned back in his chair as if Nikolas was nothing but an old friend saying hello. Footsteps came closer. Ada winced at the sound.

"And just what do you think you're doing with my sister?" Nikolas's voice was too close. He was directly behind her. "You might order the queen and country around, but I do believe I have precedence in my own family."

She gripped the chair and squeezed her eyes shut, grateful for the darkened theatre. She would give anything to disappear.

"Lady Ada is my guest." Edwin motioned to the stage where the instruments began playing. "I believe it is obvious what we are doing."

"Where is our mother, sister mine?"

Ada kept her face forward. She would *not* stutter in front of Nikolas. She would control her own body. Her own mind. She was not mad.

Girard stood, his stance defensive, a panther ready to pounce. "This is a private box, Rochelle. You'll have to find another place to spew your poison."

"I'll leave you to your stimulating conversation." Rochelle forced a laugh, the same sound he'd used as a boy to taunt Ada. "You are having a conversation, correct?"

Girard ground out. "What happens in this box is none of your concern."

"She's my sister. It is very much my concern."

Ada jumped to her feet. "S-s-s-stop."

"Some things never change." Nikolas laughed, hard and cruel. He folded his arms. He'd lost weight while in the queen's custody. The slender frame should've been less frightening, but all it did was send waves of fear through Ada. Nikolas could be tied to a chair and bloodied—and she would still be scared.

Girard leered at him. "I believe I ordered you from this box. If you violate your terms—"

Nikolas held out his arms. "Not everyone believes I'm the violent criminal you've painted me."

"Or we're tired of protecting a cheat." Girard scratched his head and forced a yawn. He waved his hand in the air as if Nikolas were nothing but an inconvenience. The ease at which he flipped through emotions reminded Ada too much of her brother. "Rochelle, you've been stripped of the homes you supposedly won and can't access your money. So eat, drink, and be merry while your enemies welcome you home."

Nikolas aimed a finger at Girard. "I could challenge you to a duel, here and now, for accosting my sister."

The duke sighed. "You want to challenge me—an adviser to the queen—to an illegal duel? You've gone mad, Rochelle. Why don't you ask your sister if she was accosted before adding another crime to your sheet, another noose around your neck."

Nikolas threw back his head—he'd always been the actor. "You and I both know she'll never answer."

Ada winced. She slipped behind her brother and retreated to the shadows. Her lungs were heavy, and her tongue stubbornly still. She needed to leave. She'd learned her lesson. Ada belonged in the shadows, not the light. She stood. This was her brother's world. Ada was foolish enough to get caught up in it.

She reached the corridor. Two beautiful ladies, each with rings donning their fingers and gold glittering their necks. They cackled and teased each other. Ada felt a surge of jealousy. She'd never had a friend to call her own. Her father was the closest, but Ada had never felt comfortable confiding with anyone.

The women turned to Ada expectantly. They both wore white. The taller one had full, chestnut hair while the other had white-blonde curls. The darker one gave a shallow curtsey. "Your Grace."

Ada glanced around, sure the woman was speaking to someone else. The blonde smiled sweetly—a glint in her eye. "Apologies. We assumed you were related to the duke. He never uses his box. Or comes to the theatre."

"Oh." It was the safest answer. Ada was slowly gaining control over her tongue but didn't want to risk anything more than one syllable at a time.

"Good evening, ladies," Nikolas drawled, appearing at Ada's side.

She stepped away from him, her heart in her throat. He looked at her—then past her. His eyes narrowed. She stepped once more, and felt a hand at her back. She spun around and into the duke. Girard's jaw was tight, his gaze on Nikolas. With surprising gentleness, he lowered his voice. "Would you mind terribly if we came another time?"

I need to leave. The words wouldn't come. Ada gripped his arm.

Girard gave a subtle nod. He glared at Nikolas, turning his dark look to the ladies. "We are leaving."

"And what does Ada want?" Nikolas *tsk*ed. "Or are you so much of a brute that you'd ignore her wishes?"

The ladies gasped, but not before sending furtive glances at her brother. Even with her hand on the duke's arm, Ada was alone. Girard didn't know of her fear or her stutter. Nikolas was cruelly aware. She blinked, terrified that her brother would see her fumble. She turned from her small audience and walked toward the entrance. It was an unwitting cut to Nikolas—*and* the duke. The ladies would gossip at Ada's horrendous behavior. A tear slid down her cheek. Footsteps ran after her. She picked up her skirts—her reputation was already in shreds—and ran.

"Ada ..." the duke called.

His voice made her pause. He would give her a set-down like no other. She closed her eyes briefly, straightening her stance. She deserved whatever came.

Girard was at her side, offering his arm. A rush of warmth came over her. She was foolish. She shouldn't be comforted by him. Without a word, they began walking. She peered up at him, his face hard. He called for his carriage, asking her nothing. With a sinking realization—Ada knew the reason for his silence. Nikolas had told him of her stutter.

12

Edwin Harrison, Duke of Girard

IN AN UNGODLY HOUR OF THE MORNING, EDWIN URGED HIS GELDING forward. He needed a bruising ride to match the pounding in his head. He'd thrown the newspapers in the fire—the gossip pages were drowning in questions of the Dark Duke and his captive beauty. One author went so far as to say Girard had bribed Lady Ada to attend with him, releasing her brother as a reward. At least, the cartoon spared him. Art had been a comfort to his father.

Edwin regretted speaking to either Whitworth. The sister was temptation reincarnated while Rochelle was the devil himself. The two of them—were they in league?

Edwin rounded the bank at the edge of his property. He'd gone to his Westminster estate, needing more space from the Whitworth family. There was something amiss between Rochelle and his sister, and he'd be damned if he couldn't get to the bottom of it. When Lady Ada wasn't twisted inside herself, she was witty. Charming, even. But for a brief moment, Edwin could have sworn he saw fear in her eyes. Not toward him, but her brother.

His horse fidgeted underneath him. Edwin guided him back toward home, another woman now on his mind—his mother. Edwin's parents were past their prime when he'd come along. He was the apple of their eye—the late duke finally had his heir. It'd only taken three wives and forty years of trying. Duties were pounded into Edwin since birth.

He would never forget the disappointment on his father's face when, as a young boy, he'd been caught trying to steal a kiss from the neighbor's daughter. Or rather neighbors. And daughters.

He'd not dallied with a woman's affections since. His stomach twisted. He'd completely lost his head last night. He'd kissed Lady Ada. He groaned at the memory. Of all the ladies to seduce, why the Earl of Rochelle's sister? He promised to never let it happen again.

Edwin was raised to carry the Harrison line, to uphold the title and responsibilities of those he cared for. He winced. The truth of the matter was he rarely spoke to his siblings. Granted, they shared a father and nothing else. Edwin was born after every one of his sisters had left the nest. He was sure they thought him spoiled.

His horse tossed his head, annoyed at the slower pace. The gelding had needed a longer ride, but Edwin's schedule wouldn't allow it. Not today. Not when Edwin needed to speak to the queen about Rochelle. He pushed thoughts of Lady Ada from his mind. He dismounted and stared at his hands. The feel of her hair was like nothing he'd felt before. Her touch brought life into his being. She was pretty enough, but there was something about the wild nature of her curls. And the feel of her lips—gads, Edwin was in trouble.

More than that, there was the queen's international ball that Edwin had not yet received word on security measures for. He'd failed—again —to convince the queen to abandon her plans. France was on the verge of another revolution, and all he could bloody well think about was the feel of Ada's lips against his. Brief or not, the kiss was a shadow that followed him. He was someone else in the woman's company.

Cursing, Edwin gave the reins to his footman and entered his home. He needed to change, horse hair and mud covered his lower half, but his ride had taken longer than normal. His world needed less Ada and more order.

His butler greeted him. "Your Grace, Mr. Miller is in the living room."

"Show him to the study." Edwin had needed a change of clothing, but if Miller had come to Westminster, there was a reason. He paused in his step. If it had to do with last night, Miller might ask questions Edwin wasn't ready to answer.

"Already done, Your Grace."

Of course, the butler had shown him into the study. Edwin slowed his pace. He didn't want to face Mr. Miller just yet. He respected the man, not that Edwin's opinion meant much. Lord Pichon had Edwin's respect, but that didn't mean he hadn't wanted to throttle the baron. But Edwin kept a schedule on purpose. He could not unwind mysteries if his own life was in chaos. Sighing, Edwin entered the study.

"Up so early, my lord?" Sarcasm dripped from the solicitor's words. He furrowed his brow. He didn't wait for an invitation but sat on the sofa opposite the desk, a package tucked under his arm.

"I could say the same thing, Miller."

"Yes, well, today promises to be extraordinary."

Edwin rubbed his neck and sat at the desk. "Dare I ask why?"

Miller smiled ruefully. "Oh, where to begin."

"Spit it out." Patience had never been Edwin's virtue. He was exhausted from restless sleep and the nation's worry. The last thing he needed was a cheeky solicitor.

"I think it's better to show you." With that Miller stood.

"Fine, hand it over." Edwin held out his hand for the package.

"The package isn't for you." Miller rolled his eyes, looking half his age instead of twice Edwin's. "I'm not sure you're aware but I do have clients other than yourself."

Edwin murmured, "Impertinent fool."

"I quite agree." Miller held out his arm. "Shall we?"

Leaving the house, Edwin asked, "Where are we headed?"

"To dear old Mr. Thomas." Miller beamed as if he'd been bursting with the news. He was an odd lot.

Edwin wondered again why he liked the older man. "I've already visited him."

"Quite. But we're visiting his home, not his office." Miller climbed into Edwin's waiting carriage.

"You told my butler to have my carriage ready?" The gall of this man was more than Edwin could manage. He was worse than a meddling mother. The thought made him pause. His mother couldn't meddle. She didn't recognize her own son, nor had she for several years.

"Could you close the door, Your Grace?" Miller gave a dramatic shiver.

"You should have been an actor, not a solicitor." Edwin climbed in and shut the door.

"But then I would have missed your performance last night."

Edwin glared at the man. "Spill it."

The carriage lurched forward. Mr. Miller shrugged, a grin creeping along his lips. "Surely you had to know you would be the talk of the *ton*."

Edwin flexed his hand, turning his gaze to the window. "I didn't think about that."

"At least the *Tales* cartoonist spared you this time." Miller cleared his throat. "Although, whoever the artist is, he seems to not think highly of your favorite earl."

"No one thinks highly of Rochelle." The one consolation in all of this mess.

"The Tailor seems to." Miller's voice had grown serious. "I do not mean to be an alarmist, but not a single victim of Rochelle's gambling cheat will come forward now."

"They're on the verge of destitution. You said the men came to you—"

Miller nodded. "They did. But every last one of them has had a change of heart. A rather fearful one."

"What of Mr. Thomas? Why are we headed to his home?" The carriage neared St. James's Square. They'd made excellent time at this early hour and were only a few short streets from Lady Ada's townhome. Had she slept well or was she submerged in regret?

"His office was ransacked." Miller leaned forward, lowering his voice. "A fire was started but quickly put out by the neighbors. The one perk of being in the center of St. James's."

"And you believe it has to do with Rochelle?" Another puzzle piece. Edwin had retraced the bloody twit's steps for nearly a year. Lord Pichon had given Edwin a letter specifically indicating Rochelle and two other gentlemen. The other noblemen had suspiciously disappeared. Edwin feared they were six feet under. But Rochelle had been especially slippery. Lord Pichon's mother went belly up the moment evidence was introduced. She was packed and shipped off to Australia—much to Pichon's relief. Or perhaps the relief of his new bride. Anyone within a mile radius of his mother heard her cry of outrage.

"I believe Rochelle has risen in status to the Tailor." Miller frowned. "And I'm not sure why."

"Even if the victims don't come forward, the estates are still in possession of the crown." Edwin had hoped freezing the earl's income would put more pressure on the clod. Apparently, Edwin was the fool, not Rochelle. "We are still no closer to finding out who the Tailor is. I doubt even Rochelle knows."

Miller shrugged, nodding to the house up the street. "Perhaps his sister knows."

Edwin's gaze snapped to the solicitor's. "Are you sure?"

"All I know is that there is growing pressure. Something is on the horizon, and I don't know what."

Edwin sat back in the seat. "The exhibition needs to be delayed until security is changed. I could get a few months at most."

"What measures are being taken for the queen's ball?"

A draft of fear crept into the carriage. The ball was an old English tradition, but Victoria had expanded it, inviting gentry from other countries as a show of good faith. Edwin was against it—and accused of being anti-change. His job consisted of keeping the crown safe. If that made him a bore and a brute, so be it.

Following Miller's lead, they entered the four-storied home on the outer edge of St. James's, half a mile from his office. And there on the sofa lay Mr. Thomas, an enormous goose egg on his forehead and a shiny black eye directly beneath.

"Heavens, Thomas. What happened?" Edwin barked.

Thomas winced at the outburst. "I'm not sure." Gingerly, he swung his legs over and sat up. "Did you bring it?"

Miller circled Edwin and offered the package.

"Thank you." Thomas turned over the package but not before Edwin read *T&T* on the front in a decidedly feminine handwriting.

"What is that for?"

"A client," both solicitors said at once.

"Oh, bloody hell to you both. I can't help if I don't know what's going on." Edwin stalked to the nearest sofa. He felt rather childish. Both men had known his father—their careers and families well established before Edwin was born.

"This particular client is dear to me, and I wouldn't dream of causing harm," Thomas said softly. "But what I can say is Lord Rochelle is very much the villain you portray him to be."

13

Lady Ada Whitworth

Ada placed her charcoal pencil in the divot of the rosewood block, the blades of the sharpener dulling once more. She'd gone through several blades over the past few months. Her fingers appeared to be permanently stained by her constant sketching. She tapped the end of the pencil for excess charcoal and placed the sharpener back in her desk. If her hands were busy, her mind was at ease. She couldn't very well march over to the duke's house and demand a reason for the kiss. Nor would she. Ada was near certain Nikolas had confessed her stuttering to Girard. Both men could rot for all she cared.

The late earl had refused to listen to the horrific doctor who dictated Ada's stuttering a fault of an unsound mind. The next doctor believed Ada was of a weak constitution and should immediately be admitted to his asylum for delicate ladies.

Smirking, she filled in the furrowed brow of the frustrated nobleman, the great Duke of Girard. Off to the side, Ada had drawn a bandit sneaking in the distance, tiptoeing off with a finger to his lips. She'd written just above the man *Le Tailleur*, labeling him as the elusive spy.

At the bottom corner of the wove paper, she'd drawn her brother, labeling him *New Earl of Rochelle*. Nikolas wanted to be *the* earl not a *new* earl. He believed the world pivoted around him, not the other way around. *New* meant he could one day be the *old*—and no one replaced Nikolas.

Ada captured his angled jaw and Roman nose perfectly. His dark hair and eyes, so unlike her golden hair and blue-green eyes. She turned her pencil to his outstretched hands, both bound in tight knots. This was Nikolas. He was caught and yet still taunting the duke. Nikolas would never admit defeat. Instinctively, she gripped the pencil.

She tore the paper and slipped the drawing back in her desk. She wouldn't send it. She'd vowed to lay off the duke after last night. Ada would return to drawing him for *Tales* later, but she wanted to pretend a little longer that there was a connection between them. Shame and disappointment still came in waves—and had since early this morning. She'd lain awake most of the night, wishing for a different ending to their outing. Part of her dreamed that they'd never left the carriage while the other part splashed cold reality over her thoughts.

"Ada, darling?" Lady Rochelle entered the sun room, her skirts swishing. She waited at the threshold between the living room and the corridor. She wore a light blue dress, her expression hopeful.

Ada tucked her papers and tools into her desk, placing her Bible back on top. Quickly, she slipped her gloves back on her hands. Lifting her chin, she straightened her posture. Perhaps she could convince her mother to take a walk, to venture past the walls of their home.

"We have a visitor." Her mother smiled, the joy not reaching her eyes.

"A visitor?" Ada could barely move. Had the duke come? Ada blinked, focusing on her breathing. In a moment, she felt his lips on hers. Her pulse raced. She briefly closed her eyes, counting softly to herself, "One. T-t-two." She winced at her stuttering. "Th-th-three."

Blast it all. She'd been able to speak to him at the theatre until her brother had shown up.

Heavy footsteps echoed down the corridor. Ada cringed at the sound. Would the duke be cold or inviting? In the corner of her eye, her mother's posture stiffened.

"What? No embrace for your beloved son?" Nikolas's booming voice filled the room.

Ada folded her trembling hands in her lap, her heart sinking.

Nikolas *tsk*ed loudly. "Aren't you a sight?"

Lady Rochelle sat on the sofa, her smile wide. She patted the cushion next to her. "Tell me of your adventures."

Nikolas smirked and nodded at Ada. "Not a kind word for your own flesh and blood?"

"She is tired, darling boy." Lady Rochelle motioned to the housekeeper rushing in with her tea tray.

"So is the excuse. Poor little Ada is too tired to speak." He rubbed his jaw, his eyes narrowing. His presence was commanding and always had been. He wasn't particularly tall, but he filled whatever room he entered. He'd inherited his father's handsome face and his mother's soft eyes. He should provide relief to the women in his family. But all he'd ever brought Ada was pain. And terror.

With an arrogant swagger, Nikolas walked to Ada. "And what does my sister do all day that renders her so exhausted? You were rushed from the theatre so soon, it couldn't have been the opera. Is there someone occupying your nights?"

Ada opened her mouth. She would force her tongue to work. Her brother leaned over her shoulder, his finger flipping through the pages of the Bible. She sniffed. He reeked of alcohol.

"Is there something that offends you?" His voice held a warning.

Ada's eyes flicked to her mother's. Lady Rochelle sat prettily, her expression blank. Opening her mouth, Ada prayed words would come. "G-g-good—"

"I'm sorry, what did you say?" Nikolas leaned forward.

"Nikolas," her mother said softly.

"A moment, Mother." He clasped his hands behind his back. He backed up against the wall next to Ada's desk, facing her. "How old are you?"

She swallowed the fear. This was an ancient argument. She was nearly on the shelf and now, without her father, had become like a child. Old fears had chained her tongue.

"Nikolas." Lady Rochelle ran a hand over the cushion next to her. "Let us speak of other things."

Ignoring his mother, he brandished two theatre tickets. "You've been invited to a performance."

Ada's vision blurred. She would not—could not—attend with Nikolas. Her breathing came short. She gripped her skirts. "I-I-I—"

"You will attend." Nikolas grabbed her chin in his hands, inspecting her face. "Your skin is smooth. Your eyes have turned more blue." He pulled at the curl framing her face. "And your golden hair will be the envy."

In a rare moment of clarity, Lady Rochelle stood. "You sound as if you're admiring a horse. Have you returned to betting?"

Nikolas dropped his sister's hair. Ada shook her head slightly, begging her mother to stand down. Challenging her brother only led to more pain. "Has she gone hungry, Mother?"

Lady Rochelle tilted her head. Mother and son stared at each other, a silent argument happening.

Nikolas turned to Ada. "Have you a roof over your head? And dresses to call your own?" He stopped in front of her and rocked on his heels as if he—not the late earl—provided for their welfare. As if Ada had not secured their servants. Her brother had done nothing.

Lady Rochelle whispered, "Nikolas—"

He held up his hand, his face softening. "I am fighting for the future of my sister."

Lady Rochelle abruptly stood. "I will call for biscuits."

The moment she left, Nikolas slammed the tickets down on the desk. "You will attend the musicale tonight. I've sent for a dress to be made. You will wear something in fashion not that hideous, revealing thing you wore at the ball. You will not embarrass me."

The lights, the intimate crowds, the questions—Ada shrank in her chair. Last night proved what a mistake her presence was. She'd attended operas quietly. Not on a duke's arm and most definitely not her brother's. She knew Nikolas would humiliate her, use her for his own gain.

Nikolas began listing all that he paid for. Lies. That was the only language he knew how to speak.

Ada squeezed her eyes shut, wishing she was anywhere else. Ada was the one who'd hired the servants and paid the council taxes. She was the one who'd taken care of his poor mother.

And yet, she cowered when her brother was around. Her tongue became stiffer with each passing moment. Like snow, grief fell on her shoulders, lightly at first. The feeling buried her brother's words. Then a warmth—a hard fire began to burn. She was angry. If the late earl, Henry Whitworth, was still alive, her brother would be constrained. Ada might have even had a season. Or two.

When she'd stood at his coffin, her lips refused to move. She left the church without uttering her goodbye. Flowers and well-wishers filled their London home. Nikolas had pushed Ada out of the house, hauling her to notable families, her grief a noose around her neck. She shivered, remembering the threats he'd sent her way when his debts were being called—until he'd suddenly come into money after their father had died.

"Where was your maid last night?" he asked, suspicion in every word. "Since Mother doesn't care enough for your reputation." He circled the room, his temper growing with each moment. Nikolas snapped his fingers at Ada. "You are not entertaining the great Girard tonight, I presume?"

Ada said nothing, wishing with all her heart that Nikolas was still in the queen's custody. Having him away at the palace was easier.

"Did he offer you his hand in exchange for your brother's neck?" His voice had gone soft once more, danger lurking below the surface.

"W-w-w-we ..." She took a deep breath and looked down at her lap. Perhaps if she pretended he was someone else, that would help. "We did not speak of you." She felt her cheeks blush.

"Oh, do tell." Nikolas laughed too loud. He kneeled before her, his dark eyes leering at her. He tugged a strand of her hair. "Has the duke struck gold?"

Ada swatted his hand away. "No."

"Well, that wasn't so hard, now was it?" He picked at his fingernails as if he was bored. "In a few hours, you will wear a blue dress." His gaze flicked to hers. "It will be in fashion."

Focusing on her words, she said slowly, "I w-w-w-will—"

"Despite that hideous dress delighting the duke." He grinned. "What I ordered is good enough for the Conroy's musicale."

She knew of the Conroy's reputation, and the terrifying abuse he was accused of. Being a former guardian to the queen should have elevated the gentleman had his behavior gone unreported. Of course, Nikolas was Conroy's friend. "I w-w-won't go."

"Yes, you will." He clamped a hand on her arm, his words deceptively gentle. For a moment, he softened and searched her face—then it was gone. He snapped to a stand, as if he was guilty of being kind. His face hardened. "I've already spoken to a solicitor. All I need is one word and you will be sent to an asylum. Have no fear, dear sister. The location is remote. Not even your adopted mother will be able to visit." He grinned wickedly. "And you'll not be able to say a word against it."

14

Edwin Harrison, Duke of Girard

IN THE TINY SPACE BETWEEN MR. THOMAS'S CHIMNEY AND WHERE he lay on the sofa nursing his swollen eye, Edwin paced, a hand on his forehead, the other behind his back. Miller was suspiciously quiet on the other end of the sofa. Edwin had begun the day with thoughts of Ada in his head, and now he was swimming in theories of her family.

Edwin desperately needed to get both his investigation and his day back on schedule. He'd unraveled mysteries before, hadn't he? He led the inquiry into Sir Conroy, the slippery eel, who tried time and again to prove the queen promised him a leadership position. The plonker was nothing more than a bully who needed a set down on a regular basis. Rochelle should be an easy target.

The walls of Mr. Thomas's home seemed too large. The space cramped. Mr. Thomas's home was more tall than wide. If Edwin stepped too close to the wall, he could hear the neighbors arguing. Other than university, the duke had never lived so close to another family. Although he had siblings, he'd not been raised with shared walls. The idea of arguments and differing opinions within the same family was fascinating. He'd wanted to go undercover earlier this year when the rumors of a French spy first began, but Queen Victoria refused to let Edwin put himself in danger. Little did she know just how hands-on Edwin was in his investigations.

Edwin was updating the queen tomorrow on Rochelle's financial link to the French spy. But with Miller rushing him over to Mr. Thomas's, Edwin's day was ruined. Edwin had promised his half-sister he'd visit his mother.

Edwin paused in his pacing, the blasted walls feeling more like a cage. He'd skipped the last few visits with his mother. He was grateful for his half-sister's tender care toward his mother—the woman didn't recognize her own son, only her stepdaughter. Edwin's appearance was always quite a shock to the poor widow.

"If you don't sit down, I'm going to tie you to a chair." Miller crossed a leg over the other. His sardonic nature did nothing for Edwin's sense of urgency.

Edwin needed to move. He had far too many things to accomplish before he could sit about. The massive decorating at his Westminster home for the upcoming ball wasn't quite complete. In fact, none of the tasks Edwin had set out to tackle the last year had been done. The thought fell like an anvil on his shoulders. His pacing became faster, his mind racing with a fear—an anxious feeling he'd not felt before. And like a snap, it pierced his stomach. Edwin Harrison was scared—at nearly thirty years, he was going to fail for the first time. Something he touched would be left undone. His breathing came short. He pulled at his cravat, the room deucedly hot.

"Counting to three." Miller held up a finger. "One ..."

"Enough," Edwin snapped. "I'm trying to think, and all you can say is sit."

Miller dropped his hand. "Your brain isn't thinking any clearer than it did last night."

Edwin sent him a scathing look. Miller shrugged. The only people who knew Edwin had kissed Ada were not inclined to share the news. Miller was not one of them. There was no reason the solicitor should be saying such things. Edwin rubbed the back of his neck. What if someone *had* seen him? He couldn't bloody well marry Rochelle's sister. That was akin to treason—the earl was under suspicion.

"The duke wasn't anywhere near my office, Miller. I wasn't planning on being there either." Thomas gingerly touched his swollen left eye. "I'm just grateful I'd already moved most of the files here."

"I was referring to Girard taking Lady Ada to the theatre." Miller blinked innocently as Girard tossed him another glare. "All of London knows it. If the veritable Mr. Thomas didn't already know, he would soon enough."

Thomas sat up with a snap. "You did what?"

Edwin rolled his eyes. "I wanted information."

Pointing a trembling finger, Thomas stood. A strange fury had washed over him. His lithe frame trembled with anger. "I told you, she was innocent. You had no right to accost her."

"Accost her?" Edwin scoffed. The solicitor must have taken a serious hit to the head. Edwin wasn't a rake. His stomach twisted. His behavior—normally—was above reproach. "I took her to the theatre, not the guillotine."

"She's an innocent." Thomas's voice cracked as he stood.

"And what am I?" Edwin bellowed. He waved a hand in the air. "Don't answer that."

"Oh, please do." Miller smirked.

"Lady Ada ..." Thomas shook his head, wincing at the movement. "She is not like her brother."

"Why does she meet with you?" Miller asked gently, his voice soft. He was a seasoned solicitor, dealing with death and business with gentleness. "She might not be like her brother but what does that mean? She could hate the earl but still do his bidding."

"She wouldn't." Thomas's voice was firm, but his stance began to wobble. "She would do anything—*anything*—to get out from under his threats."

"What threats?" If the girl was under the earl's thumb, that would prove useful for Edwin. He could offer her freedom in exchange for information. And protection.

Thomas glanced between Miller and Edwin with his unswollen eye.

He clearly trusted his fellow solicitor over the duke. "She was ... exploring other possibilities."

"Such as?" Edwin was running out of time. He needed answers not vague ideas.

Again, Thomas's eye flicked between the two men. "I'd rather not say."

"Your office was ransacked, and you were attacked." Miller tossed his head in the direction of the package he'd brought. It laid innocent on the end the table with the feminine handwriting written across the top. "I think it might be helpful to give us just a bit of information. Whatever is spoken in here, will stay here."

Thomas eyed the duke. "Do I have your word?"

Edwin held out his hand to shake. "I swear to it, Thomas."

"I will not tell you the majority of the services I provide for her." The solicitor straightened to his full height. "But I will say, I was urging her to marry. I provided a list of prospective suitors."

"Marriage?" Edwin recoiled. The man had crossed a line. That was Lady Rochelle's privilege to steer her adopted daughter toward matrimony. Not a solicitor. "Did you speak to any of these *prospective suitors?*"

"Regrettably, I might have let it slip to a gentleman that the Whitworth house could possibly be in search of a husband." Thomas sat back on the sofa. "There is a concern that Rochelle might twist a marriage into another opportunity to line his pockets."

"That is why everyone was whispering." Edwin leaned an arm against the mantle. The gossip had bothered him more than he cared to admit. It was one thing to be sketched into a cartoon for doing his job, but to be the center of a lady's marriage scandal was quite another.

"I doubt the entirety of the *ton* gave a fig about Lady Ada's sudden interest in marriage," Miller said dryly. "Their tongues were wagging because Rochelle's sister was on your arm. You are, in fact, the man charged with uncovering *le Tailleur*, are you not?"

"I am not the one on trial," Edwin ground out.

Miller sniffed and turned to Thomas. "Who was the gentleman interested in a Whitworth wife?"

Thomas waved a hand. "Mr. Lydcombe"

"Who?" both Miller and Edwin asked.

Thomas perked up. "He's from a genteel family. Kind." He touched his swollen eye once more, wincing. "More than anything, he's my age. His name could protect her."

"Protect her how?" Edwin hated the concern in his voice. It was only a stolen kiss in a carriage, but his thoughts kept turning to the feel of her hair. For over a decade, he'd gone from task to task, thinking the assignments would complete him. But from the moment he spied Ada on the doorstep of Thomas's office, he'd felt a quiver of excitement. It was irrational, that Edwin knew, but still, he felt like his life had been the midnight hour and her appearance had been the sun, breaking the long darkness with a brightness he'd never experienced before. He shook his head. He'd lost his head. "I don't see how the man could protect her."

"Mr. Lydcombe could keep her from her brother's reach." There was a lilt at the end of Thomas's statement, an almost-question. "I had hoped to write up a contract keeping her assets separate."

"What assets?" Edwin didn't miss the wary look in the solicitor's eye. "If she is hiding Rochelle's assets for him, I need to know."

"No," Thomas said emphatically. "I told you. I do not work for the earl nor would I." With a sigh, he added, "I was hoping to retire at the end of the year but cannot, in good conscience, do so if Ada's affairs are not in order. She needs me and ..." Another sigh. "I will not abandon her."

Miller leaned forward, his elbows on his thighs. "Are you aware that Rochelle has sent inquiries to lady asylums?"

"For Ada or her mother?" The color drained from Thomas's face. "Lady Rochelle's not been well since her husband died. I thought I had more time."

Edwin hadn't noticed anything amiss with the mother. She'd seemed a bit scatterbrained but nothing hysterical. "How would throwing a relative into an asylum benefit the earl?"

"The townhome is a separate estate. It belongs solely to Lady Rochelle." Thomas pursed his lips. "But if she were deemed incompetent or perhaps, if she died ..." He swallowed hard. "... the home would belong to him."

The entire idea seemed horribly cruel. Edwin's mother had left reality behind, but he'd no sooner send her to an asylum than he'd send a horse to slaughter. He'd wanted his mother to live with him, but every time she saw him, she shrank back. He'd become a stranger. And so he cared for her from afar. "And if Ada were shipped to an asylum?"

Thomas opened his mouth, only to close it. He glanced around the room and slowly sat back down. "She would lose everything she worked for."

"What has she worked for?" Miller whispered.

Thomas's gaze flicked to Edwin. He shook his head. "Independence."

"Independence?" Edwin was missing something. Independence for a woman—what in the blazes did that mean? He stepped back and nodded to both solicitors. "I am needed elsewhere. As promised, nothing said here will be divulged."

"Even to Lord Rochelle?" Thomas's voice was weak, a plea in his eyes.

"Especially to Lord Rochelle." Edwin gave a farewell nod and marched from the house. He signaled his footman. Edwin would find out what the Whitworth chit was up to. She might fear Rochelle, but Edwin knew firsthand what desperation could do to a man. Or woman.

Miller pulled on his arm, dragging the duke around. "What is in your head?"

"Do you know this Lydcombe?"

Miller smirked. "He's a simple man. Retired a few years back. His sons run his shipping company." He jutted his chin toward Edwin. "Better question is why do you care so much?"

"I wonder if he's a willing informant."

Miller pinched the bridge of his nose. "That is your first reaction to what we've heard?"

Edwin motioned to the home where Thomas was laid up, then back to the carriage. "We've learned nothing today. I've wasted a perfectly good morning to be in the exact same spot I started. I've spent night after night trying to nail that dullard to the crime. All I've got is one bloody letter with Rochelle's name on it. We still haven't a clue who the author is. We don't know why or what the hell is going on. There's an international ball in less than a month. And the queen wouldn't hear of cancelling it. The most she'd consider changing is having the blasted thing at my Westminster home instead of the palace. We know Ada Whitworth is scared of her brother, which only makes the case for chaining him to a crime. Any crime, at this point. But she's got a secret as well. Between the two of them and every other bloody countryman—"

"Are you finished?" Miller opened the door to the carriage and climbed in. Waiting for Edwin to follow, he closed the door. "Rochelle was sniffing around his mother's home last night after the opera."

Edwin narrowed his gaze. Must everyone he knew keep secrets? "You know this how?"

"Lady Ada's maid left for her home, forcing Ada to interview prospective replacements, at least, as far as your belle knows."

"She's not my belle."

"Apologies." Miller did his customary shrug. "You could do worse. Not better, but definitely worse."

Edwin's mouth hung open. The man was mad. "Is that all?"

Miller furrowed his brow. He appeared to be frustrated that Edwin couldn't read his mind. "Rochelle has lost access to funds. He might still own the properties he'd won through card games—"

"He cheated."

"Will you permit me to finish?" Miller sent him a pointed look. "Rochelle still cannot acquire the rents, buy, or sell properties. His funds with me are frozen. He has nothing."

"And?"

"It takes all of a minute with Thomas to know of his affection for Ada. He would protect that woman at all costs." Miller lowered his voice. "If he has no access to funds, he could easily ship his mother off to an asylum as well as Ada."

Edwin tapped the glass, signaling the driver to return home. "What does that change?"

"If Rochelle sends them off to an asylum, you and I both know he cannot pay the bill. They will be discarded to a workhouse for an unpaid bill. He will be officially free of his family while owning everything."

"Everything?" Edwin scoffed. "A house without an income is worthless."

Miller patted Edwin's shoulder, *ts k*ing loudly. "Have I failed as your solicitor?" Edwin opened his mouth. Miller quickly added, "Ada would not be meeting with a solicitor if she didn't have something worth protecting."

15

Lady Ada Whitworth

The afternoon sun peered through the bay window, the only light in an otherwise gloomy afternoon. Ada had spent the morning interviewing maids, and with each passing woman, she felt the loss of her former servant. The call of Mr. Lydcombe did nothing to boost her mood. Ada squirmed for the fifth time. The awkward silence of Lady Rochelle and Mr. Lydcombe was stifling at best. The elderly man had come at the behest of sweet Mr. Thomas. The solicitor meant well, but Mr. Lydcombe appeared a few years older than Lady Rochelle, never mind Ada. His lanky frame sank into the couch.

Mr. Lydcombe pointed to the portrait of the late earl on the mantel. "That is a wonderful painting."

Ada held her breath. Her late father was the worst topic. She waited for Lady Rochelle to disappear inside herself.

"Ada painted it." The countess beamed at her. "She's a talented artist."

Ada froze. The comment was like a splash of icy water on a

summer day. This was not the Lady Rochelle she'd been raised with. Ada had never been given the slightest praise—she still was not permitted to call the countess by her given name, Margeurite. Ada's late father had loved his wife's name. She was unwittingly named after a crystal, and no one loved geodes and crystal more than Henry Whitworth.

"You must be so proud of your daughter." It was Mr. Lydcombe's turn to beam at Ada.

She stiffened, unused to attention. The last time someone praised her work—other than the newspapers—was her father. She blinked, praying her emotions would stay in place.

"My son always wanted to paint." The man's eyes crinkled. "He dreamed of attending the many art schools in France."

"So have I," Ada whispered.

Mr. Lydcombe nodded. "With my daughter coming out, it was a bit too much to afford."

Lady Rochelle clasped Ada's hands. She froze, unsure if the gesture was for affection or punishment. The countess leaned forward. "My husband believed in Ada's talent. He paid several tutors to come to our house."

Mr. Lydcombe grinned, nodding once more. "That is a mark of a dedicated father."

"He is—he was." Lady Rochelle's smile faltered at her correction.

"The tea was lovely, dear ladies." Mr. Lydcombe stood, his stance a bit wobbly. He must have sensed the change in the countess. A tuft of white hair peeked out from below his hat.

"Thank you for coming." Lady Rochelle followed suit, motioning for Ada to stand as well. "I ... well, I suppose ... I should apologize."

Ada's gaze snapped to hers. The countess was still engaging in true conversation. Fear crept up Ada's spine. If Lady Rochelle was returning to her true self, Ada would no longer have space in the countess's thawing heart.

"Apologize?" Mr. Lydcombe folded his hands behind his back. His expression was soft, kind. He tilted his head to the side. "I know the loss of a spouse, Lady Rochelle. Never apologize for grief. Or for love."

Nodding, Lady Rochelle blinked back tears. She swallowed hard, the welling of moisture slowly returning to normal. "Thank you."

Mr. Lydcombe reached for her, pausing halfway. He let his hand fall back to his side. "I suppose it is I who should apologize. I didn't mean to be so forward. Perhaps I shall call again?"

Lady Rochelle's voice turned wistful. "Please do."

Without so much as a glance for Ada, he bowed and left. Ada stared at the countess, unsure of what had just transpired. She had spent her life at the knee of the late earl, his voice forgotten in her mind. She couldn't remember the sound of his laughter or the feel of his hand on her shoulder. She'd long pictured Lady Rochelle as the pining widow, nothing more. A dizzy feeling circled inside Ada, a mixture of anger and fear. Lady Rochelle as a mother was cold. Calculating. Cruel. As a widow, she was withdrawn but kind. Shame began filling Ada, squashing the other emotions. Ada should be wishing for Lady Rochelle's happiness, not worrying about her own. A thought wiggled in. Her father was a giant of a man. And he'd fallen in love with Lady Rochelle. He saw something in the countess just as he'd seen something in Ada.

Lady Rochelle wrung her hands in front of her, her voice soft and childlike. "I hope I did not embarrass you, Ada."

Ada froze. "Embarrass me?" Her voice was shockingly high. She didn't know what to say or how to act. This was new territory for them both.

Lady Rochelle's gaze was downcast, her shoulders hunched. "I worried over every word. Nothing felt quite right. I suppose I've forgotten how to be a lady."

Her words tugged at Ada's heart. "I can honestly say, I understand."

"It's been so long since I've truly entertained anyone." Lady Rochelle smiled sheepishly. "I'm horribly out of practice." She turned, pausing a moment before offering her profile. "Thank you, Ada."

The words washed over her. Ada stood in the center of living room, emotions swirling once more. She felt as if she was at sea, the horizon hidden by fog. Ada didn't know how she felt. The countess wasn't privy to why Mr. Lydcombe had spontaneously called. Ada would keep that secret. Mr. Thomas had sent him. Doubt crept in. Ada lifted her skirt and ran up the stairs. Earlier in the week, Mr. Thomas had sent a copy of his letter to Mr. Lydcombe.

She entered her room, ignoring the dress Nikolas had sent over. Ada had refused to try it on for the poor modiste who'd dropped it off. The dressmaker only wanted to ensure a good fit which was precisely why Ada would wait until the very last minute to slip on the dress. If the measurements were off—and Ada was nearly sure of it—she would either opt out of the event. Or wear something of her own.

Ada went to her desk. Mr. Thomas's letter to Mr. Lydcombe was simple, proper—Ada stiffened. He had invited Mr. Lydcombe to visit the Whitworth women as there were talks of entering matrimony. Mr. Thomas did not distinguish which woman was searching for a spouse. Ada sat on the bed, the letter shaking in her hand. She should be happy for the countess, but she'd spent her childhood never knowing the woman's mind. She was either curt or brooding.

Thank you, Ada. Lady Rochelle's words echoed in Ada's mind. The countess was more alive in that moment than she'd been in years. She had thanked Ada, not condemned her. Hope began to blossom.

Ada glanced at the clock. Nikolas would be there in an hour. There had to be a way to invite Lydcombe and the countess to the performance tonight. Or perhaps—she smirked—the duo could take her place.

There was a knock on her bedroom door. She went to open it, but Nikolas strutted inside. His suit was tailored, outlining an athletic frame. His face was dark, eyes haunting. Ada's confusion turned to anger. Nikolas had barged into her room. She could have been changing. She felt vulnerable—in a blink, she was the child again and Nikolas the brutish older brother.

Ada pointed to the door. "G-g-g-get out."

"And here I thought my sister would be obedient for once." He leaned against the doorframe. "I heard a little rumor that you wouldn't try on the dress." He nodded to someone in the corridor. The same modiste scurried in, her back hunched.

"No." Ada shook her head. This was crossing the line. She would not be cowed into a plaything. She was not her brother's doll to dress as he wished.

"Give us a moment." Nikolas didn't bother looking at the dressmaker. With his foot, he shoved the door closed. He pulled a letter from his coat jacket. "Do you know what this is?"

"I d-d-do not care what—"

"Allow me to inform you." Nikolas clicked his heels together and cleared his throat. Like a town crier, he lifted his chin and peered at the letter. "Hear ye, hear ye—"

Ada snatched the letter from his hand. Skimming the sentences, her heart sank. Every word was in French. At least she thought it was French. She didn't know for sure. She recognized *docteur* and *folle*. Ada scowled, wishing she'd learned French like Nikolas. *Folle*. A lump formed in her throat. She knew that word, French for insane. She'd been called mad one too many times for her to ever be comfortable with doctors. Nikolas had written *folle* on a few of her sketches as a child. He'd cross out her name, scribbling the word over and over again. This wasn't the first time, nor would it be the last. The threat had lost its poison. Ada had figured out a way to have an income. The asylum was just another obstacle. She needed only a few more weeks before she'd come of age. She would soon be out of Nikolas's reach.

"It's a doctor's recommendation," he whispered in her ear.

She jumped away from him. "You're c-c-cruel."

"Better to be cruel than crazy." He gave a little shrug and folded the letter, slipping it back into his jacket. "If I were you, I'd wear the dress."

Ada had spent her life in fear of him. A memory washed over her. There was a moment, a few years ago, when a light had blossomed in Nikolas. He used to hum to himself and spend hours whispering to an excited Lady Rochelle. Ada had thought he was in love and they were making wedding plans. But then the earl died, and Nikolas snapped back to the same wicked man he'd always been. The same man he always would be.

Exhaustion settled on her shoulders. She took a deep breath. "N-n-no."

Nikolas arched an eyebrow. "I beg your pardon?"

Ada closed her eyes and wished for courage. "No."

"No, what?"

"I-I-I ..." She forced her pulse to slow. "I." She did it. She'd spoken without a stutter. "I will." Her tongue slowly loosened. "I will not wear—"

"Oh." Nikolas patted his jacket where the letter was. "I don't think I was clear. This delightful correspondence was not just for you."

"Who?" She waited, watching his expression change.

A flicker of grief appeared on his face, followed by regret. He grinned, swallowing the emotions. There was only one person alive who Nikolas would grieve for. Lady Rochelle.

Her pulse raced. "You wouldn't."

He narrowed his gaze. "Put on the dress."

"H-h-h-have ..." Ada clenched her fists at her side. "Have you lost your mind?"

He tilted his head to the side, pursing his lips. "That would be ironic, would it not?"

"H-h-have you no shame?" Anger welled inside her. Lady Rochelle was like a child without a defense. She did not deserve the harsh treatment. "Th-th-the woman who raised you, nurtured you. *Loved* you. Y-y-you would throw her into an asylum? She's not insane, she's in pain. She's grieving the l-l-loss of your father."

"Well, well, well." Nikolas clapped his hands in a slow, patronizing motion. "You *can* speak."

"H-h-how could you do this?" Her voice cracked. "Sh-sh-she defended you. S-s-s-stood b-b-beside you when—"

"She betrayed me," Nikolas snapped, his eyes wide. The polished facade was nowhere. A vein ticked on his neck, his teeth bared. Pain and fury flowed from him. This was not the charming rake of the *ton*.

A wounded animal stood before her. Ada stepped back. "She what?"

Nikolas straightened, his face smooth once more. A chill entered the room. If anyone had lost their mind, it wasn't Ada. He pulled on the ends of his sleeves and ran a hand through his hair. In an eerily calm voice, Nikolas said, "Put on the dress."

16

E dwin Harrison, Duke of Girard

EXHAUSTED, EDWIN STARED AT THE ENORMOUS FRAME OF LORD Pichon with an unexplainable fury. He'd never liked the beast of a baron, but the man could be tolerable—so long as each nobleman stayed in his respective positions, the duke as the queen's advisor and Pichon as the queen's cousin. And yet, Edwin had the feeling they would be at odds once more. Pichon indulged the queen no matter the risk. Edwin had made no secret of his concern for safety with the upcoming ball and exhibit. He had little doubt the enormous man sitting opposite him was aware of Edwin's opinion.

They sat in the old castle across the great lawn from Buckingham where Queen Victoria held confidential conversations. Edwin was not small of stature. His shoulders were broad and his stance towered over most gentlemen. *Most* men did not include the baron. He stood several inches taller than Edwin. Several years before, the baron's body was marred by a fire. In an ironic twist of fate, the fire was started by his wife. But as Edwin stared at Pichon, there was a softness he'd not seen before. The baron's face was still a quilt of puckered skin. His sardonic smile still looked more like a scowl, but there was something different about him.

The queen folded her petite hands in her lap, resting her gaze on Edwin. Her lips tugged to an amused smile, her eyes flicking to her cousin. "Have you finished your staring contest?"

Edwin straightened in his chair. He was not a silly boy. And yet, a smile crossed the baron's face. His shoulders relaxed. "No, Drina. I believe we've just begun."

Drina. The familiar jealousy rankled Edwin. He'd dedicated his life to the queen and his country, but he'd never be so familiar as to call the queen by her childhood nickname. He should chastise the baron for the informality, but he couldn't wipe the joy from Victoria's face. And there it was again. The odd feeling that had begun to pierce Edwin. He'd felt it the day he first saw Ada on Mr. Thomas's doorstep—granted, Edwin didn't realize he was watching a traitor's sister—but he'd felt a hint of loneliness.

And here again, he was a spectator of a close family. Edwin had a family, of sorts. His father had been good and kind. So was his mother. But with one parent in the grave and the other now a stranger, Edwin felt untethered. He'd told himself being a relative orphan didn't bother him. But suddenly, it did. With Lady Catherine engaged, his carefully planned future was looking rather forsaken.

"Are you alright, Edwin?" Queen Victoria asked gently, her brow furrowed.

Edwin. It'd been an age since someone addressed him by his given name. Before his father had died, he'd been a courtesy viscount. Your Grace had always felt a bit formal. To be honest, he'd once loved the deference.

"Oh." Lord Pichon leaned forward, his elbows on his knees. His smirk should have been frightening but the mirth in his eyes softened the expression. "Has the Dark Duke lost his potency?"

Edwin rolled his eyes. "Is there a reason I was summoned?"

"Have you turned American on us?" Lord Pichon was not done

with his teasing. "Nothing but business. Where are the manners of our country?"

"How was your morning, Pichon?" Edwin ground out the question. He didn't have time for Pichon's foolish games. Marriage had turned the man's brain to mush. Edwin's missed the baron's former gruff behavior. It was deucedly more efficient than banter.

"My morning was delightful." Lord Pichon chuckled. The blasted baron laughed.

Edwin pulled at his cravat. The room was becoming hotter by the minute. This was a complete waste of a morning. Edwin had rescheduled his appointment with an elusive informant, which was a feat considering the Welsh soldiers prided themselves on secrecy. The duke made it a point to keep all his appointments. It was truly the only proper way to run a life, especially one as hectic as Edwin's. He sniffed, his frustration rising.

"Edwin?" The queen's voice pierced him. She shook her head at Pichon, turning once again to Edwin. "When is the last time you slept?"

Edwin folded his hands in his lap, hoping to buy some time. He'd been summoned by the queen and yet, she wanted to know of his sleeping schedule. He counted to three in his head. Then ten. By jove, he was going to lose his temper in front of the bloody Queen of England. He'd lost his mind.

"If we don't move along, he'll explode," Pichon offered. The mirth was gone from his eyes. He rubbed his jaw, the scars pulling at the movement. "It's time to let him know."

"Let me know what?" Edwin didn't bother hiding the fury in his voice. He flinched at his tone. There wasn't a true reason for his anger. He was the queen's advisor. She had claim to his schedule and could do as she saw fit. He sighed and sat back against the chair.

"A truce," Victoria said. Her voice was hesitant. She didn't meet Edwin's gaze. "Of sorts."

Edwin turned his stare back on the baron's smiling face. "What truce?"

Pichon held up his hands. "It was not my idea."

Edwin's mind raced with all the different ideas that Victoria could have decided. She was far too willing to look the other way when it came to her safety. "But you're in favor of it?"

"No." Pichon's expression sobered. He glanced at his cousin, quickly adding, "But I support her."

"My job—quite literally—is to *support* her." Edwin's voice rose. He'd spent the last year searching for the spy who'd threatened to dethrone Victoria. Each day and night were dedicated to the support of the crown.

"No one is negating that fact." The queen didn't raise her voice. She didn't pout or slink back. She—as she always did—simply spoke. Her words were measured. Careful.

It was enough of a set-down. Edwin felt the shame as if he'd committed a crime. "You are the Queen of England. I will—"

"I am aware of your concern." Again, her voice was neither high nor low, raised nor quiet. And yet, Queen Victoria spoke with an unexplained power. "I appreciate your worry and your insight. I do." Ever so slightly, she titled her head to the side. "And with you here, I have begun to worry about you. And the burden that has been placed upon your shoulders."

Edwin stared at the baron across from him. Whatever the queen was about to say, she'd already made up her mind. She'd invited Edwin *after* she'd made her decision with Lord Pichon instead of before.

"Other than Albert, there is no one else I trust to be at her side," Lord Pichon added. Unlike the rest of the *ton,* Lord Pichon was unaffected by Edwin's stare.

"Prince Albert," Edwin blurted. He couldn't help himself. The queen's husband was a prince and should be addressed as such.

The baron smirked once again. "Yes, *Prince* Albert."

"I've decided to limit the attendance of the International Ball." Queen Victoria's voice dropped. A few days before, she refused to entertain the idea of a smaller event.

"Which countries will you exclude?" Edwin dared to hope she'd see reason and uninvite France. There was enough chaos without adding a revolutionary-infested country.

"None." She didn't meet his gaze. "But we will have a committee go over each invitation, limiting the number of foreign ambassadors."

"None?" Edwin couldn't move past that word. "We know—for a fact—of a French plot."

"We know of a spy who we believe to be French. The current leadership has no ill will toward the monarchy." Lord Pichon was entirely too calm.

"How can you sit there?" Edwin stood with a snap. "Rochelle kidnapped your bloody wife. He knows who the blasted *le Tailleur* is and yet holds his tongue. For all we know, Rochelle could be the spy. He eludes every trap we've set. We know he needed a locksmith." Edwin motioned to the baron. "Or a locksmith's daughter. What else could he—Rochelle or the Tailor—be planning?" He gestured toward the queen. "We cannot risk the queen. Not for a ball. Not for an exhibit. Not for anything."

"The ball is more than a silly party, Edwin." Queen Victoria didn't stand. She didn't meet his rising fervor. "It's an act of goodwill. More than that, it's to show the world that when evil tries to penetrate our borders, we rise above. We do not cower. We do not attack. We are the United Kingdom. And we stand like the dignified country we are."

And there it was. Edwin's opinion and concern were just whispers between cousins. He was in a room with other people, two cousins and guards at the door, but he was very much alone. The feeling pierced him. He stood where kings and queens once had, and yet, was completely untethered. Groundless. He nodded to the queen. "Yes, Your Majesty."

"This was not a set-down." She stood, announcing the end of their meeting.

"It would not be the first nor last, if it was indeed a set-down." Edwin tried mustering a smile, but the pity in the queen's eyes showed how sad his expression must've been.

"Your attendance will be needed at the ball." Worry filled her eyes. She glanced to her cousin before returning to Edwin. "It will be a high-profile event."

"I'm aware." The ball was taking place at his Westminster home. Of course Edwin's presence was required. She was hesitant in her delivery. There was more in this announcement than the words spoken. In a rush, he felt the weight of his exhaustion. He was simply too tired to care.

"You'll be attending a royal event." Lord Pichon waved his hand, as if that somehow would explain the hidden meaning.

"Again. I'm aware." Edwin rubbed the bridge of his nose. The baron had the audacity to accuse Edwin of losing his potency. Pichon had misplaced his venom. "And yet, apparently, I've completely missed what you're saying."

"You'll be hosting an international ball when Lady Catherine is now betrothed to a Frenchman." Lord Pichon sighed. "And *I'm* the difficult one?"

"Betrothed," Edwin repeated. This would have been the perfect event to take Lady Catherine. Escorting her to a royal ball would have been akin to announcing their courtship, or rather, their impending engagement. Edwin was already plastered in the *Thames Tales*. Before his sudden infamy, it wouldn't have mattered who he escorted. He rarely danced or made himself available on the marriage market. He was the elusive Dark Duke, omitted from the gossipy lips of the *ton*. But all that had changed.

"It's not as bad as you're imagining. But you should at least pay attention to some other ladies. You are the queen's senior advisor. You, of all people, cannot look the fool." Lord Pichon's low voice rolled over Edwin. He dusted phantom dirt off his breeches. "I dare say, a lady might even out your faults."

"Dom," Victoria warned.

Lord Pichon smiled. "Did you not say the same to me when Georgiana burst into this very room?"

Edwin turned his gaze to the window, unable to watch the tender look between cousins. The fact remained, there was no Georgiana or Lady Catherine. There was no one coming into Edwin's life. It'd never been a problem until now. His focus had been to keep the queen safe. Not find a lady. The only woman he'd been in contact with—other than his sister and mother—was the sister of a traitor. His prospects were rather dire.

"Girard." With one word, Queen Victoria had his attention once more. She lifted her chin. "I do not mean to cause you more worry. If it is too—"

"I will be there." Edwin cut her off, ignoring the chuckling baron. Edwin had never interrupted the queen. He was the pinnacle of nobility. Until today. "I will pay attention to all the eligible English ladies." He nodded once more. "And all will be secure."

17

Lady Ada Whitworth

The hired carriage bumped along the road toward the Conroy's estate, but Ada refused to speak a word to her brother. She didn't give a fig about the Conroy's musicale. The last time she'd ridden across from her miserable sibling was when the late earl had passed. They'd ridden in the carriage with the family crest emblazoned on the side. The horses and carriage were sold last year when Nikolas's debts were called in. She would not participate in whatever scheme Nikolas had planned.

Ada was a tool, only valuable to him if she could be used. Fear and fury sparred for dominance in her mind. She was terrified of what Nikolas had planned but angry that she was in the carriage at all. If Nikolas was a man of character, he would ensure the safety of his mother and sister—adopted or not. But he cared for only himself.

Even now, he fidgeted and preened on the bench opposite her. He'd taken care to match her blue dress. The fabric was similar to the silky, gold dress at the masked ball, but that night had felt entirely different. She could speak. She felt powerful. She had chosen what to wear and where to go. And for a moment, she had felt safe.

Ada clenched her hands in her lap. She'd felt this way before, the night her father had died. Nikolas spent hours threatening her, belittling her every move. At the time, she pitied him, assigning his cruelty to grief. But the months and years passed by, and he never changed. This was who Nikolas was—cold and calculating.

The carriage stopped in front of the modest stone house. The Conroys were on the outer edge of nobility. Sir Conroy once held heavy influence over the queen, positioning himself as Victoria's impending regent—until her uncle died just after Victoria reached the age of majority. Victoria's first order was the quick removal of Sir Conroy. He'd been on the outskirts of the *ton* ever since. If Ada wasn't coerced into attending tonight, she would have been tempted to include the man in upcoming gossip sketches.

The footman opened the door. Nikolas paused, the arrogant smile falling. For a moment—so brief Ada thought she'd imagined it—he appeared scared. Timid. He quickly narrowed his gaze. His features hardened once more.

"You don't want to do this," Ada whispered, more to herself than him. She didn't know Nikolas's plan, but he wasn't the clever mastermind he pretended be.

Instead of answering, he descended from the carriage and extended his arm for her. Ada hesitated, not wanting to touch him. She placed a gloved hand on either side of the door opening. She could do this without the help of a selfish brother. She stepped down. Her boot caught on the underside of the crinoline, pulling her forward in a rolling motion. Nikolas swung around, righting her without breaking a sweat.

Ada recoiled from him. "D-d-do not—"

"Do not what?" he snapped, teeth bared. From the snarl of his lip to the bite of his words, the man was drunk with malice, his eyes brimming with barbaric ill humor.

Her tongue lay flat in her mouth.

"Do not what?" Nikolas leaned in, challenging her to speak.

Her throat went dry, her mind blanking. Words abandoned her. Her heart pounded in her chest. Once again she was the little girl with tears streaming down her face. Like before, her brother was taunting her while her father was gone—her adopted mother cold and unavailable.

"Oh, you cannot speak?" Nikolas covered his mouth in mock sympathy. "You poor dear. It would be a shame if others witnessed your fragile mind. Your delicate constitution."

Her lips parted. Nothing came. She willed her tongue to move—to speak, to do *something*.

Nikolas's eyes widened, taunting. "Do you think they'll suggest you see a doctor? Perhaps a hospital for those of your ilk?"

"N-n-n-no." A rush of relief came over her. She'd spoken. Ada took a deep breath. She would regain control over her body—for her sake, for Lady Rochelle's.

A trio of sisters came up on them, circling them to enter the Conroy estate. Nikolas flashed a disarming smile. The oldest of the sisters, a dark brunette, returned the expression, a dimple winking back.

He waited for them to look the other way before whispering, "No? And what do you mean by no, dear sister?"

Hope was fleeting. Ada could squeak out a single word. Not a full explanation, not to Nikolas. She tried once more, opening her mouth. Nothing came.

Ada's heart sank. She could have told him all the reasons why she wasn't mad. She should have listed all the ways Lady Rochelle had loved him and refused to see only the best of her son. She could have told him how much she missed those years when Nikolas was kind. Dozens of thoughts ran through her mind. But her tongue stayed silent.

Smug, Nikolas gripped her arm and hauled her forward.

Lady Conroy greeted them, her smile taut. "Welcome Lord Rochelle." She curtseyed and turned to Ada. "And who do I have the pleasure of meeting?"

Ada blinked back the welling tears, a lump forming in her throat. "M-m-m-my …"

"May I have the pleasure of introducing my sister, Ada Whitworth?" Nikolas kissed Lady Conroy's gloved hand. The woman didn't appear shocked or offended. She simpered, purring at his inappropriate attention.

Ada glanced around for Sir Conroy. He was nowhere to be found. His wife was left alone to greet the guests. Ada had not been to many social events, at least not since the earl had passed away. Either the *ton* had changed their rules on social engagement, or Nikolas was running with a different kind of nobility. She breathed in, exhaling slowly. "Thank you." She paused and smiled, allowing for another slow breath. "For inviting us."

"I'm delighted." Lady Conroy nodded but didn't take her eyes off Nikolas.

He dropped the woman's hand. "Has it already started?"

Lady Conroy's smile fell, her eyes hardening. "Yes." She gave a subtle wave toward a corridor off the main living room.

A chill crept up Ada's neck. The Duke of Girard had warned Ada, threatening her if she aided Nikolas in anyway. And here she was, unwittingly a part of whatever scheme Nikolas had hatched.

His fist at the small of her back, he pushed her forward. She felt helpless and alone. She searched the crowd for a friendly face. The brunette sister from earlier broke off from the main group surrounding the piano. She nodded to Nikolas and made her way toward them. Pearls were sewn along her neckline and on the flounces of her raspberry skirt. Ada instinctively reached for her single pearl on her necklace. It was small and misshapen, nowhere near the polished beauty on the woman's dress. And yet, for a moment, she felt as if her late father was near. She blinked back tears—hating that her emotions would betray her. Ada needed to be strong. Nikolas would twist her vulnerability to his advantage. He needed little encouragement.

The woman sauntered forward with a boldness that should have torn her reputation to shreds. She lifted her chin and said, "If it isn't Lord Rochelle?"

"You have the advantage." Nikolas's eyes crinkled, his smile beguiling.

If Ada hadn't known him all her life, she would have been tempted to believe the warm expression in his soft eyes, the ever so subtle smile in his tone.

"I always do." Like Lady Conroy, this woman simpered, eager for his attentions.

Ada's mouth turned sour. She retreated from them, her stomach twisting. Henry Whitworth must be turning in his grave. He'd raised both Ada and Nikolas to lift their sights, to improve their lives—not degrade their name and character to flattery.

Nikolas nodded toward Ada and gave a shrug, as if Ada was the one in the wrong. He left the brunette and came to Ada, his hand gripping her arm. She winced at the pressure.

Through clenched teeth, he said, "Is it all a game to you?" He didn't wait for her response. "It appears convenient when you cannot speak. And then, suddenly." He waved his hand in front of her face. "Like some magical little gift, you can talk."

"A game?" Ada managed to say. Her entire life, she'd struggled to speak, the letters bumping along her tongue. She'd spent years with doctors, some kind and others cruel. The late earl had confided that he once stuttered. He was treated horribly by his nanny—who was promptly sacked. He'd retired several governesses before his own father was satisfied with the treatment. Henry Whitworth took Ada's faults as his own. He spent many hours showing her subtle tricks, running a finger along her other hand to focus her breathing. He taught her to inhale slowly. Anything to match the cadence of her tongue with the letters. There wasn't a game or an intrigue at work. It was Ada's life. She'd thought she'd mastered her stuttering—but it'd come back in full force when the earl was laid to rest.

She blinked back tears. *Is it all a game?* The moisture in her eyes blurred her vision. Even if there was a friend in the crowd, she wouldn't recognize her. Bits and pieces of conversation swirled around her. She would never be included in their world—daughter of an earl or not. Her body was broken. Or perhaps Nikolas was right, maybe her mind was not sound after all.

His hand on Ada's arm, he guided her toward the side door.

A woman in a plum dress stood at the piano, singing a simple parlor melody. Ada didn't recognize the tune. Lady Rochelle once sang for company. But that was before. Ada swallowed the emotion, stumbling next to Nikolas.

It'd been years since the late earl died. Part of Ada was frustrated that Lady Rochelle hadn't moved on and part of her was jealous of the countess's ability to truly grieve, to let herself fall apart. Ada had never succumbed—she didn't have that privilege. Not when her tongue refused to work and her only way toward freedom was quite literally by her own hand.

They were nearly at the door when Ada pulled back, whispering, "Wh-wh-what are you doing?"

Nikolas didn't answer. She'd spoken four words to him. He didn't care.

She wiped an errant tear off her cheek and tried again. "I asked y-y-you ..." Blast it all. She'd done so well just a second ago.

Nikolas grunted and walked into the room, slamming the door behind them. Two men sat at a circular table, papers strewn across the top. The older of the two sat with his back straight and an aura of confidence. He was a handsome man, his clothes well-tailored. If he was not gentry, he must be wealthy as he completely outshone the younger man to his side. In a flash, Ada inhaled sharply. The gentleman was Sir Conroy.

The room was a dimly lit study, the walls donning dusty bookshelves. The servants must not be permitted in his room. Not even the fire was lit nor did it appear to have been cleaned in a decade.

The men stood with a snap, their eyes dark and angry. The younger one pointed at Ada. "And just who the—"

Nikolas pulled an envelope from his jacket. This one different from the one he'd shown her earlier. "Ada Whitworth, if you please."

The younger man opened the envelope, the lettering familiar—Ada's handwriting. Several sketches fell from the envelope. Ada swallowed the rising panic. This was the letter she'd hoped would find its way to Sir Lyell. Not Nikolas.

Sir Conroy flattened the letter on the table with his hand, *tsk*ing loudly. He pointed to the profile of the queen.

The younger man chuckled. "Well, would you look at that?"

Sir Conroy sat back down, his eyes scanning Ada. She shivered, wishing she could hide. Her plan had been to reignite the late earl's legacy. She'd hoped it would be anonymous. But Nikolas must have seen her work. He was there when his father presented her portrait of Sir Lyell.

"The artist appears to want a job." The younger man grinned, his white teeth flashing in the darkened room. "Isn't that brilliant?"

With a finger, Sir Conroy drew the papers closer. He peered over the letter before settling back in the chair. He folded his hands on the table. Silence filled the room. Sir Conroy turned his attention to the map on the wall, dots and circles covered both England and France. Dread filled Ada.

"Why is your name not on the letter?" Sir Conroy asked, his voice smooth. Alluring. He peered up at Ada with soft eyes. This was man unused to rejection.

"She is a woman." Nikolas shrugged, appearing a dandy instead of a shrewd brother. "She cannot offer her services as the gentler sex."

Sir Conroy held up his index finger, not bothering to look at Nikolas. "I will ask one more time, why is your name not in the letter?"

Nikolas smirked and slid to the side, leaving Ada alone in her plight.

Ada opened her mouth. She should confess her true reason for the letter, to anonymously draw for Sir Lyell's exhibit—and sneak in profiles of her father. "I-I-I ..."

Sir Conroy narrowed his gaze, flicking between the siblings. He rubbed his jaw. The younger man said nothing. He appeared to be the employee, eager to do his boss's bidding.

Ada breathed slowly, fighting against her racing pulse. "It w-w-was f-f-for my father."

Sir Conroy offered a sad smile. "Your father?"

She nodded.

He grunted. "Or the late earl?"

His words splashed over her, shoving into her chest. Ada retreated, backing against the wall. Conroy had stripped Ada of the one thing she'd clung to—her link to Henry Whitworth. He was the only father she'd ever known. Her lips trembled.

Sir Conroy nodded to Nikolas. "And what if it doesn't work?"

Nikolas smirked. "They won't be able to trace it." He pointed to the queen's profile. "Her work is impeccable. Lyell hasn't seen the letter. No one's seen her work. And if they do, she won't be able to speak a word against us."

18

Edwin Harrison, Duke of Girard

THUNDER CLAPPED WITH A LOUD BOOM, RATTLING EDWIN'S carriage as it raced toward the Conroy residence. The rain would begin any moment, the final act of a rather dreary day. The sun had barely set before the storm rushed in. Edwin had spent the day with informants, the Welsh variety. Each man had a different version of a Welsh dragon tattoo on his upper forearm. They'd sworn their allegiance to queen and country just like Edwin had done. He'd admired the lot of them, but today, conversations left him drained.

Names were never exchanged, but each tattoo was slightly different. The last man today had two Welsh dragons, end to end. Edwin had aptly named him Twice Over. Although Edwin doubted he would see the soldier again to remember. The Welsh soldiers rotated the informants regularly. They'd saved the country once before. Edwin ignored their eccentricities. He was grateful for the help.

Twice Over was tasked with installing a maid at the Whitworth's residence, but Ada had proved difficult. He'd reported that Ada was easily distracted and noncommittal. Twice Over had made sure that every maid sent over was loyal to the cause. But as of yet, no woman was hired.

It was another strike against Ada Whitworth. Edwin couldn't help the suspicion. Ada might fear her brother, but she was unaffected by the duke. If a woman didn't fear someone as ominous as the Dark Duke, why would she fear her sniveling brother? Rochelle was a coward of the first order. Edwin pulled his cravat loose. He had been heading for his Westminster home at long last—at least until he'd been given information of Rochelle's newest friend, Sir Conroy, a man whose status was raised briefly before Queen Victoria was crowned.

Edwin's carriage was now turning back toward the lower end of London, on the tip of respectability. As far as the duke was concerned, Sir Conroy's neck should be fitted for a noose. The last time Edwin caught him, all evidence went up in flames. The committee's building was ablaze, devouring his crimes. He'd been caught trying to defraud the crown with phantom railroad invoices. Edwin's eagle eye had found the fault, earning Sir Conroy's eternal wrath. The man was not French, nor was he a spy, but he was not to be trusted. Rochelle's friendship with Sir John Conroy—the man who tried to coerce Queen Victoria before she was of age—had added another layer of suspicion for the earl.

The driver slid the carriage in line with the others and stepped down. As practiced, the driver spoke loudly to the other drivers. "Have you been here long?"

"Aye," several men answered back from varying distances, covering the sound of Edwin's escape.

He kept to the shadows, watching couples depart—one every few minutes. With the night ending, Edwin didn't have much time. He circled the back of the house, trying to remember the instructions his informant had given. Sir Conroy had a room on the north end of the main which was off limits to everyone, including his wife and servants. Edwin had never been inside the man's home and would have to guess the exact whereabouts.

Half a dozen dresses and suits were still conversing in the great room, glasses in the hands of the men. Edwin crept toward the north end. The first room was completely dark. The second room was dimly lit. He heard voices and snuck closer to the window. The Earl of Rochelle picked at his nails, pretending to be bored. Edwin had seen that look before. The man moved, revealing Ada behind him. Her eyes were wide and her skin drawing paler by the moment. Her eyes flicked between two men sitting by the window. Their backs were to Edwin. He waited—and was rewarded with Sir Conroy's profile. The man murmured something, triggering Ada to retreat. The woman was scared. Terrified.

And Rochelle didn't care. He nodded and shrugged in agreement or some sort of acknowledgment. If Ada hadn't looked horrified, Edwin would think Rochelle was having a leisurely conversation about trivial matters. Lord Rochelle finally waved his annoying hand about like he'd decided on quail for dinner instead of lamb. He ushered Ada from the room. She winced, making Edwin wonder if Rochelle had been a bit rough in his guidance.

The two men snuffed the lights after the siblings left. Edwin waited for the sound of the door clicking shut before picking at the window lock. It didn't budge. He tried another window. The light flicked on, revealing Lady Conroy. She peered in, her eyes searching the room. The light shone through the window. Edwin saw the sill; the windows were nailed shut on the inside. Sir Conroy had wanted to keep the room secure.

Lady Conroy stepped inside. Edwin crept along the outside of the wall. He would need to return or have an informant slip inside. Sir Conroy was keeping a secret, and Edwin wanted it. With Rochelle as the link, Edwin knew *le Tailleur* was at the center.

He stepped around the corner and caught a flash of blue inside the room. Peering through the glass, he leaned in. A map of England and France was on the wall. *Blast.* This was enough to tighten his focus on both Lord Rochelle and Conroy.

He scurried toward the front of the house and blended into the noblemen and women spilling out toward their awaiting carriages. The outdoor lights cast eerie shadows along the walkway. Edwin's boots crunched along the gravel drive.

"And just when I thought you'd forgotten about me," Lord Rochelle called out, Ada next to him under a flickering outdoor light.

Edwin straightened his stance, turning toward the voice. Rochelle had his sister by the arm, his smile wide, while her gaze was on her boots. "Lady Catherine is not here. But you probably knew that, didn't you?"

At the mention of Lady Catherine, Ada came to life, her eyes snapping to Edwin's. The fear subsided, replaced with curiosity. Edwin felt the frustration fade. She parted her lips but said nothing. She blinked. With a subtle shake of her head, her gaze returned to her boots. There had been a private argument in her head, and Edwin wished he'd been privy to it. He was drawn to her vulnerability. The slump of her shoulders, the quiet resignation, reminded him of his mother when she'd first realized her mind was leaving her. It wasn't long before she forgot her son and the lines between past and present blurred.

"Oh." Rochelle threw back his head and laughed, the sound caustic. He seemed oblivious to the stares he garnered. He sobered and covered his mouth in mock apology. "How could I have missed this? You weren't here to win back your once betrothed. Oh, how indelicate of me. I'd supposed you were the only one who thought you two were to be married." Rochelle nodded dramatically. "Poor man."

Ada shook her head and pulled her brother forward. She was eager to leave.

"Oh, no. Ada, darling." Rochelle released her grip. "Don't you see? The Duke of Girard has cast his net. He aims to snag a defenseless maiden, one who can't deny him."

Ada's mouth fell open. Edwin stared at the twit. For a moment, the facade crumbled. Guilt and regret showed on the earl's face. It disappeared as quickly as it had come. It was enough to hold Edwin's tongue. There was more to Rochelle than Edwin had thought. Perhaps he was just another tool.

Edwin shifted his gaze to Ada. "How did you enjoy the musicale?"

"She found it exhilarating," Rochelle answered smugly.

"Which song did you like most?" Edwin stepped closer. Her eyes were wild, flitting about. Her lips parted only to shut once more. The arrogance he'd seen before wasn't there. Or perhaps he'd read her wrong all along. She again opened and shut her mouth, looking like an adorable fish. Edwin shook the thought. She was very much the prey, and her brother had placed a rather large hook in her. He shifted his stance, his back shielding Rochelle's view. He whispered quickly, "Say the word and I will help."

Ada covered her head in her hands, a cry escaping. He froze. He'd thought offering assistance would comfort her, not undo the poor woman.

Rochelle edged Edwin out of the way. For the growing crowd, he shouted, "The Dark Duke has a way with women, does he not?" He whisked her away in the carriage.

Edwin unleashed a round of curses. Gasps erupted behind him. He spun around and saw the smug expression of Sir Conroy. He'd witnessed the entire thing. Edwin growled, relishing the immediate scattering of the crowd.

A few paces away, he heard the distinct voice of Sir Conroy. "She'll not say a word."

19

Lady Ada Whitworth

On the carriage ride home, Nikolas sat silent on the bench. He'd not apologized for his behavior or the rough treatment to Ada. Not that she would expect it. Just before the earl died, he'd visited her in their childhood home. He'd fidgeted for a while before hesitantly confessing his faults as a brother. Ada had said nothing, waiting for his laughter to come. Surely he had been joking. But the laughter never came. The weeks following had been glorious.

And then her father died, taking the warmth of the family with him.

At night, in the quiet of her room, Ada grieved for him. She screamed into her pillow. She didn't cry at the funeral. Nor did she confide her loss with Lady Rochelle—no, the woman was crippled by her own grief. Ada waited for the return of an affectionate brother. But she was alone.

Nikolas deposited her at the front door like a brute. He did not enter the home and greet his mother—Lady Rochelle was asleep. A part of Ada wondered if he knew that. Or if he was still angry at some betrayal he'd mentioned.

Ada had walked with a heavy heart to her room. Without a maid, she undressed and readied for bed. The room was cold, not from the lack of a fire, but from her future. She sat on the bed and stared at her hands. The late earl had given her a gift, a talent to improve the world around her. She'd wanted to share his legacy, not bring shame to her family.

Nikolas had somehow stolen the letter she'd had a servant give to Sir Lyell at the masked ball. She didn't understand how a sketch could be used for a nefarious purpose. She only knew it had to do with France and England—and worse, her brother. She was now ensnared in their plot.

Ada groaned, her head in her hands. Nikolas had never shown an interest in her art. He'd been rather repulsed and critical. He—like Lady Rochelle—had made their dislike clear. Neither wanted the expense of her tutors and supplies. Never mind that Ada carefully refused the late earl's offers for new dresses. She was very much aware of how much she cost the household.

Both Nikolas and Sir Conroy had pointed to her sketch of the queen. She'd drawn the royalty's portrait next to Sir Lyell's. The first time they pointed, she'd assumed it was to Lyell's. Why would Nikolas have need of an artist?

She went to her desk and gathered her latest sketches. This time she would include a few of the duke. Ada felt a twinge of guilt, but any cartoon including Girard sold at a much higher rate. A sketch of her brother used to garner more sales, but she'd overdrawn him. *Thames* readers no longer cared about the rakish earl.

Ada slid her sketches into the package, her fingers trembling. If Nikolas had stolen her letter to Sir Lyell, he must have kept a careful watch at the ball. She wouldn't be able to sneak off to see Mr. Thomas, even if she'd hired a maid. She couldn't trap Mr. Thomas in her family's affairs. The poor man had helped her enough.

Girard had asked her what she thought of the music outside the Conroy's estate. He'd known something was amiss. But she'd been silent. Again.

Ada touched her throat. She'd failed to speak. Her future had felt so promising just a few days before. Pencils, brushes, and different wove papers were littered on her desk in front of her. At the far end were small lumps of lava and wood coal, one from a faraway land and the other from an old Welsh mine. The late earl had gathered the little treasures for Ada to draw. She'd run up to her room to sketch, only to be surprised by the very desk she sat in now. Most ladies had gilded vanities while Ada had a desk. She ran a hand along the wood, wishing the late earl was able to surprise her once more.

A tear fell down her cheek. With the back of her hand, she brushed it off. She could hardly afford to fall apart now. She wrote a note to Mr. Thomas, telling him this would be the last package for a while. Ada didn't bother signing her name. She didn't quite know how to send the parcel. She couldn't exactly walk up to his office with Nikolas lurking about. And Girard—she pinched the bridge of her nose. He was just as much a concern as her brother. Neither man could know of her income. Not for a few more weeks.

She dug through her trousseau for her hidden stash of bank notes. She would pay double the price for a runner to deliver her sketches to Mr. Thomas. She pulled out the crisp notes—and froze. In the top right corner of the note was a portrait of Queen Victoria. The very same likeness she'd accidentally drawn in her letter to Sir Lyell, her father's onetime expedition partner. Ada stared at the note, her hands trembling. Her mind connected the pieces. Girard had made it clear Nikolas was in desperate need of money. The duke believed Nikolas worked for *le Tailleur*, the famous French spy. The map on Sir Conroy's study had marks all over England and France.

Nikolas needed an artist to print bank notes. The curl of Nikolas's lip, his arrogant smirk, emerged in her mind, his words haunting her. *She won't be able to speak a word against us.*

She dropped the money and scurried backwards. She wouldn't do it —she *couldn't*. Her hand went to the pearl on her neck. Her father believed there was beauty in the misshapen, charm in the ugliest of circumstances. She could see nothing good from helping her brother. Ada would be a traitor to the crown.

Until the first rays of the morning, she paced in her room, toying with different plans—each becoming less plausible by the hour. Ada dressed slowly, a needle in her hand. She pinned the last of her hidden bank notes on her crinoline. Quietly, she snuck through the house, gathering every portrait she'd drawn of the queen, including the sketches in her package to Mr. Thomas. She wanted nothing left behind that would link her to Lyell's letter.

With both parcels under her arms, she descended to the living room. Lady Rochelle was perched at the window seat, a hand on the glass window and a stack of letters by her side. The woman sent enough communication to command an army.

Across the street was the same carriage with the advertisement of Sir Lyell's discoveries. Ada stepped closer. The portrait seemed to taunt her. Perhaps she'd dreamed too big.

"Ada?" Lady Rochelle peered up at Ada, her eyes crinkling. The sight sent Ada back. The countess was not crying nor did she have the haunted look in her eye. Lady Rochelle appeared happy. Rested.

"Are you well?" The words came out of habit.

Lady Rochelle donned a cream dress, ready to tackle the morning without her dark mourning wear. She stood and, with outstretched hands, reached for Ada. "Did you and Nikolas have fun last night?"

"Your hair." Ada's voice cracked. She'd not seen the countess change anything, her hairstyle or her clothes, in years. She no longer looked like a widow. She was a woman. Ada forgot about Nikolas, her parcels dropping from her hands. Lady Rochelle furrowed her brow in question. Ada blurted, "It's different."

Lady Rochelle patted her relaxed chignon, loose coiled curls hanging. "How was Sir Conroy?"

"Good." Ada kneeled and gathered her parcels. She should not have lied. This was her moment to tell Lady Rochelle the truth. Clutching her parcels, she took a deep breath. "You were not up when I came in last night. I would have liked to share a few things."

Lady Rochelle's eyes welled with hope. "You wanted to share a few things?"

Blast. The woman was turning sentimental. Ada would have loved this moment weeks ago—days even. "Yes."

The countess wrung her hands and pursed her lips. "I was tired. I had company."

"You had company?" Ada dumbly repeated. "I thought you were in bed."

Lady Rochelle's gaze flitted about. "I should have been." Her attention was pulled to the bay window. "But Mr. Lydcombe had stopped by unannounced." She kept her profile to Ada. "He brought his niece along. As a chaperone of sorts." She tipped her head, her eyes on her boots. The cold and proper mother Ada had grown up with was nowhere to be found. "She reminded me of you." Her hand made a little circle. "Of who you were years ago. As a little girl. Years. Years ago." Lady Rochelle nibbled her lip and swallowed hard. "Years. It's been years, Ada."

"It has been years." There was a lilt to Ada's statement, almost a question. She didn't understand where this conversation was going. "Lady Rochelle."

"Mother." The countess faced Ada. "Please call me Mother."

"Mother?" A lump formed in Ada's throat. She'd dreamed of this moment, or rather, she used to have visions of this fantastic, surreal blip in time when Ada would be fully accepted by the countess and Nikolas. In her mind, Ada would be gathered in, embraced by Lady Rochelle. They would sit together as a family with dazzling conversations and secret jokes known only to the four of them. That day was today. But Ada stood there—and felt nothing. She had to tell the countess of her son. Ada shook her head. She didn't want the answer. "Nikolas is in trouble."

Lady Rochelle grinned. "Nikolas isn't *in* trouble. He *is* trouble." She looped an arm through Ada's and squeezed.

Ada offered a weak smile. The countess thought all was well. Nikolas wasn't just a trickster. He was a criminal. She pulled back and faced Lady Rochelle. "He's in serious trouble."

Lady Rochelle's grin didn't fall. Her eyes still held the naive hope that her son was still the sun of her world. She patted Ada's hand. "You two were always competitive."

Competitive. Years of cruelty had been dismissed as simple sibling rivalry. Nikolas had taunted Ada, reducing her to tears.

The countess squeezed her hand, her eyes lighting up. "I remember when you were little and how Nikolas would try to interrupt your lessons. You would scream." She beamed, looking past Ada to a memory existing only in Lady Rochelle's mind. "Oh, how you both would get the other in trouble."

Ada straightened, memories racing in her head. All of them included her punishments from Lady Rochelle while Nikolas sat victoriously in the corner. "That is not quite how I remember it."

Lady Rochelle shrugged. "Oh, to be young again. A lovely time."

Ada had just a few weeks left before she would be of majority. There was nothing lovely about waiting for freedom, with the threat of Nikolas on Ada's shoulders. Ada's pulse hummed in her ears. She could not stand in the living room—miles away from her childhood home—and pretend that their history was full of laughter and love. The very reason Ada and Lady Rochelle were under this London roof was because of Nikolas's selfishness.

Frustration blossomed in the pit of Ada's stomach. She gripped the back of the sofa, her tongue threatening to thicken. She took a deep breath in.

"Henry would have loved to see it." Lady Rochelle continued on, completely unaware of Ada bracing against the furniture. "You and Nikolas going to the Conroy's together."

Ada shook her head and blurted, "He's under suspicion for treason."

The countess reached over and patted Ada's hand. "Oh, come now. What are your plans tonight? Will you invite the duke to join you and Nikolas?"

Ada ripped her hand back. "The Duke of Girard is the man who's investigating Nikolas."

Lady Rochelle furrowed her brow. She glanced at the parcels below her on the sofa. "There was a mistake. You and I know Nikolas could never do anyone harm."

Frustration turned to sorrow. Ada stared at the woman, dressed in denial. "I do not think we know the same Nikolas."

The countess *tsked*. "Come now. You two have had your spats. Let us be a family again."

Again. Ada had never been a part of Lady Rochelle's family. Not too many years before, Ada would have begged for a kind word, a warm embrace. She had once longed for approval from both the countess and her son. But that was before. With money pinned to her crinoline, Ada was leaving. She would never see this poor woman again, and with any luck, she'd never see Nikolas. Or the duke. Her heart sank at the thought.

20

Edwin Harrison, Duke of Girard

Across the square from where Ada and her mother slept, Edwin rummaged through Lord Rochelle's rented rooms. The earl had not returned to the boarding house since dropping off his sister. From the complete disarray of the room, Edwin doubted Ada and Lady Rochelle knew of the earl's close proximity. It'd taken Edwin weeks to find the place, and at that, it'd taken a hefty bribery to get the exact location. Edwin had a man placed at each end of the hall—or rather, a man and a woman. Edwin preferred the gentler sex as spies. They were far more clever at absorbing details than the men.

The supervisor confessed Rochelle paid for three months ahead of time, and he'd not seen the poor sop in days. A touch convenient as the end of his three paid months was yesterday. Rent was due, and Rochelle was nowhere to be found. Although, he'd not signed in as Lord Rochelle, he'd gone by his father's name, Henry Whitworth. Edwin searched all the usual hiding spots, under the bed, in the closet—checking for false bottoms in the desk and dresser drawers. There was nothing. If the residence had not been confirmed several times over by separate informants, Edwin would believe this room nothing more than a young gentleman's straight out of university. Not a man plotting to overthrow the queen with a French spy. There was nothing untoward about this room. No papers or secrets anywhere.

Perhaps the location itself was the secret. Edwin went to the window and stood in the very center. Directly across the way was the Bank of England. Edwin stepped to the left, a direct view of the Whitworth townhome. He went to the far right of the window, a direct shot to Mr. Thomas's office—Ada's solicitor. Rochelle was keeping tabs on his sister and her visits to Thomas. The solicitor vehemently denied helping Rochelle but rose to the sister's defense with valor.

Edwin braced himself against the windowsill, the wood creaking. He kneeled and ran a finger down the seam between the sill and the wall. The seam was cracked. Edwin gave a gentle push, and the wood opened with ease, revealing portraits of the queen, some polished and others horribly concocted by talentless artists. At the very bottom was a letter addressed to a *Miss R. D.* with Rochelle's signature at the bottom. A quick skim—the letter was a proposal. The earl had a fiancé, if the letter had reached its intended target. Edwin emptied the sill, gathering everything. He doubted Rochelle was returning. He would set up shop somewhere else.

Rochelle was in love with someone. Edwin checked the date of the letter. The proposal was a few years back, before the late earl passed away. If Rochelle loved someone, there was a glimmer of hope. If he'd loved someone before, he was human. Empathetic. It also meant Rochelle had a weak spot.

Edwin left the room, sending word for Miller to meet him at White's. The club was closer than Edwin's London home, and Edwin had a feeling he would not be in the city for long.

For what seemed like days, Edwin waited for Mr. Miller on a freshly upholstered armchair. He'd caught sight of his reflection in the club's window and pulled the chair to face away from the front. Just yesterday, his valet had remarked twice on his dark circles and his shriveled aura. Fidgeting in the chair, the fabric squeaked with his movement. He glared at the eyes drifting toward him at the sound.

Edwin had enough temper to go around if someone had the audacity to make a comment. Social niceties would have to wait. Edwin needed to find a certain lady and chase Rochelle's past. If he could find the woman—she might be able to shed light on the earl's friends. And with some hope, Edwin might find the identity of the Tailor.

Pulling his watch from his waistcoat, Edwin checked the hour. He was running out of time. He needed to be on the road. The queen's ball was in a few weeks, and he was no closer to securing her safety than he was a month ago. He knew Rochelle was at the heart of it, but everything surrounding the earl was anything but clear. His character was as murky as his past. For a brief moment, Edwin wondered if Rochelle was the Tailor. But that didn't quite add up. The Tailor appeared out of nowhere a few years ago, blackmailing his followers. He'd coerced Lord Pichon's mother before Rochelle became involved.

"And what color is your sky, Your Grace?" Miller asked with far too much humor.

"Sit." Edwin didn't have the patience for small talk.

Miller slid the day's *Thames Tales* across the table and sat. "Notice anything?"

Edwin was in no mood to look at gossip cartoons. Before he'd sent the message for Miller to come, the solicitor had been on a mission for the duke. "Was there a link between Ada and Conroy?"

Miller flicked the paper over and pointed to the gossip section. The duke was on the left, Rochelle on the right, with the Tailor in the middle reading a book—Sir Conroy's name as the author of the book. "Seem a bit odd?"

"Did the paper hire a new artist?" Edwin rubbed his eyes instead of playing Miller's game. The sketch seemed different than the rest, but newspapers would hire and fire at will.

Miller cleared his throat. When Edwin didn't meet his gaze, the solicitor tapped the paper. "Why would an artist draw Conroy? That's a bit out of the ordinary. He's not been featured in any gossip—column or cartoon."

"The same reason we are investigating him." Edwin glared at a butler coming to offer drinks. The poor man backed away without a sound. Edwin turned his stare on the solicitor. This conversation was quickly becoming a complete waste of precious time.

"Put it away before you go from Dark Duke to Brooding Duke." Miller sat across the duke with a huff. Another butler approached. Miller rejected the man with a quick shake of his head. Leaning over the table, Miller asked, "It's a bit strange. Who would link Conroy to Rochelle and you?"

Edwin shrugged. He needed a bath and a change of clothes, both of which he wouldn't have the luxury of getting until he was at his ancestral home. "It could be anyone who was at their musicale." Edwin had questioned Ada in front of the Conroy house for all to see. The artist could have been anyone. The thought made him pause. "He's a peer."

Miller smirked, taking full credit for Edwin's realization. "And if the artist is a peer—"

"He could be our link." Edwin leaned forward. The day was looking much brighter. "We need a list of the families invited that night."

The solicitor nodded. "We should have that by the end of the day."

End of the day. That was too much time wasted. Miller wouldn't have come to White's to deliver that message. "That cannot be your only offering."

"Your powers of observation are astounding." Miller sat back.

"Miller," Edwin warned. The solicitor looked behind Edwin. Edwin refused to turn around and look at whatever had caught Miller's attention. "What else did you discover?"

"I was going to tell you that no one has seen Lord Rochelle since the musicale." Miller pursed his lips.

Sighing, Edwin turned in his armchair. "What is it now?"

In full view of the grand front window of White's stood Lord Rochelle, arm in arm with Lady Catherine. Her shawl was trimmed with exotic furs and her plum dress had crystals lining the seams. Lady Catherine's leather gloves were new and appeared supple. From her fashionable hat to her fine half-boots peeking out her hem, this lady was the picture of refinement. Her dark hair was pulled back under her hat, loose curls framing her face.

Edwin should be overcome at the sight of her, yet, he felt nothing.

Her face was alive in animated conversation with Lord Rochelle, no doubt about her impending nuptials. Edwin waited for the envy, the jealousy, to take hold. Instead he stepped closer, wondering how Ada would look in the expensive dress. Ada was taller by a hair or two. But she had a presence. There was something warm and inviting about Ada that Edwin didn't feel from Lady Catherine. He'd spent his life believing he'd marry the woman outside. He supposed, in a way, she was pretty. In fact, with her fine clothes, dark complexion against porcelain skin—she should be the talk of the *ton*. Edwin flexed his hand. He'd touched Ada's golden hair. He felt a warmth creep up his neck. He'd kissed her, ever so slightly. He'd never stolen a kiss from Lady Catherine. And he'd never felt alive in the lady's presence. He'd never really lived until Ada.

Perhaps this was why the woman had found another to share her life with. Lord Rochelle tapped the window. He must have known Edwin was within. The earl waved, beckoning the duke to join them.

Edwin wiped his face, murmuring, "Bloody hell."

21

Lady Ada Whitworth

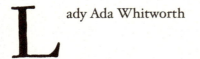

With a parcel stuffed with her *Thames* sketches and another full of portraits, Ada waited around the corner of the stairs for Lady Rochelle to sit down for breakfast before slinking from the townhome. Nikolas would arrive soon. He'd not specified the hour, but Ada had seen the desperation last night. He needed Ada to help his criminal aspirations. Her heart quickened. She was very much alone in the world. Lady Rochelle was quite stubbornly refusing to believe her son was capable of anything untoward.

Ada took the back way around the house, careful to avoid the dining room windows. She'd not yet hired a maid but would soon be scurrying down a busy street without a companion for all to see. She'd skirted social rules the last few weeks. If Nikolas was going to make a case for her and Lady Rochelle's insanity, he would need to only point out Ada's complete disregard for her social rules.

Hopefully, the early hour would be her saving grace. No one of consequence should be up and about yet. Unfortunately, that also meant Mr. Thomas, but Ada couldn't leave anything at the home, not with Nikolas lurking about. She didn't know what today or tomorrow would bring. Last night, Sir Conroy did not seem overly concerned for Ada's welfare, only her ability to draw the queen.

Ada packed enough sketches in one parcel for the next ten papers. She'd already snuck a hint about Conroy yesterday—published this morning—but that was a shot in the dark. It was a moment of frustration with her brother. She'd not realized they were in league with each other.

Unfortunately, the drawing she'd packed about Conroy wasn't very good. She didn't have time for proper shading or dialogue, but it would have to do. She'd at first thought she'd slip in the sketch toward the end of the stack, having the drawing published on the tenth day. But she'd written a note asking for it to be in today's paper. If she could get to Thomas's early enough, London would continue to gossip about the Conroys. She knew the papers would eagerly publish it. Every time Ada drew a new character, sales would soar.

Ada pulled her shawl over her head, hoping to cover her signature golden hair. She clutched the parcels tighter. In truth, her hand was more honest than her tongue. Her mouth had a history of betrayal, her sketches never lied.

She neared the building and froze. The windows were boarded up, and scars from black smoke marked the brick above each window. Ada stood at the door, her heart sinking. She needed to get these packages to the paper but could not do that herself. A tear fell down her cheek, her mind racing. If she were ever to escape Nikolas's clutches, she would need the income. *Thames Tales* could replace her in a moment. But she would not be able to find another paper—or solicitor.

A man stepped from the shadows, his dark jacket too big and his hat tugged low on his head. Ada retreated. He could be a thief or a simple jakesman hired to empty the privy. Either way, Ada wouldn't stay to find out.

He held up a hand. A red Dragon tattoo peeked out in the skin between the sleeves and gloves. He signaled to someone in the street. Ada followed his gaze but saw nothing. They were alone.

In a thick Welsh accent, he asked, "May I help you, my lady?"

Ada shook her head, her pulse settling slightly. The dragon tattoo made sense. The stranger was at least patriotic to his country. She prayed her tongue would work. "I need to speak to Mr. Thomas."

"Aye." He nodded. He was tall but not overly lanky. He was roughly the same age as the duke, perhaps a year or two older. There was a rough quality to him. He'd either served in a war or was a sailor—not that Ada had much contact with either type of men. Until a few weeks before, her circle of men was limited to a solicitor, the florist, and her brother. "Mr. Thomas is home recovering."

"He was in the fire?" Ada's voice cracked. Her thoughts immediately ran to Nikolas. Was he the cause of this? She sighed. No. Nikolas was cruel, but he didn't know about Mr. Thomas. No one did—yet. She knew the duke was sniffing around. Mr. Thomas had warned her.

"He's not burned." The man was careful in his words. He eyed the street.

"What are you looking for?" Ada didn't bother hiding her panic. She was paranoid, as any sister of Nikolas would be.

"A carriage, my lady." He tipped his head out of respect, but his eyes showed no humility.

"Who are you?" She retreated. "Whose carriage?"

"I am here to keep thieves from the building." He tipped his head again.

"Who are you?" Her tongue began to thicken. Fear was starting to take control of her mouth. She needed to know if this man knew Nikolas. This conversation could condemn her.

"I am a friend." He held out a hand. "Would you like me to help carry your packages?"

"No." She clutched them tighter. "They are for Mr. Thomas."

The sound of a carriage approaching sent her nerves on edge. She spun around, her heart in her throat. If Nikolas gained possession of Mr. Thomas's parcel, he would know everything. Her income would be gone. The future she'd thought was hers would be destroyed.

"You have no reason to fear, my lady." The man stepped closer. "Your brother does not know you are here."

Your brother. The man knew who Ada was. Her pulse raced, pounding in her ears. She needed to leave. *Run.* Mr. Thomas lived nearby, but she'd only been to his house as a child. She didn't know how or if she could find it. The carriage came to a stop—a crest emblazoned on the door. She turned, breaking out into a sprint.

The Welshman stood in front of her, his hands out. "I mean you no harm, Lady Ada."

Lady Ada. His words were a cold slap to her face. "Y-y-y-you know who I am."

"Aye." He nodded, keeping his arms outstretched. "I know you fear your brother."

"N-n-no." Ada was not weak. She was terrified of Nikolas, but she would not admit that to a stranger.

"He is not here." He took a step closer. "Let us take you to Mr. Thomas."

"Us?" From the corner of her eye, she saw a familiar frame exit the carriage.

Without a sound, the Duke of Girard came to her, his boots eerily quiet. Dark circles underlined his eyes. His face was haggard. The sight of him rooted her feet to where she stood. The fear subsided, replaced with something else. Ada should run from him. He was eager to throw her brother in jail. He'd been quick to condemn her as well. And yet she stood. A quiet came over her—a comforting peace.

"Are you well?" Girard's low voice woke her from her stupor.

Ada nodded, not trusting her voice.

Girard pointed to the parcels clutched to her chest. "And you were here, delivering those to Mr. Thomas?"

Again, she nodded. Ada should be running, fleeing from the duke. And yet she stayed.

He glanced to the Welshman. "Thank you."

The soldier bowed and tipped his hat. "I'll stay my post, Your Grace." He spun on his heels and disappeared from view.

"Would you allow me to deliver those to your solicitor?" Girard wasn't asking. His steely gaze was rather commanding. He held out his hand.

Ada retreated. The fear in her chest roared back to life. Girard knew Mr. Thomas was her solicitor but hearing the words made her nervous. She didn't know who to trust. Sir Conroy was supposed to be on the outskirts of the *ton*, and yet he showed no fear or deference toward the duke. Girard was supposed to be the most powerful man in England, an advisor to the queen, and yet Nikolas had bested him time and time again. Was Girard secretly in league with the *le Tailleur*? Dozens of other scenarios littered her mind, each one worse than the other.

"Have I given you reason to fear me?" Girard had come closer. He'd need only to reach out, and Ada would be in his grasp.

"I-I-I-I ..." She cried out in frustration. Now more than ever, she needed her mouth to work. She could create an income, a rarity for her sex, but she could not speak to the duke. She could remain anonymous for years as the artist, but could not speak her mind. If she could, just for a moment, be the master of her own body, she would be free. A tear slid down her cheek.

"Please, Lady Ada." Girard pulled a kerchief from his jacket and offered it. His face had softened.

Ada glared at him. She could not take the kerchief with both hands full. It was a dirty trick that she would not fall for. She'd spent her life being a puppet to her brother's temper. She would not drop her parcels for the duke to snatch up.

"Shall we deliver your parcels to Mr. Thomas together?" He stepped back. "And then you can decide whether or not to trust me?"

Ada didn't have much choice, but she didn't know if the duke would be true to his word. She hesitated, fidgeting in broad daylight.

"Did you choose Mr. Thomas because your brother could watch you deliver the packages?"

"What?" Ada snapped, surprised the word came.

Girard motioned to the square, toward an enormous complex more than a hundred acres wide that included offices, hotels, and theatres. "Your brother rented rooms straight across the square. Surely you knew that."

Ada felt the color drain from her face. The fire. Nikolas would have watched it. Had he caused the damage? A chill crept up her neck. She spun in a circle—twice—feeling vulnerable. And watched.

"You didn't know." The duke's expression was stoic.

Ada didn't know if he'd given a statement or a question. Either way, she wouldn't answer. She couldn't risk it, not with Nikolas threatening to throw her in an asylum. She would have to be careful.

"Would you care to stay here on the doorstep where you can be watched? Or shall we make haste toward the Thomas residence?" Girard stepped to her side. She flinched, but he did not pull a parcel from her arms. He simply waited for her to start walking.

He stood next to her with his back straight and complete confidence on his face. His steely gaze was intense, intimidating. The paranoia gave way to frustration. He was like a soldier and she the criminal. She disliked being ordered about, especially by an arrogant, insufferable duke.

She turned, glaring at him with what she hoped was complete fury. "Why would I trust you?" She gasped. Shocked that her mouth obeyed her.

Girard held out an arm. "Shall we go?"

"No." Ada looked at her boots, praying it would keep her tongue obedient. "Give me a reason to trust you."

She risked a glance, peering up at him.

He folded his arms, his gaze boring into hers. "I've dedicated my life to the queen and spent every waking moment trying to keep her safe. You're either in league with your brother or you're terrified of him. I've not yet decided which. I believe the question should be, why should I trust you?"

22

Edwin Harrison, Duke of Girard

For the second time since this morning, Edwin stood before a Whitworth under an afternoon sun. He'd extricated himself from an awkward conversation between Lord Rochelle and Lady Catherine. The earl was all too willing to speak of the many merits of Lady Catherine's French beau. She hadn't changed since she was a child. Her manners and words were practiced. She was everything a nobleman should want in a wife. But Edwin was bored stiff.

Until now. Edwin had received the warning cry from the Welshman and left Miller to deal with the foolish earl. Edwin's carriage had come barreling down the square. He'd thought Lady Ada was in trouble, his mind filled with horrible thoughts, but he'd arrived at Mr. Thomas's office where she was holding two packages. She was not in danger. Nor did she seem particularly pleased that Edwin had come to her rescue. Either that, or she wasn't in fact in danger like the Welshman had thought.

His frustration should have taken over, but he'd felt relief—she was safe. His concern had shocked him. Even now, in her presence, he felt a growing sense of purpose.

Edwin needed to remedy the communication before he made a fool of himself. The stubborn woman to his right was making the last week of little sleep feel like an eternity. He desperately wanted to know what was in the parcels. He'd been present when Mr. Thomas had received another. Edwin had already peered over her shoulder; the same feminine handwriting was on the front. She was the one who'd sent the packages to Mr. Thomas last week.

And like a plonker himself, he'd just shouted at the poor lady. He would never get her to confide in him now. With time running out, he needed answers.

Ada glared at him, her fury evident in her clenched grip and straight back. The emerald color of her day dress complimented her hair. A breeze tugged on her golden tresses, releasing curls from her loose chignon. A strand fell, framing her face.

Blast, she was a beautiful sight. He could not pull his gaze from her. The wild glint in her eyes held more personality than Lady Catherine's entire being. Ada's lips were drawn into a taut smile. Edwin had offended her, and yet Ada refused to back down. She was alive in a way Edwin had never seen a lady become. His mother—long before she'd forgotten who she was—had been meek and kind. So had Edwin's sisters. But Ada had a fire in her, a streak of stubborn that a mule should be jealous of. Edwin's sex would mark her as difficult. The *ton* would believe her unmarriageable if her pedigree hadn't already discredited her. Ada was the adopted niece of the late Lord Rochelle, not the daughter. A fact the new Lord Rochelle would use to his advantage.

"Mr. Thomas can offer you a valid review of my character." Ada marched to the carriage, her chin lifted and arms gripping her packages tightly.

Edwin followed, tucking his smile away. There was something admirable about her temper. In truth, Edwin rather liked getting her feathers ruffled. The movement of her brisk walk undid her remaining hair, her golden curls swinging. With her hair undone, Ada would draw unwanted attention. The sooner Edwin delivered her, the better.

He climbed into the carriage after her, shutting the door softly. The memory of the last time they were in a carriage together was at his forefront. His hands became balmy. He was the Dark Duke, the man with a reputation as rigid as his schedule. He was without so much as a whisper of scandal—until Rochelle and Ada came into his life. He'd kissed the bloody woman. His world had been twisted. He'd let it happen—no, he'd been the one to brush his lips against hers. Edwin had lost control. He flexed his hand, remembering the feel of her hair.

Ada was against the far side of the carriage, leaning away from him. He wondered if she shared the same memory. A flush of shame washed over him. Perhaps she would hold that kiss against him. She groaned and fiddled with her hair. Edwin didn't dare offer his assistance. No. He was here to serve the queen, not steal a kiss.

"A lady without a companion is visiting her solicitor." Edwin kept his voice low, hoping the accusation was hidden. "Am I allowed to be suspicious of this?"

Her fingers wrangled her curls into a quick plait. Without looking at him, she answered, "My maid turned ill. I've not replaced her."

"Lady Rochelle could not accompany you?"

Her arms stiffened. "No."

"And why is that?" He turned to her, desperate to see her eyes. He needed to know if she was hatching a lie. He had no other reason to see her face. That wasn't true. His silent lie didn't sit well. There was something alluring about the woman next to him, and he couldn't understand it. She was the sister of a traitor, and she held her tongue at the most inconvenient moments.

Ada finished her hair, pulling the braid into a tight bun. She kept her profile to him. "Mr. Thomas is my solicitor. Not the late earl's."

Her words were too careful. Edwin leaned forward. Surely she would look at him now. "Your solicitor?"

"Yes." She swallowed hard.

Edwin narrowed his gaze. She was purposely avoiding him. The lack of sleep pulled at his mood. He caught his reflection in the window. He was by no means a handsome duke. Rochelle was the man with a pretty face. But Edwin was not hideous. He did not bear scars of a former life. He was plain. He paused. Lady Catherine had seemed simple to him compared to Ada. Perhaps he was the same. The thought rankled him. He grunted, his temper flaring. "And just why would a lady have need of a solicitor?"

Ada stiffened, tension rolling from her. "Does a lady need to justify every action?"

"When her brother is accused of treason, yes." His voice began to rise. He was a blasted fool, but this woman had awoken something inside him.

Ada turned to him, a parcel falling from her lap. Her eyes were ablaze in anger. A strand of golden curl fell, touching her cheek. "I am not my brother. I am trying to get as far away from him as I can." She grabbed the parcel from the floor. "Mr. Thomas is assisting me with that goal." She sniffed. "I hardly think my efforts warrant the attention of a duke."

"And that is where you're wrong." His attention was very much needed regarding the Whitworth family.

"Ever the gentleman, aren't you, Your Grace?" Her eyes narrowed at *Your Grace*. "Interrogating a lady without a companion, without a guardian."

"You and I both know you're not a lady."

Her mouth opened, her face draining of color. Her lips trembled.

Edwin cursed under his breath. He'd gone too far. "Blast it, that was uncalled for."

She said nothing.

"Lady Ada, I apologize for my behavior." Edwin pinched the bridge of his nose.

Her shoulders hunched.

The air in the carriage had turned dark, matching the storm brewing overhead. Guilt pounded in his head. If his father were alive, he'd give Edwin a tongue lashing he'd not soon forget. And Edwin would deserve every moment of it. "I was raised better than this. I ..." He shook his head. The words seemed so inadequate. He'd injured a lady. And not any lady, but the only woman who made him feel alive. "I've hurt you. I am sorry."

Ada said nothing. She opened and closed her mouth a few times, each time twisting the guilt inside of him.

CLARISSA KAE

"How can I make this right?" Edwin had turned into a poor sop indeed. But what he would give to see the fire in her eyes once more. "You're more of a lady than—" He nearly said Lady Catherine. He'd not completely lost his head. Only a plonker would utter another woman's name to win an argument. "You are the last person I'd want to harm."

Edwin clenched his hand into a tight fist. He shouldn't have confessed that last part, but the words were true. There was a quality about Ada that drew him to her. There was a need and she the balm.

Her gaze flicked to his, a question in her blue-green eyes. She blinked and looked away.

The carriage stopped in front of Mr. Thomas's house. Edwin groaned and pointed to the solicitor's door. "He will hang me."

"Mr. Thomas is kind," Ada said softly to the floor of the carriage.

"You inspire him to be protective," Edwin whispered.

She pursed her lips and waited a beat. "He is more than that. His wife loved roses. When she died, he continued to care for them." She wrung her hands and seemed to focus on her breathing. "He would give me yellow roses to match my hair."

Edwin grinned. He was not the only man infatuated with the golden curls. "I bet he did."

Ada tucked her chin. "He always remembers my birthday."

The words she didn't say pulled at his heart. Edwin had little doubt Rochelle forgot his sister's birthday. The earl was too selfish to see past his own desires. Lady Rochelle was a shell of a woman, unable to look past her own grief to a mourning daughter. The splendid woman next to him had been forgotten. And from her bowed posture, the slight had been repeated.

"You deserve to be celebrated." Edwin's exhaustion had turned him soft. He should be interrogating this woman but found himself wanting to see her smile. He'd rather hear a laugh than a confession. "You deserve to be protected."

Ada offered a hesitant smile. She spoke to her hands instead of him. "You should be careful, or you'll lose your reputation of the Dark Duke."

"Ah, the Dark Duke." Edwin chuckled. There was a time he'd

relished the nickname, but next to Ada it felt heavy. And misplaced. He rubbed his neck. "Well, I do have dark hair. Dark eyes. Perhaps I am the Dark Duke after all."

"I think it had more to do with your soul." Amusement tugged her lips, a whisper of a smile.

Edwin wrapped a finger around her errant curl, giving it a playful tug. "Maybe I need some light to help it."

"I try to tame it. I promise I do." Ada rolled her eyes. She blew the strand with a puff. The small movement pulled another curl from its plait. She glanced at Edwin. "I can't help it."

"Don't." His voice cracked, breaking the word in two. "Don't try to tame it."

Her eyes widened. Without a sound, they held each other's gaze. A current snapped between them. He was aware of her, every breath. Every move, down to the dusting of her lashes on her cheek. Edwin caressed her cheek with the back of his hand. Ada closed her eyes. He leaned forward.

23

L ady Ada Whitworth

The duke's hand was on Ada's cheek. A feeling of comfort rushed through her. She closed her eyes, wishing to hold onto the memory. She didn't know what tomorrow would bring. She didn't know what *today* would bring. But for a moment, she felt safe. Protected.

The carriage came to a stop. Girard's hand became rigid. Ada's eyes shot open. He was still looking at her, all of her. He stared at her, searching her face. Her pulse raced.

"What I would give to know your secrets," he whispered.

Know your secrets. She felt seen. Not as Rochelle's sister, not as anyone other than Ada Whitworth. No. It couldn't be. The duke wanted to know her brother's secrets. "My secrets?"

Girard smiled, sparking a warmth in Ada. Gently, he whispered, "Your secrets."

She blinked, her mouth parting. She was dreaming. He ran a thumb across her bottom lip. His gaze never wavered. Steady. Consistent. She leaned into the touch.

The door opened.

A flicker of grief crossed Girard's features. He dropped his hand with a sigh and descended from the carriage. She felt a draft from his leaving. She touched her lips and shivered from the loss. For a moment, she was warm. And seen.

Ada focused on her breathing. Her heart was racing but not from fear. From something else entirely. She pinched the bridge of her nose. She needed to focus. She'd shared a moment with Girard. That was all.

She knew his goal—protect the queen. If that meant prison for a silly girl with golden hair, so be it.

Nikolas was lurking about. Her brother needed Ada, that fact was a shadow. If she turned quickly enough, she might be able to see Nikolas. It was just a feeling, but the quiver of her lips, the pulse pounding in her head, felt real enough. She gathered her parcels, only to leave the one filled with portraits on the bench. She didn't need Mr. Thomas to know of her brother's plans. At least not in front of the duke. She paused at the carriage door.

Girard stood ready, both hands extended, but his eyes were not on her face. Her hair had fallen from her plait and cascaded over her shoulders. He stepped closer as if he was going to touch her hair.

"Your Grace? Lady Ada?" The worry in Mr. Thomas's voice pierced her.

She scrambled down toward the old, lanky man. His eye and nose were swollen and his gait unsteady. Ever the gentleman, Mr. Thomas's suit was pressed and his face freshly shaved. From the dirty gloves on his hands, he was tending to his late wife's roses.

The sight brought a rush of feelings. For a moment, Ada was a little girl at her father's side, her tiny hands around the late earl's finger. Mr. Thomas bent on one knee, offering her a rose.

Ada ran to her solicitor and wrapped her arms around him. She squeezed her eyes shut, wishing with all her might that her father was still alive and that he was the man bringing Ada to Mr. Thomas's doorstep.

"Oh, child." Mr. Thomas patted the back of her head. He stepped back and gave her a once over. "Come in, Lady Ada. Come in."

With Girard trailing, she followed Thomas, one arm holding her parcel, the other in Mr. Thomas's hand. She felt rather childish, but she didn't dare let go.

Mr. Thomas ordered for some tea and motioned for Ada to sit on the sofa. The house had not changed since Ada was a child. The same sofa with the red striped fabric. The hearth that once matched Ada's in her late father's home. The mahogany armchair next to the fire. The portraits and curtains—all of it brought a wash of memories, not of Mr. Thomas but of the late earl, Henry Whitworth, a man Ada had yet to forget. He'd once sat on the same sofa. The memory pulled at Ada's feet, guiding her toward the furniture piece. If she sat where her father had, would she feel closer to him? Ada had watched Lady Rochelle give in to her emotions, the grief swallowing her completely. And yet, Ada would gladly give in to madness if it meant she could remember the sound of the late earl's laughter.

Girard cleared his throat, ripping Ada from her thoughts. She quickly sat and folded her hands in her lap. Her brother was building a case against her, keeping the threat alive to throw her into an asylum. Ada didn't need another gentleman witness.

"Your Grace." Mr. Thomas motioned for him to sit on the sofa next to Ada. He brought an armchair toward the sofa. "I fear I cannot sit anywhere but here. My back has seen better days."

"Who hurt you?" Ada reached for his hand.

Mr. Thomas frowned, patting her hand. "That remains to be seen."

"I found Lord Rochelle's rented rooms." Girard sat stiffly next to Ada. Gone was the tenderness from just a few minutes before. He pulled at his sleeves. He was once again the Dark Duke assigned with the queen's security. He nodded to Mr. Thomas. "Depending on where I stood, he had a clear view of your office." He tipped his head to Ada. "And of your mother's townhome." He didn't quite meet her gaze. The man fidgeted and cleared his throat once more. He refused the offered tea.

"Are you well?" Ada asked. In the carriage, he'd exuded confidence.

Girard only nodded, but again, he didn't meet her gaze. His eyes flittered about, landing on Mr. Thomas, the hearth—everywhere but Ada.

"I did not think Nikolas was capable of doing such things." Mr.

Thomas wiped his face, wincing when his hand went over his eye. "He showed such promise."

"I saw him earlier today." Girard's posture became even more rigid, his frown severe.

"Doing what?" both Mr. Thomas and Ada asked.

The duke fidgeted again, crossing his left leg over his right, and then changing for his right to be over his left. "He was speaking to a woman."

"Lady Rochelle." Ada felt the betrayal. She knew the woman would always be Nikolas's mother before anything else. She'd hoped the countess would at least wait a day, or even a few hours, before confessing Ada's accusation. Ada shouldn't have told Lady Rochelle that the duke was investigating Nikolas. Of course the countess would take her son's side. She would defend Nikolas. She always had, always would.

"Uh, no." Girard swallowed hard. "Lady Catherine."

"Oh." Ada blushed, the heat rushing down her neck. She was wrong. She'd assumed the worst of her adopted mother. Only Ada would be this petty. "Is Lady Catherine important?" The name sounded familiar. She'd heard it recently but couldn't remember where. Ada wondered if that was the woman Nikolas had loved all those years ago.

Mr. Thomas glanced between the duke and Ada, a question in his eyes. He said nothing. Ada had seen this look before. He was gathering information. Ada turned to the duke, wondering what he could possibly be doing to hold the solicitor's attention in such a way.

Girard tugged at his cravat. He groaned, murmuring, "She's a friend of my family."

"A friend of the family," Mr. Thomas repeated, his expression unchanging. He was still very interested in Girard's behavior.

Ada's skin prickled. She'd been betrayed by her own brother. She should not be surprised that this stranger, a man who said pretty words when they were alone, would hand her over. He had no obligation, no loyalty, toward the traitor's sister. "What kind of friend?"

"She was a childhood friend." Girard's words were sharp. Scowling, he added, "I was promised, in a way. But she's engaged to another man, and your brother wants to rub my face in it."

"Oh." Ada had jumped to an irrational conclusion once again. First with Lady Rochelle and now with the duke. "That is why you were a little ..." She kept the rest of the words to herself.

Girard was missing the woman he'd lost. And loved. The touch of her cheek, the tug of her hair, that was all misplaced. For the third time, Ada had missed the mark. She was talented at sketching people, portraying expressions and gossip with finesse. But she did not understand people. Not even her family.

"Lord Rochelle has mastered the art of social warfare." Mr. Thomas adjusted the pillow behind his back.

"Lady Catherine has taken the worst of it." Girard scowled and shook his head. "In truth, we'd not spoken in a decade." He grimaced. "Possibly longer. It was a promise between our parents."

"It was an unofficial arrangement?" Mr. Thomas quirked an eyebrow.

"Yes." Girard's face screwed up in frustration. "That is what I cannot understand. Not many people knew of the arrangement. How would Lord Rochelle, of all people, know?"

"Nikolas seemed rather desperate," Ada said quietly. She couldn't confess what she'd discovered. Not in front of the duke. She needed to tell Mr. Thomas about her meeting with Sir Conroy and what she believed they were planning. Even Girard admitted Mr. Thomas would protect her. He may be the only man who would.

"When?" Girard leaned forward. "At Conroy's?"

"Sir Conroy's?" Mr. Thomas's mouth was slack. "You took Lady Ada to Sir Conroy's?"

"No." Ada squirmed, knowing how he'd react. "Nikolas came, demanding that I accompany him to their musicale."

"At Sir Conroy's?" Mr. Thomas stood, wincing as he unfolded to his full height. "The man has no shame."

"Which one?" Girard gave a sardonic laugh. "They both should be hanged." He cringed. "Apologies, Lady Ada."

She smoothed the paper on her package, feeling the weight of it. She'd wanted to deliver her sketches in private, not in front of the duke. She'd left the portraits in the carriage. She would have to hide them elsewhere. She couldn't leave them at home. Nor could she ask Mr. Thomas to keep them here. Ada had already asked so much of the man.

"Why would your brother bring you to Conroy's?" The solicitor braced himself against the mantel. He turned and nodded to the package on Ada's lap.

She shook her head. She blushed fiercely. She could feel the heat from her head down to her toes. Girard watched it all.

"I promise you, Lady Ada, I will not harm you." Girard's voice was low. And firm. He motioned to the package. "But I cannot protect you if I do not share your confidence."

"It is a private matter, Your Grace." Mr. Thomas tilted his head, his eyes narrowing. "Lord Rochelle is not trying to marry you off, is he?"

Girard stiffened at her side. Ada shook her head. "No." She rubbed her temples and whispered, "Nikolas was hoping I would do a favor for Sir Conroy."

"A favor?" the duke ground out.

Shouting erupted outside. A gun went off. Horses neighed. Another gunshot.

Girard jumped to his feet and ran through the house. He rushed outside, Ada behind him and Mr. Thomas on her heels. The carriage was a few yards off, both doors open, papers waving in the wind, one landing by the duke's boot. He reached down and picked it up.

Ada winced, her gaze drifting to Mr. Thomas. The solicitor glanced over the duke's shoulders and shook his head. "Oh, Lady Ada."

She retreated, knowing the portrait Girard held in his hand. Her hands trembled, her throat thick. She felt exposed, vulnerable. Girard would never look at her the same. Protecting the queen was his main goal—not protecting a traitor's sister. Or rather, with her forced participation, she would cross the threshold. She would be a traitor as well.

The duke turned to face her, his brow furrowed in confusion. "Why would you have sketches of the queen?" He motioned to the garden where dozens of portraits, from palm size to portrait, were scattered. Most were of the queen or other famous British leaders.

Mr. Thomas bent over and picked up a drawing of her late father. He frowned and handed the paper to her. "Take this, child."

With shaking hands, Ada took the paper, unable to look Mr. Thomas in the eye. She couldn't face his disappointment. Not today.

Mr. Thomas turned to the confused duke. "I have no doubt that Rochelle tried to take your carriage, thinking Ada was inside or her portraits."

"Her portraits?" Girard narrowed his gaze. A storm was brewing. His countenance darkened. Tension fell from him, piercing Ada's chest. "Why would you have portraits of the queen? Why would Lord Rochelle have need of you—of them?" His voice rose with each word.

"I-I-I-I," Ada lifted her chin with the last ounce of courage she had. She inhaled sharply, too quickly. "I-I-I-I ..." Not now. She needed to defend herself, but the portraits flittering along the walkway were far too suspicious. The evidence surrounded her. She was an accomplice—a reluctant and unwitting one—but she was guilty.

"What am I missing? What is going on?" The duke held up a paper of the queen sketched to perfection, her royal profile exact. Girard towered over Ava. "It feels a bit convenient that you're out of words—"

"Your Grace," Mr. Thomas snapped. "She is in need of your assistance not your condemnation."

"Bloody hell, I'll give her assistance. I'll give her anything if she'd answer a real question for once." Girard glared at the servants running to their master's aid, gathering the papers. "Answer me, Ada. Now."

"I-I-I ..." She cried out in frustration.

"She can't." Mr. Thomas stepped between the duke and Ada.

"Blast it all, she can." A vein on Girard's neck bulged. The dark circles under his eyes deepened. "Tell me the truth."

Mr. Thomas gripped the duke's shoulders. "Are you so blind you cannot see the lady suffers from a stutter?"

Girard recoiled, his eyes wide. Ada slumped, covering her face in her hands. The future was dark indeed. The duke would soon piece together the information, linking Ada's portraits to Nikolas's need for money. And now the man knew. Her tongue was wicked. Girard would never look at her the same. She was worse than a traitor. She was mad —unable to control her own tongue.

24

Edwin Harrison, Duke of Girard

EDWIN HARRISON, THE GREAT DUKE OF GIRARD, WAS A BLOODY plonker. He didn't deserve the title of gentleman nor would his father be proud of the man Edwin had become. He placed a hand to his forehead and wished to hell that he could disappear. Edwin's driver and footman had fought off whoever had tried to steal the outfit and were calming the horses, steering the carriage back to the house.

Ada sank to the ground, her head in her hands. Her shoulders shook. The lady was crying, and it was Edwin's doing. He'd been cold. And cruel.

Mr. Thomas stood before him, the words still echoing in Edwin's mind. *Are you so blind you cannot see the lady suffers from a stutter?* Edwin was more than blind. "I'm a mumbling cove. A heater."

"Your Grace," Mr. Thomas warned.

The duke scowled. He hadn't meant to say the foul words out loud. He wiped his face and tipped his eyes to the sky. How had he fallen so far from his noble upbringing?

Mr. Thomas grabbed the duke's elbow, his eyes hard. "She needs your help."

Edwin nodded. "I ... didn't ..." Words failed him. He was the worst sort of man, as wretched as Rochelle.

The solicitor's hand dropped, his expression softening. He whispered, "Tis only one of many secrets she keeps." He glanced back over at the woman, her golden curls spilling over her shoulder. "She's not been given the softest landing in this life."

"I thought ..." He couldn't finish the sentence. His thoughts became jumbled around Ada, long before she ever stuttered.

"Take her." Thomas nodded to the carriage, his lips in a severe frown. The man aged a decade with the worry written on his face. "Lord Rochelle knows of my affection for her. She's not safe here. She can't go home. Lady Rochelle will always defer to her son."

Girard stifled the laugh. He respected the solicitor, but Thomas was daft. Girard could no sooner house Lady Ada than he could Lady Catherine. He was an unmarried man with no relation to either woman. "You must see the madness in that plan."

"Th-th-the parcel?" Ada voice pierced him. She came to Thomas's side, keeping her back to Edwin.

Thomas placed a hand over hers, nodding. "I'll make sure it's delivered."

She smiled at her friend, her eyes lighting with gratitude. Edwin felt a twinge of jealousy. She'd never looked at him like that. Guilt pricked his conscience. Edwin had never been her champion like Mr. Thomas. Edwin had ridiculed her when she was weak. He picked at her, prodded her, when she needed mercy.

Ada turned from them both, walking toward the carriage. Edwin panicked. He couldn't take her to his home. He shouldn't take her anywhere.

"Thank you." Thomas's eyes welled with moisture. "I will meet with Lady Rochelle. There are some things she needs to know." He left with a nod and entered his house.

Edwin stood in the garden, unsure of what to do. He'd never dealt with the tender feelings of a woman, his sisters long grown before he was born. *Sister.* Edwin nearly jumped for joy—like a clod. He would take Ada to his sister's house. She would be well-kept. And far from his wicked tongue.

He opened the carriage door—empty. He slammed the door. Ada had walked toward the carriage a moment before. Running to the front, Edwin called for the footman. A few yards off, he saw the retreating form of Ada, her curls waving in the wind.

"Blast it all." He motioned to the footman. The servant would bring the carriage around. Edwin's long stride covered the gap between Ada and him.

She didn't glance over her shoulder as he approached. Ada lifted her head higher. "Whatever you promised Mr. Thomas, forget it."

"I am sorry." Edwin was at her side. By jove, the woman could keep a brisk pace. Her legs were half the length of his, but she kept the march swift. "I should not have said those things."

Ada sniffed, refusing to look at him. "You'll have to be more specific, Your Grace. There's a great many things you should not have said."

"You're an impertinent chit, aren't you." Edwin chuckled. He loved the sight of her, the glint in her eye. Blast it all, he was only alive in her presence. Had his life been so dull until he'd met her—even if she couldn't meet his gaze directly.

She spun around, an accusing finger pointed at him. "I am an impertinent chit?" Her eyes were glorious, filled with fury. She spoke to his chest instead of his face. "Who is the supposed gentleman that cannot keep his honor? Cannot hold his tongue? But I—*I*—am the impertinent one?" Her nostrils flared, reminding him of an adorable puppy. She narrowed her eyes. "Are you smiling at me?" She growled and spun on her heels.

"I'm sorry." Edwin grabbed her elbow. "You've said more words in the last hour than you've spoken to me in a day."

"I believe Mr. Thomas already explained the reasoning." Ada yanked on her elbow.

Edwin held his grip. "I have said everything wrong. And I don't know how to make it right."

"It isn't up to you to make it right," she shouted. Groaning, she tried again to pull her elbow free. "You made the cut. Why would I allow you to stitch me up?"

Her question caught Edwin off guard. He dropped her elbow and stepped back. His release made her pause. He stood in the middle of the street in full view of various neighbors. Edwin should be embarrassed. He was a duke, a bloody gentleman, and was arguing with a woman he'd only known a few weeks. He pulled on his cravat and watched his carriage approach.

"Lady Ada—"

"You and I both know I am not a lady." Ada spat out the words.

The carriage stopped behind him, and like a clock, his servants stood at their post. Everything in Edwin's life—aside from sniffing out spies—had been predictable. He knew the names of every man and woman in his employ. And that of the queen's. And yet he knew almost nothing about the creature in front of him.

Edwin bowed deeply and said, "My name is Edwin Harrison. I am the fifth Duke of Girard. There are a few other titles I hold, but most of them are French. My family hails from the border between Spain and France. I am the youngest of five children, the only boy. If you were to ask the ladies in the family—including my mother—they would have you believe I'm spoiled." He was awarded with the beginnings of a smile. Edwin dramatically placed a hand over his chest. "It wounds me, of course, because I was a perfect child."

Ada rolled her eyes. "You've gone mad."

"Yes," Edwin said with too much fervor. There was a desperation welling inside him. A need was growing to make this woman with a tangled mess of emotions and curls happy. He held out an arm. "I am not a sentimental man by any means. I spend my days ferreting out the darkest secrets of my English countrymen. I have never been ashamed of my service to the queen." He bowed once more. "Until today."

She shifted her weight as if deciding to believe him. "Wh-wh-wh-what?" She clenched her hands at her side, her head falling back, her eyes closing.

"How can I help?" Edwin whispered. He wanted to reach her—hold her. Do *something* to stop the frustration.

Her eyes snapped to his. "Help?"

Edwin didn't know if he'd said the wrong thing. He scratched his neck. "How can I help you?"

Ada's mouth fell open. She recovered quickly, but the surprise stayed in the slack of her lips. "I ... don't know."

"Has no one offered to help you?" Edwin held his breath. This woman could not be this ill-treated. "Does a doctor help with it? A teacher?"

"A doctor?" Ada folded her arms across her chest. Her stance was defiant. "What is your opinion of those with a stutter?"

"I've no opinion." Edwin had stumbled upon troubled territory. He'd taken the wrong path. "You're the first person I've met who struggles with this."

She dropped her gaze.

He noticed she cut off eye contact when the words became difficult. He motioned to her head. "Does that help?"

She met his gaze, her brow furrowing.

"When you don't have to look at me, does that help the words come out?" Edwin stepped closer, slowly, as if she was a frightened foal. "My father never learned to read properly." It felt like a betrayal, delivering a deeply guarded family secret. But he'd have given her a crown if it'd help her speak clearly.

Ada quirked an eyebrow but kept her silence.

"He was treated poorly. He struggled at university, and my grandfather spread a fantastic rumor that his health was poor. He was allowed many tutors throughout his studies." Edwin shrugged it off. "He was a great man even though he couldn't read and write like his peers. He married kind women and relied on them, mourning them terribly when they died. He relied on them not just to keep his secrets but to be his eyes. His partner."

"He couldn't read." Ada looked down at her feet and bit her lip.

"He could read but not well at all. He once told me that letters got jumbled." He shoved his hands into his pockets and took another step closer. "My grandfather protected his secret. We all did. I have dozens of letters and accounting, all in delightfully feminine handwriting."

The grin appeared on Ada's lips. "Delightful?"

"I can recognize feminine handwriting—even if it's numbers—

anywhere." Edwin brushed phantom dirt off his shoulders. "Ada Whitworth, I've injured you. I've no right to ask, but please allow me to make it right."

"You owe me nothing, Your Grace." She shook her head, the last of her hair breaking free.

"Are you scared of Rochelle?" Edwin was close enough to see the swirl of colors in her eyes.

Ada swallowed hard. "Yes."

"Has he threatened you?" Another step closer.

Her lip trembled. "Yes."

"Does Lady Rochelle know?"

She shrugged and rocked on her heels. "Yes. And no."

"What does that—"

Ada hesitated, her eyes flitting about. "She doesn't believe me. She never has."

Edwin cupped her elbow. "Where were you going?" He tipped his head toward the street. "Just now. Where were you going?"

"I-I-I ..."

"I'm sorry." Edwin dropped his hand. "I do not mean to cause you distress."

"I don't know," she blurted out in a breathless rush.

He nodded to the footman. "Ada, look at me."

She peered up at him, her lashes dusting her cheeks. A breeze toyed with her curls and rustled her skirts. Edwin paused—if she'd asked him for the keys to his castle, he would hand them over. The thought twisted in his stomach. He was on dangerous ground. He would need to tread carefully. There was no future with this woman. She was the adopted sister of a traitor. Edwin knew his responsibilities.

"I have watched my brother hand out promises like the florist gives bouquets." Ada shook her head. "I am well aware of the situation I am in. Do not patronize me because I am a woman—"

"Let me help."

"No." Ada held up her hand. A monogram was stitched on the edge of the glove. His mother's monogram—his mother's gloves. The calf leather from the same shop his family purchased all their gloves.

Edwin grabbed her wrist. "That's my mother's."

"Oh." Ada squirmed.

"Why do you have her gloves?" Edwin asked. He was a fool, softening at her pretty face. She was not a lady in distress. She was a con artist like her brother. He'd bought her theatrics. "I will ask only once more. Why do you have my mother's gloves?"

Her eyes were wild like frightened prey, her mouth opening and closing.

Edwin pulled her to the carriage door. "Get in."

25

L ady Ada Whitworth

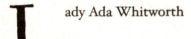

The carriage ride to her London townhome was tense and silent, punctuated only by the sound of busy city dwellers and horses clopping over stoned roads. The duke refused to look at her after demanding she climb into his carriage. He didn't offer information on where he was taking her, nor did he divulge his plan to keep Mr. Thomas's promise of protection.

With surprising gentleness, he helped her descend the steps. Edwin paused a moment before releasing her. He opened his mouth to speak but squeezed her hand instead. Ada didn't know if it was a peace offering or a threat. Their dance had been both tense and tender—much like her family relationships. On shaky legs, she entered her home, eager to change her clothes. Her tongue was too stiff for her to explain why she had his mother's gloves. Purchasing clothes from the secondhand store had never been a problem before. Ada didn't run in the same crowds as the original owners. The idea had seemed so foreign, rather absurd.

Until today.

Ada ran the household here in London and had more communication with jakesmen cleaning the privy or the knocker-uppers than dukes and queens.

As they entered the home, Ada's head ducked and her shoulders slumped. The duke would tell Lady Rochelle what had happened today. He would have to, thinking the countess would ensure Ada's safety. Lady Rochelle met them with a warm smile. Her brow furrowed in confusion, her earlier conversation with Ada forgotten.

"Your Grace?" Lady Rochelle motioned to the butler for tea.

"Apologies for the abruptness of the call." Nothing about the duke was apologetic. His face held the sternness from earlier, his eyes a steely glint. "I interrupted Lady Ada's visit with Mr. Thomas and—"

Ada sighed. Girard cut himself off, glancing back at her. This was not at all how she'd planned the day to go. She bit her lip to keep from crying. Her emotions were too close to the surface. Lady Rochelle would have a host of questions.

"Mr. Thomas?" The countess gestured to sofa. "We've not seen him in ages."

Ada held her breath. This would be the final blow. The Dark Duke would plant another round of doubts, and the cold Lady Rochelle of Ada's childhood would return. Ada had already overstepped this morning with her accusations toward Nikolas. Ada took in the room, memorizing the details. This was the last home she would share with her family, adopted or not. Ada had been angry when she'd arrived at the threshold. Nikolas had sent them away, allowing Ada to take only one trunk. She'd packed a lifetime into the simple box, taking only the bare minimum of memories. Her hand clasped the pearl on her necklace. Ada had taken an old charcoal stump and a small geode. She wasn't allowed to take the portraits she'd painted for the late earl. Ada had made her new ones. Her first large purchase from her sketches was a beautiful wood frame encasing the new portrait. She wouldn't be able to take it with her now. Ada had pinned the last of her money to her crinoline under her skirts, the rest of her savings in an account Mr. Thomas guarded.

Lady Rochelle flashed a smile, looking so much like her son. "You are so good to call on that sweet man, Ada. Mr. Thomas was always a gentleman."

Girard arched an eyebrow, his gaze flicking between Ada and Lady Rochelle. "And I was so rude to interrupt your daughter."

The countess beamed at him. "And you are too kind, Your Grace."

"I am rather selfish, my lady." Girard tipped his hat. "And would like to extend an invitation for you and your daughter to accompany me to my ancestral home."

Lady Rochelle gasped and quickly covered her mouth. She appeared entirely too hopeful in the invitation. Girard must not have been around enough debutantes or their eager mothers. Lady Rochelle would expect an engagement after the house party.

Ada quietly stepped to the duke, placing a hand on his arm. She whispered, "You do not have to do this. I will be quite fine on my own."

He dipped his head, but his eyes were on the gloves. Ada snatched her hand back, her face flushing. She needed to rid herself of these gloves.

Girard lifted his head, speaking loudly. "Lady Rochelle, I must confess. There is a ball to be held in a week's time, and although you'll be needed back in London by that time, I would like for Lady Ada to help me host that evening. I fear I am need of a feminine touch."

"I've haven't the foggiest idea on how to host, Your Grace." Ada groaned. This man was impossible.

Lady Rochelle snapped to attention. "Oh, dear." She placed a hand on her middle, the other to her forehead. "She's not had a proper wardrobe in years. We could not leave for—" She paused. "Where do you live, Your Grace?"

"Wales, my lady," he answered.

"Oh ..." The countess murmured to herself.

Ada didn't know who surprised her more, Lady Rochelle for suddenly caring about Ada's wardrobe or the duke pretending to court her. She held out her hands, her *gloved* hands, and felt the weight of her deceit. Secrets kept her company when her family didn't. It'd given her a sense of control. She felt powerful, working on her own future, hiring her own servants. She'd wanted to move from the city but was still dependant on her frequent visits to Mr. Thomas.

"Would it be so terrible if I sent for a carriage to bring your trunks later?" There was a confidence in his tone. He wasn't truly asking.

Lady Rochelle had a hand on her hip. She'd begun pacing in front of the hearth. Her face drained of color. Ada had seen this look before. The countess couldn't leave her cave. This home had been a sanctuary since the passing of the earl. Not once had Ada seen the woman cross the threshold in years.

"Your Grace." Ada stripped her hands of the gloves and held them out to Girard. She was the reason for Lady Rochelle's distress. "I do not think we can accept your invitation."

The duke didn't take the gloves. Instead he whispered, "I am the bearer of many secrets. If you would trust me with one, you'd find my talent as a vault."

"She cannot go." Ada was too exhausted to keep her voice low. "And it would be improper for me to leave without her."

Lady Rochelle paused in her pacing. "Perhaps if I had more time?"

"We do not need to go." Ada offered the gloves once more. Hope began to blossom in her chest. She would soon be rid of the duke and would escape the townhome. With the money pinned to her skirt, she would find herself in a new town. Her accounts were kept in the Bank of England. She could bide her time before siphoning money. Perhaps she could escape to France and visit the art schools where her father had dreamed of sending her had Lady Rochelle not insisted she have tutors instead of boarding school. Freedom seemed too bright a temptation. She curtseyed to the duke, a lie on her lips. "I am perfectly content here."

"Lady Rochelle." Girard took the gloves and held them up. "I gave these to my mother as a Christmas present."

The countess covered her mouth, her eyes shifting between Ada and the duke. Ada wanted to melt into the floor. She'd underestimated the man.

He gently took Ada's hand. "Do they not fit her brilliantly?" He placed the gloves between her hands and winked.

Ada glared at him. He had the audacity to wink at her. Frustration began to boil. Winking at her plight was a trick Nikolas used often.

Lady Rochelle came to both of them, moisture welling in her dark eyes. "This will be a joyous occasion."

"No." Ada backed away. "The duke is teasing."

"Am I?" He gave her a beguiling smile. "Those are my mother's gloves, are they not?"

Blast. She fidgeted under their scrutiny. She would sort this out, somehow.

"Oh, Ada, don't be shy." Lady Rochelle gasped again and pointed to the small portrait on the mantel. "You should have Ada paint your mother a portrait. She's a bit out of practice, but she was enormously talented before—" Her voice cracked. She glanced around, appearing to be at a loss for words.

Girard's head turned to Ada. He searched her. Another blush. She brought a hand to her face, hoping to buy some time. She needed out of this conversation. Out of this house.

He held up her hand, his eyes on the stain between her finger and thumb. "Charcoal pencil?" Ada pulled on her hand. He held it fast. "The portraits. They were yours?"

She tucked her chin.

Lady Rochelle plucked the framed sketch of the late earl from off the mantel. "All of them, Your Grace."

With both hands, Girard held the portrait. A grin turned to a wide smile. "You have his eyes."

"And his hair." The countess's voice shook. "She is a Whitworth."

Ada's pulse raced. *She is a Whitworth.* Lady Rochelle had never uttered those words before. Ada felt rudderless, her legs shaking beneath her.

"Henry had quite the mess of curls." Lady Rochelle backed into the sofa, forcing herself to sit. Her expression was far away, drowning in memories. "All the Whitworth boys had golden hair." She dug her elbows into her legs. "None of his children did."

Her words were a cold splash to Ada. She bristled—the slight wasn't intentional. Ada knew that, but the hurt was still very much alive. She curtseyed and without another word, fled from the room. A boot on the first step, and a hand caught hers.

"I meant what I said." Girard placed the gloves in her hand. "I would like you to stay with me. Help me with the queen's ball."

"Stop." She offered only her profile to him. "The true reason is you'd like to keep watch over me. You've led Lady Rochelle to think you favor me."

"Would you rather I accuse her son?" His hand was still on hers. "The woman is still in mourning."

"I'm well aware of her grief." Ada had been reminded of the woman's loss every minute of every day for the past four years. "I know what she can and cannot handle."

"You manage the household." There wasn't judgement in his tone, only a softness in his eyes. "Can we trade a truth for a truth? I have a mother who cannot handle the real world. She does not recognize me."

"I didn't agree to your game."

Girard smiled. He was a handsome man when he let his humor in. "Where did you get the gloves?"

"Petticoat Lane." Ada dared the man to mock her.

"Where is Petticoat Lane?" He arched an eyebrow.

"It's a secondhand store, Your Grace." She emphasized *your grace*. Of course Girard wouldn't know of it. He'd never been second best in anything. He was a duke. The world was laid out for him to take. "It's where my ilk can purchase items just out of fashion so we can keep our precarious grasp on the lower rungs of nobility."

Girard burst out in laughter. She fumed and tossed the gloves to him, racing up the stairs. He caught them and took the steps two at time, beating her to the top. "You cannot blame me when that is the greatest line you've ever said to me. More than that, I believe that is your new record for the most words you've strung together." He placed a hand on his chest. "At least to me. You've spoken to Thomas easily enough."

"I'm glad my poverty can be a form of amusement for you." She circled him. "Perhaps you should visit the workhouses instead of the opera."

Girard shot out an arm, stopping her. "You do not trust me enough to tell me your secrets, but I know Nikolas is a desperate man. Desperate people place others in grave danger. I believe you fall in that lot." He held up the gloves. "I am a cad for how I behaved."

Ada pushed his arm away. "Which time?"

He winced. "All of it?"

"You cannot ask me to help host the ball." She sighed and leaned into the wall. "You have no idea what you're offering. What that would mean, what that would imply." When he made to speak, she shook her head. "I need you to leave. You're making knots out of my already complicated life."

Girard's face turned somber. He folded his hands together in pleading. "Stay with me until the ball, and I assure you, I will leave you alone forever."

"No." Ada held up a finger. "I will not be on your arm for the *ton* to judge. To criticize. And then mock when I am no longer paraded about—"

"Paraded about?" The duke groaned. "Bloody hell, woman. I'm trying to help."

Ada whispered softly, "And yet, I am left feeling hurt. Not helped."

26

E dwin Harrison, Duke of Girard

THE LONDON HOME OF THE HARRISON FAMILY WAS FOUR LEVELS, five if the small attic room used for storage was counted. The building was renovated when Edwin went away to university, the grounds updated with ornate embellishments, the classic return of a quintessential English garden. Manicured hedges and clean lines were revived. Garden rooms were divided by gravel walkways with splashes of color on each side. The modern landscape was a gift to Edwin's mother who loved the quiet greenery in Wales. The late duke had purchased the neighboring homes, turning one into a stable and the other into an orangery. The Harrison home was one of only a few buildings not inundated with the growing stink of a city stuffed with people. Edwin's father had gone to the exorbitant expense of installing water closets.

Standing in his late father's study, Edwin had his view of the expansive gardens littered with servants decorating for the upcoming ball. He felt far away from the bustling filth of London, the epicenter of the world. He was council to the most powerful monarch, the guiding light for a maturing globe—and Edwin couldn't behave like a gentleman.

He leaned against the window in his study. Miller had helped himself to the port on Edwin's desk. From where he stood, Edwin could see the roof of Buckingham Palace. As a boy, he would visit this home when his father served in parliament. He'd loved living in the country on the Welsh border as well as London. Edwin didn't have the same bittersweet memories like his sisters, each one determined to be a different parent than they were given. Edwin thought his upbringing was idyllic, but his sisters had reminded him of his risen status. He was born an heir, giving him a lift in the eyes of society. And their father's.

"Are you going to sit down or continue contemplating all your life choices?" Miller poured another glass and joined Edwin at the window, a glass in each hand. "Is this how the next generation of dukes waits for God?"

Edwin took the offered glass, swirling the dark liquid. He should welcome the solicitor's companionship but having a witness to Edwin's mistakes made them all the more real. "I'm a vazey ratbag."

"And this is a surprise? Has anyone ever accused you of being a saint?" Miller sipped his port and grimaced. He coughed and set down his drink. "Did this come from your privy? This is awful."

"Not one for mincing words, are you?" Edwin left the window, setting his glass on the desk.

"Rich, coming from the Dark Duke." Miller leaned his back against the window and crossed his ankle, his drink set on the sill next to him. "I spoke with Thomas."

"Bloody hell." Edwin rubbed his tired eyes. This day had gone on far too long. He'd insulted Ada, faulting her for having a stutter. And then gave judgment instead of compassion when she wore his mother's discarded gloves. "If Rochelle was standing before me, I could tear his character apart. For hours, I could lay into him, cut him down with every sin he's ever committed."

"You would not be the first, nor the last, to feel this way toward Lord Rochelle." Miller picked up the glass bottle of port, squinting at the label.

"I'm a bloody duke and acted like a spoiled cad." Edwin had been wrong at every turn with Ada. He'd taken her to the opera unaccompanied. He'd kissed the chit—the very thing a lady's companion would have prevented. "I told her mother ..." He cursed again. "I wanted Ada to be my guest at the ball. Help me host."

"Oh." Miller set the bottle down. "The ball as in *the* ball?"

"After I invited both of them to stay with me." Edwin braced himself on the desk. He couldn't sit—the chair reminded him of his father and all that the man had taught Edwin. He couldn't pace, the movement tugged at memories of his mother teasing him for his constant fidgeting. Every room, every wall, was covered in tokens of his family's history. The character that should have existed in Edwin's flesh was nowhere. He'd been honored to serve the queen but now questioned if he'd truly done anything of merit.

"It's not the most hideous of ideas," Miller said carefully. "It might do well to invite other young ladies to fend off the gossips. Your attention would be split amongst many pitiful creatures."

Edwin scoffed. "How am I to get Ada to trust me with other people around?" He pushed off the desk and folded his hands behind his head, his gaze on the ceiling. He needed sleep—a year's worth. Time wasn't something he had in spades. "She keeps her cards close."

"Wouldn't you?" Miller threw his hands in his pockets and rolled his shoulders. He was twice Edwin's age but was limber like a university lad. "Pretend you're Ada. Your mum and father die when you're an infant. Your uncle adopts you—much to the chagrin of his self-centered son." He *tsk*ed to himself. "And then your body betrays you, tying your tongue."

"You knew of her stutter?"

Miller's smirk fell. "It did seem rather obvious."

His words pierced Edwin. He was the fool, not Lord Rochelle. "I was cruel, Miller." Edwin was no better than Lord Rochelle, a man the duke was supposed to catch in a crime. Edwin was failing.

Miller frowned and shrugged. "Girard, listen. We've scoured Conroy's office. There's nothing there. The map you saw is gone. We need her to talk. The only people who know what happened in that meeting—"

"She won't tell me." Edwin didn't blame her. "Blimey, I've made a mess of everything."

"There's still hope." Miller placed a hand on the duke's shoulders. "Shall I come with you to gather the women?"

The duke shook his head. "I've dug my own grave. I might as well lie in it."

"Do you know for certain Lord Rochelle was the man who tried to steal your carriage?"

"I cannot think of anyone else." Girard returned to the window. "It was a ghost for all I know. This spy, this Frenchman, is he even real? Or is it an elaborate game of intrigue for a bored earl?"

"Rochelle is clever, but only in playacting. He mucks everything up. He's not some mastermind."

Ada had developed a future using her solicitor. If she could control her tongue, she would have a better chance than Rochelle at manipulating countrymen. It would be easier for Edwin if she was behind the schemes. He could ignore the growing tenderness for her. "But his sister?"

"We already know the answer to that. I'd keep that to yourself. If Thomas heard your suspicion, he'd confess to a crime he didn't commit." Miller gathered his hat. He was off to update the Welsh soldiers who would increase their numbers and their watch. "Did Lady Ada offer any insight into the sketches?"

Edwin turned and mirrored Miller's earlier stance, leaning with his back to the window and ankles crossed. "No. Lady Rochelle was eager to talk of Ada's talent."

"But Lady Rochelle had no idea Ada was visiting Thomas?" Miller was now repeating what they'd already discussed. They'd gone in circles, discovering nothing.

"No. Sadly, the woman does seem a bit mad. I think the loss of her husband was too much."

Miller pursed his lips. "Thomas had hoped Ada would be married or at least engaged. That she would have a sense of freedom."

Edwin pulled at his cravat. The idea of Ada marrying bothered him. He knew it was a silly infatuation. There could never be a future with her—even if she'd want him. Ada had kept her distance. And from what he witnessed, from everyone. Except her solicitor. "Why Thomas? What is it about him that she trusts?"

"He was a friend of her father's." Miller tapped a finger on the desk. "Thomas has wanted to retire for quite some time. He's referred most of his clients to his junior partner but not Ada." He narrowed his gaze. "He was not surprised by the portraits?"

"He seemed to almost expect it." Edwin had built his reputation, his success hinging on small details. Her skill felt like a nugget worth searching. "There were dozens of portraits but Ada was the only one who appeared bothered. She didn't want to talk about her talent. Thomas seemed to know much more than her mother."

"The sketches were in the carriage?"

"She had them in the parcel." Edwin straightened. He rubbed his thumb along his forehead. This had to be the link. "She had two packages. One was left in the carriage. The other she gave to Thomas."

"She's delivering portraits to a solicitor?" The doubt was evident in Miller's tone. "There's no value in sketches. Lord Rochelle wouldn't steal a carriage for something he couldn't use."

"What value is there for a portrait?" Edwin began pacing. He was on the cusp of something, an answer or another trail to follow. Edwin didn't know. "There were sketches of her father mostly. And the queen."

"Why steal them?" Miller pulled a banknote from his pocket. "Any Englishman can see the queen's portrait any day of the week."

Edwin froze—the pieces coming together. "Lord Rochelle is going to—"

"Print money." Dazed, Miller backed into the chair behind Edwin's desk, forcing him to sit. "I'm not sure if that's brilliant or completely mad."

"There is no possible way the Earl of Rochelle is doing this alone." Ada's portraits on the walkway were damning evidence, but he couldn't speak the words out loud. There had to be someone else. Ada could not—would not—be a true traitor. A heavy dread grew in his chest. Forced or not, Ada was a part of Rochelle's plan. She was a brilliant artist. That was the only fact Edwin knew for certain. "He must have a partner."

"Conroy." Miller stared at the banknote.

"Why would they need money?" When Miller scoffed, Edwin continued, "No, think on it. Rochelle acquired properties by cheating. There's income there—granted, they're frozen at the moment, but why money? There's an easier way to wealth than forging bank notes at five pounds a piece. The Tailor, supposedly a wealthy French spy, has plenty of deep pockets. A certificate of railway stocks or something else would be much more lucrative. Conroy is skilled at counterfeit. I nearly had him in irons for it. We're missing something."

"At least the Whitworth women won't be sent to workhouses," Miller said dryly.

"What do you mean?" The dread came back in full force. His stomach twisted. Edwin was a gentleman. His goal should be the protection of Ada, not prosecution. She was caught between her brother and Conroy.

"He's made inquiries at five different asylums. His threats to Ada are not empty."

Edwin recoiled. He'd assigned Ada with a traitorous character when she was a woman at the mercy of her brother. He wiped his face, his chest heavy. He'd doubted the golden woman who lifted his gaze, allowed him to feel—to be alive.

Miller slipped the banknote back in his pocket. "If he has money, he'll be able to keep them locked away a bit longer."

27

Lady Ada Whitworth

Ada packed her trunk at the insistence of Lady Rochelle who fluttered in and out of Ada's room like a worried hen. The countess had yet to pack her own belongings. Ada didn't have the heart to tell the woman she wasn't going to the duke's home. There would be no grand ball and no lavish party. Not for Ada. It was all a farce. She was running away.

The housekeeper entered Ada's room. "I'm sorry, Lady Rochelle, but no modiste is able to come on such short notice."

It was absolutely ludicrous for the countess to suggest a dressmaker could wave her magic needle and produce a wardrobe in mere hours. Ada had secretly told the housekeeper to not fret. Lady Rochelle's sudden interest in her adopted daughter's future was a few years too late.

The countess covered her mouth, her eyes bulging. "We simply can't send you to the duke's house without the proper attire."

"The duke?" Nikolas's voice drifted into the room.

"Nikolas!" Lady Rochelle came to him. "She's been invited to the Duke of Girard's home, and she doesn't have a proper dress at all."

He grimaced for effect, a hand on his chest. "Whatever shall we do?"

"Do not tease me." The countess sank to the bed. "She has a chance at a future, and I've ruined it. I've ruined it. I've ruined it all. I've ruined it." She hugged herself, repeating, "I've ruined it."

The housekeeper backed out of the room, worry in her eyes. Gripping the back of the chair at her desk, Ada watched the scene—an eerie sequel to four years earlier when the countess awoke to her husband's unblinking stare.

Nikolas's eyes narrowed, and his hands clenched at his sides. A vein on his neck bulged. He stared at his mother, the tension rolling from him. His gaze flicked to Ada's.

She fought the urge to wince, to shrivel at his dark countenance, but she lifted her chin. Her lip began trembling. She bit it gently to keep the fear from showing.

Without a word, he pulled his gaze, turning to his mother. He inhaled slowly and closed his eyes. The room shifted. Ada stepped closer. For a moment, Nikolas was not the terrifying elder brother. Nor was he the traitor Girard accused him of. His face smoothed. He became just a man. Nikolas opened his eyes—tired. Desperate. That was how Ada would have drawn him. She swallowed, unsure of his vulnerability. He'd spent his life pretending. Was this another game—another ploy that he'd win?

Nikolas kneeled at the feet of his mother. He tenderly entwined his hands in hers. "Mother, Ada will be fine. She has already commissioned dresses for herself."

The countess didn't seem to hear him. Her words had turned to moaning, matching the cadence of her rocking.

"Mother?" Nikolas tried again.

Lady Rochelle hugged her knees tightly. "Ruined it ... ruined it ..."

"What did you needle today, Mother?" Nikolas tapped her knee. "What colors did you use?"

She paused in her rocking.

"Blue?" Nikolas released her hand. "Did you stitch the sea?"

Ada crept closer. She'd watched the countess rock during the months after the funeral, but the countess had not picked up a needle in years. A memory came to Ada—she was little girl, her hair blowing free from its plait—the countess was murmuring in her bedchamber. Her father had kneeled before her, Nikolas at his side, holding one of her hands. They had spent hours pleading with her to come to dinner.

Ada felt around in her mind, wondering how many other memories of the countess she held. "What are you doing?" she whispered, shocked at the sound of her own voice.

Nikolas dropped his mother's hands and stood. "I do not have the patience or the time to pull her from her mind today." The tenderness was gone, replaced with the cold demeanor of before. Unfolded to his full height, Nikolas looked very much like the countess once had, handsome face included.

"She cannot go to the duke's." Not that Ada ever thought Lady Rochelle would be brave enough to leave.

"Neither will you." Nikolas brushed his hands together. He was done with his mother.

Ada kept her gaze on her boots. "Girard is expecting me."

"It is not the first time he will be disappointed by a Whitworth." Nikolas clenched his jaw, the frustration returning.

Ada had forgotten the mercurial nature of his moods. She could feel the tide shifting. The fear of a wave, the crash of whatever fury he would unleash—settled in her stomach. She placed a hand on her middle and braced herself.

"Are you frightened?" His voice was smooth. And deceptively soft. Quietly, he waltzed closer, like a cat toying with its prey. "What scares you most? Ending up like her or becoming someone like me?"

"Either way, I'm alone." Ada gripped her skirt and kept her eyes off Nikolas. Her tongue was thick but still malleable enough to speak. "I am already alone."

Nikolas paused. Lady Rochelle had stopped rocking but hadn't returned to her senses—the little she still possessed. He glanced over his shoulder at the countess. "She will never be a true mother to you."

"I am aware." But hearing the truth spoken cut her heart. She didn't need Nikolas to twist the knife.

In a big circle, he waved his arms. "All of this. The servants. The drawings. You—" He stepped closer. "Breaking your neck to make sure she's comfortable. Making your little income from the papers. It's all for naught."

Ada froze, unable to breathe. Nikolas knew. Her future was over. She retreated, glancing about the room for an escape.

"Oh." Nikolas pouted, pushing his bottom lip out. He bent down, his head at her level. "Didn't think I knew about that, did you?"

"I-I-I-I ..."

Standing, he snapped, "Stop it. You sound like my mother."

Ada sucked down a haggard breath. *You sound like my mother.* She'd thought Nikolas was the chosen son, the good child. But he scowled at the countess, the disdain evident in his voice. Ada focused on steadying her breath. "I didn't do it for her."

Nikolas arched an eyebrow. "Are you telling me you've given up your saintly ways?"

"Saintly ways?" The fear fell from Ada. She was never the golden child. Nikolas was the son, he had a perfect mouth. He could charm the devil—no, he *was* the devil.

Nikolas *tsk*ed. "It's time to leave."

"No."

He smirked. "You have no other place to go. Girard doesn't give a fig about you—"

"I'm aware of what the duke wants." She waved a hand, motioning from his head to his boots. "It's you."

Nikolas brushed his shoulders. "Well, I am a man in demand."

"I can't help you." Ada couldn't look him in the eye. If she so much as risked a glance, her mouth would disobey. "I know you plan to print money. I can't—"

"Feeling clever?" Nikolas folded his arms across his chest. "You think you solved a mystery. Would you like a party? Perhaps we can convince Girard to hold a ball, celebrate your first step into intelligence."

"Cruel," she whispered and tucked her chin. "Why must you be so cruel?"

Hands on his knees, he squatted to her level. "I am but a baby compared to the world out there."

"*Le Tailleur?*" She dug down inside of herself. Courage wasn't a house she'd ever built within herself. She was the sponge, soaking up her father's affection and turning a deaf ear to the countess. Ada had spent nights watching the opera. She could pretend for a moment. With more confidence than she'd ever felt, she said, "The great French spy that has the country chasing its tail. That is who makes you shake in your boots."

Nikolas smirked. "Well look who found her tongue?"

"If you could not mock, would you be able to speak?" Her voice shook, betraying her. Ada closed her eyes briefly.

"That was fun while it lasted." He clapped his hands together. "But it's time to go."

"N-n-n-no." Her heart pounded in her chest.

He threw back his head and laughed. With a hand on her back, he steered Ada past the countess and out into the corridor.

"S-s-s-stop." She pulled back.

Light on his feet, he circled around her, guiding her down the stairs. She fumbled and fell into the wall, knocking the wind from her lungs. He steadied her. She whimpered.

Wide-eyed, he sprang back, setting her free.

She froze.

His wide eyes settled, his face twisting from concern to frustration. He held up a finger. "Let me make myself clear. I am not the enemy."

Ada's mouth fell open. The man had lost his mind. He was very much the enemy—he'd *always* been the enemy. Words wouldn't change that. "You've threatened to take your own mother to an asylum."

"She's mad. You can't deny that." He rubbed his eyes, and his shoulders relaxed. "There is more at play here than what you see."

"I'm not a child, Nikolas." And yet, that's exactly how she felt. "I can see her grief. Same as you."

He ran a hand through his hair. Pointing upstairs, he said, "You're a fool if you think that is a result of grief."

Ada could not believe her ears. He dismissed his mother's pain like a fly in his food. She focused on her breathing. She would keep her head. She would speak. "How ... how would you know? You've never loved anyone but yourself."

"If you believe that lie, there's no hope for you." Nikolas guided her to a waiting carriage pulled next to the wagon advertising Sir Lyell's exhibition.

The footman opened the door. He bowed, the movement pulling the sleeve of his jacket, exposing a red tattoo. He was another Welshman—the same ilk that worked for the duke.

Fear took a hold of Ada, its grip twisting her spine. She felt the effects from her neck to her toes. Her legs shook as she climbed inside. Staring at the window, she felt the last of her hope fall away. She gripped her skirt, hearing the crinkle of the bank notes she'd pinned to her crinoline. She would escape, somehow. Some way.

28

Edwin Harrison, Duke of Girard

UNDER A DARKENING SKY, EDWIN STOOD ON THE THRESHOLD OF the Whitworth's townhome, soldiers and policemen searching every nook and cranny. Just a few hours before, he and Miller pieced together Rochelle's motivation of printing banknotes. As quick as he could, Edwin came calling, but when he arrived, Lady Rochelle was staring out the bay window, a haunted look in her eyes.

She'd greeted him, asking when Rochelle and Ada would return home. When questioned, she repeated herself, again and again, *I've ruined it.* Something had happened. The woman was mad—beyond repair. Edwin immediately sent for reinforcements. And heaven help him, he'd gathered Mr. Thomas to occupy the countess during the search.

There was an empty feeling to the home as if it was missing something—more than Ada. Edwin circled the home once but found nothing. Including a watching Welshman. Edwin should have been alerted to Rochelle arriving by a Welsh soldier. If *le Tailleur* infiltrated the Welsh soldiers, the queen was in greater danger than he realized.

While the rest of the house was being inspected, Edwin marched to Ada's room, leaving strict orders for anything of significance to be taken directly to him. He paused at her door. Muddy boot prints went to the center of the room, only to backtrack to the hallway. They were a man's boots, but Edwin wouldn't know if they were from a servant or Rochelle.

Edwin tried to envision Ada filling the space of simple wooden floors and pale wallpaper. Nothing screamed that an artist lived here. Only one painting adorned the wall, a landscape of what Edwin assumed was her childhood home up north. The portraits of her father and other ancestors were downstairs. The room felt bland and colorless, so unlike the golden-haired woman.

Her trousseau was tucked halfway under the bed as if undecided to leave or stay. Edwin took a trip around, inspecting the walls and window. The silence was eerie. The entire house felt dull and lifeless without Ada. Even now, in her room, he should be tearing into the furniture, tipping the contents out in a rush. But he was careful, gentle, as if she could see what he was doing. He wanted to help her, not destroy her.

His initial search brought nothing. He felt torn by his duty and his growing affection for Ada. *Blast.* He should feel nothing for her. He couldn't see a future with her—not with her brother at the center of a treasonous plot.

Edwin checked the dresser, no hidden compartment or false bottoms. Guilt pricked him once more. He was breaching her trust. She would never speak to him again if she knew he'd been in her room. Hesitantly, he peered into her closet. A swatch of gold was deep in the shadows. Pulling the hanger toward him, folds of golden silk spilled forward. Edwin let the fabric of the skirt slide through his hands. She'd worn the dress at the masked ball.

Ada was a vision of perfection that night. His mind began listing all the horrible things that could happen to a woman without protection. His chest felt heavy. He would find her.

Edwin found a commission tag on the inside, another purchase from the secondhand store. He smiled at her ingenuity. The woman had produced a relatively fashionable wardrobe at a fraction of the cost. She could teach the ladies of the *ton* a thing or two. His mother and sisters would spin around for his father, showing off their latest dresses. Edwin felt a twinge of remorse. Ada more than likely had never twirled in excitement for her mother or brother. She'd not been given a season, her father long passed before she was of marriageable age.

Edwin stepped from the closet, the weight growing heavy on his shoulders. He was determined to find the woman but wondered if she wanted to be found. She was the link to uncovering *le Tailleur* and Rochelle's plan. More and more, Edwin wanted to know just how close the relationship was between Rochelle and the spy. In his study, Edwin had asked Miller if the spy was a real person and if Ada could be his colleague. The solicitor had refused both ideas.

But Ada was nowhere to be found. The evidence against her was piling up—but deep in his mind, he couldn't accuse her. He wanted to save her. He needed to whisk her away from her cold brother and distant mother. A tease and a smile was reward enough. The thought lifted the weight. Even in his mind, she was letting light into his life. The moment passed too quickly. The facts remained. According to her servants, she was accosted by her brother and forced into a waiting carriage. The Welshman watching her house had disappeared as well. Danger was here.

Edwin needed to believe Ada's innocence, but her mysteries were piling up. Her solicitor was eager to keep her skeletons hidden for eternity. Edwin had chased villains with abundant secrets. There was an entire section in London that was too dark for society, dubbed the Abyss. Some people were beyond repair. He shook the thought. Not Ada. She was not beyond reach. If she was found to be guilty, he would remain in her corner. She would not be cast away. The thought eased his worry.

Down on his knees, Edwin tugged the heavy trousseau out from under the bed. With no lock on the latch, he wasn't hopeful it contained anything of worth. The lid squawked as he opened it. Several newspaper clippings were bound together. At a closer glance, the entire bundle consisted only of the gossip cartoon. He frowned. He'd thought better of her until that moment. He'd met a cartoonist once—a cranky old man with a belly as large as his ego. Ada had not seemed interested in simple gossip before. The *ton* had empty heads and busy lips, something she'd never appeared to have.

Perhaps Edwin was wrong about her. She was an artist, according to Lady Rochelle. Perhaps she only held an admiration for the *Thames* cartoonist.

Below the clippings was a sketch on wove paper—of him. He was in the corner of a room, donned in the suit he'd worn at the ball. His brow wasn't furrowed like how the gossip artist had always drawn him. His eyes were full of wonder, the way he'd felt when she'd entered the ballroom. This was how Ada had portrayed him. The warmth came back, his pulse humming as if she was in the room. There was no title or wording depicting the foolish Dark Duke. No, she'd simply drawn him as Edwin. To the queen, he was an advisor and to the papers, he was a vengeful duke. But Ada had drawn him as a simple man. The paper trembled in his hand.

Did Ada know the power she held? There was potency in beauty— many an empire was felled by vixen. Ada was tempting enough, the way the sun lit her hair. She was almost angelic when the breeze toyed with her curls.

"Have you found anything of use?" Miller interrupted Edwin's thoughts. Edwin hated how the solicitor could sneak up on him. Miller frowned. "There's a broken clay pipe found in the bushes. I don't think that came from our Welshman."

"I don't remember smelling tobacco on any that I met." Edwin set the gossip cartoons aside. Below the portraits were a geode and a tied bag. He undid the bag and rolled a piece of charcoal into his palm. "Why would you keep a piece of charcoal?"

"According to Thomas, her father was an avid naturalist with Sir Charles Lyell. They traveled and documented loads of things." Miller peered over Edwin's shoulder. "Lyell is expected to have a large showcase in the exhibition. He's on several advertisements throughout the city."

"Sir Lyell is on the continent." Edwin repacked the trunk and slid it under the bed. "The queen complained last month that he was not going to attend."

Miller shrugged. "I've seen a wagon advertising his discoveries outside Thomas's office."

The wagon. Edwin rushed to the window. Just a few days before, there had been a wagon on the opposite street. Lady Rochelle had been at the bay window, her gaze on the covering. "That's how the Tailor has been one step ahead of us. He's been watching." The wagon was gone. And if Edwin had to guess, the same wagon in front of Thomas's office was no longer there. Rochelle had what he needed, Ada.

"Why go through such trouble?" Miller rubbed his neck, peeking into the drawers of her desk. "If Rochelle wanted his sister, why not just take her. He's her legal guardian. Why go through all these motions?"

"Why do any of it?" Edwin could think of a dozen other ways to spend the day. Threatening a country was not on his list. He squatted down, his finger wiping the outline of one of the muddy boot prints. Rubbing the mud between his fingers, a horrid smell wafted up.

Miller squatted next to him, his nose scrunching. "That's rather putrid."

"Smells like a privy." And something else. Edwin sniffed once more. There was a sandy texture. "A bit fishy too."

Miller cocked his head to the side. "Rochelle has not returned to his rented rooms, nor has Conroy been to his home. This could be their new meeting place."

"We need to ask the staff. This could just be a butler's boot prints." Edwin stood, exhaustion settling on his shoulders. "We need more to go on."

With a hand on his head, Miller circled the room. "We know Rochelle was in debt. And then *not*."

Edwin murmured his affirmation.

"He needed a locksmith. And then money. The locksmith fell through." Miller frowned, the lines around his eyes aging him. "At least, as far as we know. We know Ada was meeting with Thomas for something. She had an asset or an income."

Edwin shook his head. "If she had an income, Rochelle would have siphoned it already."

"Maybe Thomas kept it from him. He wasn't exactly forthcoming with us." Miller wiped his face. "What if she knew? What if she was sending her portraits to Thomas to keep for him, an attempt to keep them out of reach of Rochelle?"

The idea didn't sit well. They might be on the right track, but Edwin wasn't quite sure of the woman anymore. Or her brother. "Why keep the portraits safe when all Rochelle needed was Ada. The portrait could only go so far."

Miller shrugged. "But how could Rochelle show the almighty French spy her talent? It's not like she can announce herself. The woman becomes anxious rather quickly."

Guilt pierced Edwin. He'd been the cause of her anxiety on more than one occasion. He was not the gentleman he was born to become. He'd not helped a lady in distress. He was the cause. Not the savior.

Miller placed a hand on his shoulder. "I didn't mean to pick at your wounds."

Edwin's pulse raced. He didn't understand it. He'd chased plenty of criminals before, but he'd never been this out of sorts.

A policeman cleared his throat. "Your Grace?"

Edwin ordered, "Out with it."

The man fidgeted, his eyes flicking between Miller and Edwin. He tipped his hat and said, "We found a body, Your Grace."

29

Lady Ada Whitworth

The carriage swayed and bobbed along London's cobbled streets. Ada clutched her skirts and focused on her breathing. Nikolas sat opposite her, his expression stoic. Thunder clapped above them, the windows shivering in response. Ada's heart leapt into her throat, clinging for dear life.

The familiar London streets quickly faded, along with the stoned road. A wheel hit a divot in the street, lurching the carriage to the side. Ada gripped the bench with all her might—to no avail. She slid across the bench. Her hand raked the curtains, tearing them from the windows. She slammed into Nikolas.

Without a sound, he tossed her back to her side of the carriage. He didn't spare her a glance. He returned to his vigil of staring darkly at the passing buildings. Ada gawked at him, her tongue thick. She wanted to scream, rail against the injustice of his treatment. He sat on the edge of the bench, his leg bouncing with nervous energy. A purple streak of lightning flitted across the sky, the light spilling into the carriage and softening Nikolas's profile.

He flexed his hands, his lips taut. He was crumbling under the pressure. Nikolas deserved it, every last anxious thought. The facade of the arrogant criminal was nowhere. Nikolas could charm the ladies of the *ton* and win a verbal sparring with Girard, but he could not hide the doubt creeping across his face. Small crescent moons appeared under his eyes. He blinked, changing his expression in an instant. His brow dropped the heavy concentration. He blinked once more, tugging at Ada's heart.

She stiffened. He'd spent their childhood taunting her. The only relief she'd felt was when he'd shipped Ada and his mother from his newly inherited home. The tender affection between siblings was not a feeling Nikolas could contain. He was incapable of love.

The carriage bounced and swayed along the uneven road. A stench wafted into the carriage. Nikolas pulled a kerchief from his jacket, tossing it to Ada without a glance. The kerchief fell on her lap. She refused to touch it and kept her hands on the bench. There was a purpose to everything Nikolas did, even his kindness.

"It's not poisoned." He leaned against the bench, his hands no longer flexing. His brow had smoothed. "Not that you would believe me either way."

Ada steadied her breath and rolled her tongue around in her mouth. She was in control. "Give me a reason to trust you."

The stench grew worse as they followed along the Thames. Dozens of decaying fish were belly up on the banks. The carriage left the river, and the smell grew fouler. Ada eyed the kerchief on her lap. The temptation grew.

"You'll need the fabric in another few streets." Nikolas never strayed from his focus on the view.

"Why?" Ada's tongue relaxed. She could speak so long as only his profile faced her. "Why are you doing this?"

His lips stretched to a severe frown. "Why be a saint when you could be the devil?"

Ada traced the stitching along the kerchief. The air in the carriage had changed despite the horrid smell. "Do you know why you're doing this?"

He shrugged. "I am a selfish man. That is reason enough."

"You've dragged me from my home." Both hands were now tracing the stitching. She hadn't raised the kerchief to her nose—no, she couldn't succumb quite yet. She breathed through her mouth. She swallowed the horrid taste. There was more to the stench than overwhelming privies. The air smelled of death. And despair. "At least tell me why."

"There is no why."

Her finger found a monogram stitched into the corner. Ada paused and rubbed her thumb over the middle initial, reserved for the last name. Instead of a *W* for Whitworth, there was *D*. Squinting, she held it up to the window. The first letter was *R* instead of *N* for Nikolas. Sir Conroy couldn't be the owner, nor could his wife.

The carriage bounced along, jostling both Ada and the earl. Her stomach clenched as she fell to the floor, Nikolas's boot in her back. She scrambled to her bench, away from his feet. He would kick her without hesitation.

Nikolas was sprawled in awkward angles, his torso on his bench, his boots on the floor of the carriage. He sighed and slowly sat back on the bench. His shoulders were hunched. He wiped his face, pausing a moment over his nose. He glanced at Ada—his eyebrow arching. "What is it?"

"Nothing." Ada hadn't realized she was staring. She dropped the kerchief and turned her gaze on the window. With a hand on her stomach, she prayed it would stop tossing and turning within her. She tried breathing through her mouth, but the taste of London's filth threatened her breakfast.

"Here." Nikolas pulled a lavender sachet from his wrist and tossed it to her.

Grateful, she held it to her nose and breathed deeply. Her stomach settled. She relaxed into the bench. She couldn't remember the last time she'd held a sachet. Her daily life limited her ventures to the opera, Mr. Thomas, and the secondhand store. She had no need to travel toward the darker parts of London or for days at a time on England's roadways.

Nikolas's mouth hung open. He must have been breathing through his nose. His color paled.

Ada glanced down at his sachet. He'd sacrificed his comfort for hers. She cupped the little fabric bag, debating on whether to keep his offering. Lady Rochelle was more than likely the creator of his sachet. Nikolas had always been her cherished treasure. Ada closed her eyes, pretending for a moment that she was more than the adopted orphan and, instead of Nikolas, Lady Rochelle had filled one of her own kerchiefs with lavender for Ada. She opened her eyes. Nikolas had turned rather green. She took one long breath and tossed the sachet back to him. It hit his elbow and fell to the floor.

He started and reached for it but didn't put it to his nose. He hesitated, his thumb and forefinger rubbing the stitch. His gaze flicked to the kerchief on Ada's lap. His eyes filled with longing and regret.

Ada gently picked up the kerchief and showed him the monogram. "Whose is this?"

Nikolas grimaced, his mouth twisting into a painful scowl. "No one's."

"It's not yours. Or anyone I know."

He waved away her words, dismissing them as annoying gnats. His countenance changed. He slunk back to the bench, his chin lifted in arrogant confidence. "I can list on one hand the people you know."

She waited for the fury, the caged feeling that sent her nerves on edge. There was nothing. Ada had spent her life shrinking from the venom in his words. She'd been tied, unable to fight back. But here in the carriage, she'd seen a glimmer of Nikolas's humanity. There was vulnerability in him.

Instead of firing back a glare, she inhaled slowly. "Thank you for letting me borrow the sachet."

Nikolas's eyes widened. He'd not expected her gratitude. In a flash, the surprise was gone, replaced once more with a stony expression. "You're of no use if you're vomiting."

"And you are of no use if you care." Ada's mouth fell open, realizing she'd said the words. More than that, she'd not stumbled and stuttered her way through the sentence.

"She'll never care for you," he said quietly. Grief filled the lines in his face. "She's not capable."

"Who's not capable?" Ada asked, unsure if he spoke of the mysterious owner of the kerchief or someone else.

Nikolas rolled his eyes, the sarcasm returning with full force. "Can you truly sit there and think my mother is of sound mind? That she has the capacity to love and care for you and me?"

My mother. Ada swallowed the slight. Nikolas was her child, not Ada. "My mother ..." she repeated.

Nikolas waved his hand. "Your mother is turning in her grave."

Ada winced as if he'd struck her. He didn't have the right to speak of her real mother. He'd not been around as a brother. He'd not cared for her. There was no affection between them.

"Why do you care?" The stench filled the carriage, but she didn't care. Her stomach tossed and turned, but anger had taken hold of her. "Why bother with speaking of my mother at all? It's not as if you've ever cared about my well-being. I cannot be angry at the countess for not loving me now when she never did."

"If I cared so little for you, I would have hauled you to Conroy's years ago." Rochelle spat out the words. "I wouldn't have kept you far from me and the spy."

"What difference would it make?" Her tongue began to thicken. Soon, she wouldn't be able to speak freely. She hurried to add, "Your mother was at least consistent in her coldness. You pretended to care a few years ago, only to return to th-th-this." She cut herself off, her mouth mutinous.

"The greatest gift I could ever give you is this," he snapped, his eyes growing dark. "Never care. Never love. Or you'll become—"

Ada blurted, "Human."

"No, little Lady Ada." Nikolas sneered at *lady*. "You'll become mad."

30

Edwin Harrison, Duke of Girard

In Ada's bedroom, Edwin stared at the policeman. The officer had one foot in the bedroom, the other in the corridor. Edwin pulled at his cravat, oblivious to the growing crowd of detectives in the corridor behind the policeman. Ada was gone. Edwin didn't know who he blamed for her disappearance—herself or her brother. The afternoon light was fading along with his patience.

He pointed a finger at the policeman's chest. "You found what?"

"A body, Your Grace." The young man cleared his throat once more, his eyes flitting about. The Dark Duke had a demanding reputation.

"A body," Edwin repeated, his hands flexing at his side. *Blast*. He should have never left. If he'd stayed and helped Ada pack, she'd still be here. And there would be no body in the garden. Guilt filled his heart, his chest struggling with the weight of it. Edwin's hand twitched. He remembered the feel of Ada's hair between his fingers. And the way his mood lifted when she spoke. Edwin was not a gentleman. A true nobleman would not have left her. He'd known she was in danger. He'd thought Ada and her mother would pack. He was supposed to be whisking her away to his Westminster estate, not finding her body. With a curt nod, he followed the officer, grunting at the others in the hallway. "Unless you have some news, get back to work."

"They're only curious." Miller was at Edwin's heels. His long legs kept pace with Edwin's march. "Girard, it's not her."

Edwin quickened his stride. He refused to acknowledge the *her* Miller referred to, but his racing heart refused to be ignored. Rochelle hated his sister, that was obvious. But would the earl have killed Ada?

"Is it a woman or a man?" Miller descended the stairs and circled the officer, a hand on his shoulder.

"A man." He held out his arm and motioned to the back garden.

Miller held Edwin's gaze. "A man."

"I never thought it was her," Edwin grumbled, wishing he could believe the lie. The blasted minx occupied his thoughts more than she should. He wasn't going to admit it to anyone, even Miller.

"Are you alright?" Miller was at Edwin's side as they followed the officer.

"I never thought it was her." Edwin sounded like petulant toddler. The more he spoke, the more foolish he became. His body betrayed him, relaxing with the news that the victim was a man.

"Right." Miller didn't hide his smirk. "And you're only interested in her as it pertains to Rochelle."

"Exactly." The falsehood wasn't believable even to Edwin's ears. He was angry with the woman. She'd kept gossip articles, many of which he was featured in. It wasn't pride that frustrated him. He'd only thought more of her. She was intelligent and witty, not a silly debutante concerned with the *ton*'s theatrics.

Edwin shook his head. His thoughts were daft. How could he think more of her when she was very much the sister of a traitor? Gossip cartoons were the least of his worries. His temper flared. *She should have been home, not gallivanting with her brother.*

"Gallivanting with her brother?" Miller raised his eyebrows, his disappointment etched into every word.

Edwin cringed as they rounded to the unkempt garden. "I'd not meant to say that out loud."

"Clearly." Miller pulled Edwin back by his elbow. "You're exhausted. You've been chasing Rochelle for nearly a year."

He scowled. "No one knows this more than me."

"So we agree you're not thinking straight?" Miller's face was somber. He nodded to the officer to continue without them. After the policeman left, he said, "And that you should go home and rest."

"I am not a child, Miller." Edwin glared at the Whitworth's butler making his way toward them. The servant did a quick about-face and went into the house. "I have work to do."

The solicitor folded his arms and leaned against an overgrown hazel tree. Miller was a few inches shorter than Edwin, but the paternal look in his eye had the duke shifting his gaze away. "My dear man, you're slipping on the details. You spoke with the butler earlier, and any amateur sleuth would notice his boots haven't been near mud in days. He was not the man in Ada's room. Someone else was—more than likely her brother." Miller sighed, his voice in earnest. "Your Welsh soldier has disappeared, and you've not sent inquiries. Your head is not right. Before you take another step, at least acknowledge you need assistance."

"And just what type of help do you suggest?" Edwin snapped. His life was dedicated to serving the queen and he was failing. He tugged at his cravat, the fabric slipping from off his neck. Edwin groaned. He was becoming more undone by the minute—every precious moment lost. "Basking in pity will not—"

"Basking in pity?" Miller scoffed. A flash of anger appeared in his eyes, an emotion Edwin had not seen from him before. "Listen to yourself. Are you even human?" The solicitor wiped his face. Without another word, he left Edwin.

Like a dumb ox, Edwin stood in the Whitworth garden, his mind reeling. He felt as feral and unkempt as the surrounding garden. He should be irate and demand an apology from the insufferable solicitor. Miller had been a family friend for generations—how could the man treat Edwin this way? He leaned into the garden column, guilt pricking his conscience. Edwin had been a brute to the solicitor time and time again. He'd dismissed the man's gentle concerns.

Edwin rubbed his temples, his head pounding. He wasn't angry with Miller. No, Edwin was frustrated with himself. His heart had raced the moment Lady Rochelle had asked when Ada was returning. Edwin had foolishly thought he would arrive and whisk the golden goddess away. He'd not planned on being outwitted—again. The worst of it was his mood had lifted in Ada's company. She would never be his future, her brother had made that plain as day, but there was a light about her. She pushed him to lift his view. He held out his hands, the sunlight piercing through his fingers. Like the sun, Edwin would never hold her. And that—he swallowed hard—was the very reason he was in the foulest of moods. He missed her. They'd been parted only a few hours, and he missed her.

Miller returned with a somber look. "You need to see for yourself."

Edwin dropped his pity and followed the solicitor. He cleared his throat and offered, "Miller, I need to—"

"Your Grace." The officer nodded and waited with several of his colleagues standing in a semicircle. At their feet lay man stripped of his clothing, a working smock draped across his naked frame covering his vital parts. His left arm splayed outward, an old tattoo of two Welsh dragons in full view.

Edwin kneeled next to the man. He'd just spoken with the Welsh soldier the day before, nicknaming him Twice Over for his two dragon tattoos. Bits of red enamel were on the grass surrounding the man's forearm, but no paint on the soldier's skin. Edwin dipped a finger and rubbed the paint against his thumb. It was sticky, not quite dry. "This is only hours old."

"That's face paint, isn't it?" Miller kneeled next to him and peered at the man's face. He touched the man's tattoo with a finger and held it up. The tattoo was real, no paint. "Why would he have paint near him? He wasn't an actor, was he?"

"No." Edwin stood, the weight of the man's death like a noose around his neck. If the *le Tailleur* had infiltrated the Welsh's most sacred circle of men, England didn't stand a chance. Edwin's shoulders sagged. The brightness of the afternoon sun felt like a betrayal. The future was dark indeed.

The officers began whispering amongst themselves, their eyes drifting to the dragons on the dead man's forearm. Bent over, Miller searched the immediate surroundings. With a nod, he summoned Edwin over. In the foliage were several other cosmetic tins—black, green, and another red. There was a flash of white. Edwin peered over the overgrown shadbush to see a few pieces of paper with sketches of Welsh dragons.

He pulled the pieces of papers up, offering them to Miller. "This was planned."

"Inside job?" The solicitor fanned the papers. "The entire time we've been trying to ferret out the Tailor, he's been watching us."

Edwin tipped his head, motioning Miller to follow. If *le Tailleur* was watching, Edwin didn't want to show his cards. They circled the house and neared his carriage. "It seems our little investigation is backwards."

Miller eyed the pedestrians on the street and the carriages marching along. "They might think the prey has become the predator, but it doesn't have to be that way."

Edwin narrowed his gaze. He'd come to the Whitworth residence to whisk Ada away, and now Edwin was more concerned for both Ada *and* the queen. The ball was in a week. He'd depended on the Welsh soldiers for the better part of a decade. If they were in danger, so was the rest of England. He climbed into the carriage, Miller sitting opposite of him. The door swung open once more.

Gray Knight, the leader of the Welsh soldiers, shuffled in next to Miller, his face pale. "You found him?" Before Edwin could answer, he continued, "We're switching out our soldiers. Too many have been compromised. We don't know who or how, but someone has begun copying our tattoos." The man shook his head, a severe frown forming. "We've been training a new crop for the last few years. Pray that they're ready."

"I've never known a name. Tattoos are the only identification. If that is compromised, the imposters will be able to breach security—if their painted tattoos are convincing." Edwin cleared his throat. "I hate to ask but with the ball in a few days and foreign dignitaries coming ... we'll be vulnerable."

The soldier nodded gravely. "Your house will be secure."

"I have no way of honoring him." Edwin could grant a stipend for the man's family. There were funds for both civilians and informants.

"We take care of our own." The air in the carriage had changed. The soldier's eyes flicked between Miller and Edwin. "You asked something of me, that if we found Lord Rochelle to be a danger to the queen—"

"My word stands. I will not back down from a promise." Edwin felt Miller's stare, the questions in his eyes. "We cannot arrest without evidence. It's best if I am there to witness."

"I have no desire to become a vigilante." The soldier placed a hand on the carriage door, a vein ticking on his neck. The man was hiding something, or perhaps he did have plans to enact revenge outside of the law. "I will send word the moment I know something."

31

Lady Ada Whitworth

Under a brilliant sun, Ada's world became small and dark as the rented carriage barreled into the underbelly of London's poorest streets. The stench of overcrowding and under cleaning silenced both Nikolas and Ada. Nikolas donned a tailored suit and boots that pushed his status to the upper echelon of society, a complete contradiction to the surrounding poverty. Even Ada with her secondhand dress and worn gloves had money pinned to her crinoline.

The carriage stopped, but Nikolas didn't move, his left hand still holding the sachet to his nose. He closed his eyes briefly as if he was bracing himself. Ada should run or beg—do something to convince Nikolas of his own doubt. But the memory of Girard, his face earnest, asking what would help her overcome her stutter made her stop. She held her breath and reached for Nikolas's right hand. He flinched.

She tried to breathe through her mouth. "I don't know what caused your pain, but I am sorry that you're hurt. Is there something I can do ... is there something I can say to help?"

He snatched his hand back. "I do not need your pity."

Ada scurried back to her bench. She should have known better, but she had to try. He'd seemed torn. Or perhaps she truly was mad and only saw what she wanted.

The footman opened the carriage door. Nikolas grunted and offered his sachet but didn't meet her gaze. Grateful, Ada took it and held it to her nose. She breathed the lavender in slowly, deeply. His offering was a small kindness. Perhaps he was not so far gone.

He descended the steps and extended his hand for her. She hesitated. Offering sympathy was different than placing her trust in Nikolas. She bit her lip and thrust her hand into his. Gently, he helped her down. The road was pitted, the air thick with a putrid aura.

Her boot caught on the uneven gravel. Nikolas cupped her elbow, guiding her over the pothole. She gripped his arm. Like a gap-toothed child, the building had every window shattered. Smoke scars covered the walls on the first floor, and the garden surrounding the front was nothing but overgrown weeds.

A wagon canvas was strewn across the front steps. Another glance confirmed it was the same canvas advertising the queen's exhibition. Ada slid the pieces together in her mind. Nikolas—or Conroy—had kept watch over her using the wagons. The small spark of hope dimmed. Nikolas could never be the brother Ada needed. With a heavy heart, she continued on, her eyes taking in everything. There had to be a way to escape.

The walkway was pockmarked, puddles and filth filling each hole. The front door hung crooked and hunched over. The pitiful columns holding up the tiny porch had chunks missing as if dogs had nibbled several bites at the footings. A group of young boys peered through the fence between the neighboring buildings. Their tattered clothes and pale skin was covered in soot.

Nikolas pulled her gently to the side. Ada peered at the porch as they passed. The floorboards were twisted or smashed. The side door was missing. Nothing but a gaping hole and a splinter of wood remained. Nikolas—in his smart jacket and fine trousers—looked out of place. If Ada could memorize and draw the great Lord Rochelle creeping into a dilapidated building, she could sell thousands of newspapers. No one would believe the dapper earl would descend below the polished society of the *ton*.

One step inside, and they were greeted by steep stairs. Nikolas gripped the rail and turned his feet sideways, the steps too short to fit his boot. He tossed over his shoulder, "Stay to the right."

She took the first step and started falling backward. She gripped the rail with both hands, dropping the sachet. The stench of despair and death filled her lungs. She took another step, nervous to be alone on the dark stairs. She mimicked Nikolas's gait and turned sideways, her hip leading the climb. Her boot slipped. She whimpered.

Nikolas scurried back toward her, offering his hand. "Each step is a different height. And width."

"Why make each step different?" She stiffened. She'd spoken. She was nervous and yet she spoke. Out loud. She was in a seedy part of London with a brother she couldn't trust. Her heart pounded in her chest. She glanced at Nikolas, wondering if he could hear her panicked pulse.

"They're of servant quality." Nikolas shrugged, far too comfortable in the deserted building. "Nobody of consequence will ever see these stairs or servants' stairs. Why bother making them presentable?"

Ada swallowed the rising fear. "How do you know this?"

"I frequent more than the opera house." His voice was eerily calm. "Your life might not be idyllic, but there're worse places to live."

"Workhouses," Ada whispered. "I'm aware of what my future could be."

Nikolas gave a solemn nod. They climbed the darkened staircase, each step a haunting creak as they entered the belly of the building.

At the last step, Nikolas hesitated. He whispered, "You would not end up in a workhouse, Ada."

"An asylum." She didn't meet his gaze. He'd threatened her for too long.

"In France." He offered his arm, a large hole between the top step and the landing. "I would have kept you safe in France."

"Kept me safe?" Ada shoved his arm from her. "You've tormented me for all of my life, and now you've made plans to protect me? From whom? You?" She recoiled, knowing his temper would strike.

He placed a hand to his jacket, the same place he'd pulled the physician's letter from. "England is not safe."

"And you are?" Fear crept up her throat, thickening her tongue. By jove, he'd lost his mind. His complete disregard of reality—her childhood and the pain he'd caused—was eerily familiar to Lady Rochelle.

He held up his hands. "I am not safe." With the toe of his boot, he tapped the nearest door open. "But I am not the villain you should fear."

"Then who?" She scurried after him. "You, brother mine, are the one threatening me with an asylum. Let's not forget how quickly you'd throw your mother into an asylum as well."

The door shut with a large clap, the hinges squeaking. Ada winced at the sound. The door hung open, waving in the draft swirling into the room. The room felt haunted, shards of glass in each of the broken windows. There was a heaviness in the chipped walls and uneven floors.

The walls were littered with different, haphazardly hung portraits—each one a sketch of Queen Victoria. Two machines were slumped in the corner. Ada didn't dare investigate. She didn't trust the architecture. Where she stood—and where Nikolas stood—there were holes in the floorboards.

Rectangular metal plates were discarded in various piles on the floor. A second look, and Ada realized they were broken mint plates, failed attempts to print bank notes. Stacks of bank notes bound with twine were in every corner. She kneeled over a pile of mint plates. Conroy and Nikolas weren't just printing English bank notes. They were attempting French and American money as well.

"What have you done?" Ada whispered. She'd walked into the heart of their counterfeit scheme. "I can't do it. I won't help you. This is wrong. All of it."

Instead of answering, Nikolas walked to the empty window facing the street. "You are safer here than at home."

"I'd have given you a portrait if you'd asked," Ada confessed to the dark room. "A kind word. Even a simple request." She didn't need to be here. She couldn't manipulate medal. She was a master of the brush and charcoal, not a blacksmith.

"I never pretended to be a saint." Nikolas offered only his profile, his body still facing the window. "It won't be long, and you'll be whisked away."

"To an asylum." Ada's voice rose. Voices echoed from the stairs. A chill crept up her neck.

"It's not what you think." He turned, his eyes becoming dark. "Your cartoons will still be delivered, although at a much slower pace. You will have an endless supply of wove paper, charcoal ... all that you could need."

"Except freedom." The very thing Ada had yearned for.

"Your letter is for a retention of only three months." He pulled two envelopes from his jacket. "Thomas will have all the documentation to set you free. Although, he doesn't know it yet."

"And your mother?" Frustration filled her chest, replacing the fear. Only her brother would believe his idea, his plan, was superior to anything Ada could think of. She had her future well in hand long before Nikolas decided to care.

"Hers is a bit more complicated." He hunched his shoulders. "She has been unwell since long before my father died."

"How could you?" Ada circled the piles of mint, her nerves taking hold. "What injury did I give you? What pain did I cause that would make you hate me so?"

"There's more at play here than what you see." He slunk from the window and placed the envelope back in his jacket. "He's here."

Ada felt hope slipping through her fingers. "I had a plan, Nikolas. Without you, I would be free. I would be safe on my own terms."

"Your plan included the Duke of Girard." He *tsk*ed and smiled ruefully. A lock of dark hair fell across his forehead. For a moment, he looked deceptively young and innocent. "He might be well-intentioned, but he cannot outwit the Tailor."

"Girard is not a coward," she cried. Ada needed her brother to believe her—to trust her enough to let her go.

"His courage was not in question." Nikolas wiped his face, exhaustion etched into the lines framing his eyes and lips. "The Tailor has more power than the queen herself."

"And so you roll over? You give in?" Her voice was high, but Ada was grateful she could still speak. If Conroy was truly about to enter, she would be silenced.

The stairs creaked and the soft whispers of male conversation echoed into the room. Nikolas smiled sadly. "We don't have a choice. *I* don't have a choice."

"There is always a choice." Her breathing came shallow—and far too fast. Her throat became thick. She needed to hurry. "Why do you hate me so?"

"I never hated *you*."

"But you never loved me. You've never loved anyone," Ada whispered. Boots scratching along the steps became louder. Her mind raced to find something to hold on to, something to convince Nikolas to walk away. He'd loved someone once. "Who was the woman, the one who gave you the kerchief? You've chained me to a future. At least give me something of your past."

He closed his eyes briefly and said, "Rosalyn."

"Did you love her?" Her words were coming slow, letters harder to form.

"It doesn't matter." Nikolas looked at his hands. "Our mother rejected her. And me." He sighed, the facade slamming down his face. His lips turned to an arrogant smile. The brother was gone, replaced with the criminal.

"Our mother," Ada repeated. She stepped backward. Nikolas had never included her in their family. "She was never mine."

The curtain fell from Nikolas's face. He blinked and turned from her. "I might have failed you. But this is the only way to keep you safe."

"Delivering me to Conroy?" Her voice shook. She touched her throat, praying she could keep the words coming. "How does that keep me safe?"

"I'm not delivering you to him." He sat on the windowsill. A breeze from the shattered window ruffled his hair. "I've a plan in place."

"Your schemes do not make sense." Ada waved a hand in the air to some far-off land. Nikolas couldn't plan his own life, let alone an escape for his sister. "Sending me to France, the same country that the Tailor is from, that will keep me safe?" Ada shook her head. Her brother had gone completely, utterly mad.

"Spoken like a silly chit." Conroy entered the room, a wild glint in his eye. Half a dozen men spilled into the room behind him. One of them had a splash of red on his forearm. Ada's heart sank. The man must be in league with the other Welshmen. This must be how Girard was outmaneuvered. He'd unwittingly employed the same soldiers.

"I brought the artist." Nikolas sprang to his feet, the charming smile and charismatic chuckle firmly in place.

"And so I see." Conroy stood there, folding his hands in front of him. He tossed an envelope to the floor. "I do not appreciate demands. Do you honestly think you could outmaneuver me? Or *le Tailleur?*"

"Demands?" Nikolas picked at his nails as if he were bored. "I've made no demands. I merely wanted to meet the man himself. I've been a loyal servant. I only want to meet my master."

The pieces slid into place. Ada's gaze flicked between her brother and Conroy. Nikolas didn't know who the real spy was—he was just a pawn. He'd never been the mastermind, not that she believed the charade. The chill wrapped around her neck. Her tongue thickened. She backed away from the approaching men toward the window. She peered down below. The second floor was much taller than her townhome. This building was narrower, each floor at a higher rise than the modest house she'd lived in.

"The Tailor offers many apologies, but you'll not be having a meeting today." Conroy twirled a finger in the air. "We have work to do."

The men fanned to the periphery of the room, their heads pivoting between Nikolas and Conroy. A few of the men pushed up their sleeves. The man with the red tattoo did the same. Ada paused. His tattoo was smeared, the dragon's head nearly gone, only the back claws of the animal still clear. He wasn't part of Girard's men. Ada didn't know if she should feel relief or fear.

"Our schedule is quite open." Nikolas shrugged and brushed phantom dirt off his trousers. He was buying time just like he'd done when Ada was a child. He was a champion of wreaking havoc and not getting caught. Ada was always caught with her hands covered in chocolate, not Nikolas. "We can wait all day. And night."

A flicker of movement on the street below pulled Ada's attention.

Several men on both sides of the walkway crept toward the house, their hats tucked low over their faces. By the cut of their clothes, they were similar to the men in the room. Ada's heart sank.

"You do not have a leg to stand on, Rochelle." Conroy snapped his fingers. Each man pulled out a pistol, their aim on Nikolas.

Ada stepped in front of her brother. "D-d-d-don't …"

Conroy snickered. "I wouldn't waste your breath for his worthless soul."

Nikolas placed a hand on her shoulder, whispering, "I never planned on walking away. I only planned on you being safe."

Ada spun around, and her boot caught on the uneven floorboard. Nikolas steadied her. He squeezed her hands. "I might not be worth redeeming, but please remember this moment." He stepped to her side and faced Conroy. "I've confessed my sins."

Conroy pulled an envelope from his jacket. "This letter?"

"Is that to the queen?" Nikolas squinted, pretending to read from across the room. "Oh, perhaps that one is for the Duke of Girard."

Conroy tossed the envelope to the floor and reached into his jacket. He threw two more envelopes down. A smirk crept across his face. "Or would you like the letter you hand delivered to the police?"

Ada whimpered. Nikolas was outmatched, outmanned and outwitted. "P-p-please—"

Her brother tapped his forehead. "Oh, what about Lord Pichon, did you happen to grab his?"

"You have failed at everything *le Tailleur* has asked of you." Conroy smirked and stepped closer. From the other side of his jacket, he pulled a pistol. "Pray that your sister is more cooperative."

32

Edwin Harrison, Duke of Girard

Edwin's carriage pulled away from the Whitworth house. He rubbed his temples and felt Miller's concern from across the bench. The carriage slammed to a halt.

Edwin blurted, "What the devil?" He pushed the window open, the swivel hinge squeaking in protest. A large black carriage arrived. It was split in the middle, allowing for separation between the benches. Edwin had only seen them used for asylums or the police force.

Both Miller and Edwin rushed from the carriage. Edwin nearly collided into a spindly gentleman with a medicine bag clutched in his hand. "Who are you?"

"I was sent for." The man pushed his glasses up his nose. "I'm a physician. And you are?"

Edwin relaxed. Of course a physician was requested when the Welsh soldier was found. "I do believe your trip is wasted. The man has already passed."

"Mr. Lydcombe?" The doctor's gaze flicked between Edwin and Miller.

The hairs on Edwin's neck stood on end. There was more at play. He folded his arms. With the death of the Welsh soldier, no one was above suspicion. "How do you know Mr. Lydcombe?"

"He sent a messenger, asking that I evaluate a lady. That is all the information I am willing to give." The physician narrowed his gaze. "And might I ask, who are you?"

"He's the Duke of Girard." Miller came dangerously close to the doctor, searching his face, his chest—down to the man's boots.

The physician's mouth fell open. He dropped his medical bag. "A thousand apologies, Your Grace."

"What did Mr. Lydcombe's message say to you?" Edwin had thought it odd. "He's only recently become acquainted with Lady Rochelle." And Ada.

"I was hoping he could tell me that." The man's lip trembled. The bravado from earlier was gone. "He is not here?"

"I doubt Mr. Lydcombe knows of the morning events." Edwin rubbed his neck. He needed to notify the queen, but he didn't dare leave without querying the doctor. "How long have you known Lydcombe?"

"I don't know him." The physician's brow furrowed as if he'd been insulted. "When a call of distress comes, I do not question it. I am a man of medicine, not a detective." He winced, realizing his tone. "Apologies, Your Grace."

Edwin's mind raced with reasons for the physician's sudden appearance. He had great doubts of Lydcombe's sudden concern for Lady Rochelle's—or Ada's—health. He barely knew the women. Edwin flinched. He'd been consumed with Ada's welfare since they'd met. He'd only known her a few weeks. Rochelle was a spineless coward. He wouldn't have looked beyond his own nose. The earl would never send for a physician—unless it was to throw either woman into an asylum. Edwin rubbed his forehead. "What evaluation were you to perform?"

The doctor's smile was taut. "It's a delicate—"

Out of the corner of Edwin's eye, another Welsh soldier stood off to the side. The man gave a nod to someone across the street. Bloody hell, they had information. Edwin left the stammering doctor and marched toward the soldier.

The Welshman nodded to Edwin. "Your Grace."

"What's happened?" Edwin searched the street for the soldier's colleague. All he saw were the backs of several other men scurrying down the street.

"Just checking in, Your Grace." The man's face was stoic, not an ounce of emotion.

"You're lying." Edwin couldn't threaten him. The man would disappear before Edwin could make good on his promise of prison. "A doctor just arrived to evaluate one of the Whitworth women. Something is afoot, and I need to get to the bottom of it."

The soldier started to shrug.

"No." Edwin grabbed the man's jacket with both hands. "I cannot protect if I do not know. You've sent a signal. I am duty-bound to protect the crown at all costs."

The man narrowed his eyes. "We take care of our own, Your Grace." He soured at *Your Grace*. With surprising deftness, he peeled Edwin's hands off his jacket.

We take care of our own. Edwin dropped his empty hands. His temper flared. He took a deep breath. He needed information. "You've found who was responsible for the soldier?"

The Welshman's mouth fell open. He quickly recovered. "I've said nothing of the sort."

"I will not stand in the way." Edwin couldn't stop the words. He would promise anything to uncover the French spy. "The soldiers can deliver whatever punishment—anything—just tell me what you know."

The man shoved his hands into his pocket and rocked on his heels. "We've been ordered to trust no one."

"I am tasked to keep this bloody country safe. I've trusted Welshmen since I was a boy." Edwin held out his arm, motioning to the Whitworth townhome. "Please tell me the courage of Welsh soldiers did not die with that man."

The man stared at him, the silence deafening. After a moment, he tipped his hat. "The earl took his sister to the Abyss."

"The Abyss?" Edwin recoiled, his heart sinking. The eastern side of

London's poverty provided fertile ground for the darkest crimes. Children and women were sold to the highest bidder. The *ton* would never go near it, nor were many aware of its existence. "You can't be serious." If the Tailor's headquarters were in that part of London, he would never be discovered.

The Welshman didn't smile nor did he appear to be breathing. There was no mirth in his eyes. "Lord Rochelle will pay for his crimes, Your Grace. You can believe me or not. Either way, keep your word. We mean to handle this on our own."

Edwin's mind raced with the horrors of the Abyss. Lady Ada would be exposed—and possibly sold. Her brother would toss her over to save his own skin. "The lady is innocent—"

"We've no interest in her."

Edwin held out his hand. "Come with me. You can be witness to my word."

"I'll not abandon my post." He folded his arms and puffed out his chest. "But I'll give you all that I know."

In what felt like an eternity, the Welshman gave directions to their location. Edwin left the soldier and repeated the directions to his driver. The carriage bumped and swayed along the road, hitting the potholes. The familiar stench stung Edwin's nose long before they crossed the threshold between the working class and the starving. The Abyss was known for moral filth and the despair of souls. Edwin fidgeted. The driver cracked the whip, the horses's hooves pounding the street, but he felt as if he was in a dream.

Every sound and movement was painfully slow. Guilt gripped his lungs. He struggled to breathe. He needed to know—with his own eyes —that Ada was whole. She was life and light. He needed her to be well. He blinked, surprised at the emotion. He needed her. The thought sent him back. Edwin hadn't needed anyone. He held out his hand. For a moment, he'd felt alive. And Ada was the cause.

Shouts from outside pulled his attention. Another carriage— similar to the physician's at the Whitworth townhome—was pulling in front of a crooked house, sorrow etched in the broken windows and broken doors. And yet, its neighboring houses were sadder still. They were just a street away from where Ada was supposed to be.

Men surrounded the carriage with pistols drawn and mouths shouting. Only when they saw a physician clutching a medicine bag did they stop. The scene was eerily similar to the Whitworth residence. Edwin flipped the top of his bench up and pulled two pistols from its belly. The carriage was slowing but not fast enough. Shoving the door open, Edwin leapt down and ran toward the confused physician.

The men stripped the doctor of his medical bag. There were flashes of red as the men pointed their pistols. Welsh soldiers—or possibly imposters. The poor physician's knees trembled. He hung his head and awkwardly stuck his hands in the air.

"Let the man be!" Edwin shouted. He didn't meet any of the men's gazes but went directly to the doctor. He prayed they were loyal Welshmen and not the Tailor's army. "Tell me who sent you."

The man peered up at Edwin, his eyes wide. "I was sent to evaluate—"

"A lady." Edwin cut him off. He placed a hand on his shoulder. He could feel the glares of the surrounding men. "But who sent for you?"

"Mr. Thomas." The man's voice shook. "He sent his butler."

Edwin sighed. He doubted Ada's solicitor sent for the doctor. Whoever had ordered the two physicians was no friend of the Whitworth women.

"Your Grace." Gray Knight appeared next to the doctor. He motioned to a house farther down the street. "We need to move. They're upstairs."

Edwin swallowed his retort. The Welshman had promised to keep Edwin in the loop. Only now that he was quite clearly aware of Ada's location did Gray Knight involve Edwin.

"Stay with him," Edwin ordered the nearest soldier. The man's face was shockingly young. He couldn't be more than sixteen, seventeen. "Ask every detail about who and how he was sent."

The young soldier looked to Gray Knight for affirmation. A quick nod and Edwin was following the senior Welshman around the building. Edwin breathed through his mouth, the stench horrific.

"Jakesmen won't come near here to empty the privies." Gray Knight eyed Edwin.

"It's criminal," Edwin muttered. Twice, he'd tried to nudge parliament toward tighter standards. But Edwin couldn't convince anyone to testify of the conditions. If there were no victims, there was no need for change.

At the side door, Gray Knight kicked off his boots and motioned for Edwin to do the same. Just inside were several other Welshman, their boots missing as well. Three men were bound and gagged at the base of the stairs. Their eyes were closed. Together they silently climbed up the stairs, fumbling at the steep and irregular steps.

Light on his feet, Edwin made sure to keep pace with Gray Knight. He needed to ensure Ada was safe—even from vengeful Welsh soldiers.

"I would never send just one letter or even five. Nor would I leave it up to the police. I've notified doctors, as in, more than one. The world will be looking for her." Nikolas's voice drifted down the staircase. He was shouting as if he wanted to be heard.

Edwin placed a hand on Gray Knight, whispering. "He knows we're here."

They got to the landing as Nikolas continued, "She's been reported as missing and needing a medical evaluation. No stone will be left unturned."

"Did you really think you could force your way into a meeting?" Conroy chuckled. "The Tailor doesn't take demands."

With soldiers behind them, Edwin and Gray Knight flew through the door, pistols at the ready. Conroy shouted, "Kill them. Kill them all."

The Welshmen filled the room, firing at will. Gunshots ricocheted. Girard rushed across the room toward Ada. One by one, Conroy's men crumbled to the floor. Rochelle spun around, covering Ada. He arched his back—a shot to his right thigh. And then his shoulder. Another to his hip. He sank to the ground. Ada's eyes widened. She wrapped her arms around his chest.

Girard was at her side. "Come with me."

She shook her head, refusing to leave her brother. Rochelle blinked, his face pale. He reached a hand up, tugging on one of her curls. "This is how it must be."

Girard froze. Rochelle had planned to die. That was not the man

Girard had spent the last few years chasing. The earl was a flea, a constant irritation.

"He n-n-n-n ..." Ada wiped the tears from her face.

Rochelle squeezed her hand, blood seeping from his back into Ada's skirt. "The doctor will be here soon. Don't fight him. Go. Be safe."

She shook her head, the rest of her curls falling from her plait. Her hair encircled Rochelle, giving him a false halo.

"She will be safe with me." Girard needed Ada to trust him just one more time.

Rochelle smirked, his face turning an eerie gray. "No offense, Dark Duke, but you still think the Tailor is French. She's not safe in England. No one is."

"Stop lying," Girard snapped.

The doctor appeared in the doorway, clutching his medicine bag to his chest. His eyes searched the room. Only a handful of Welshmen were standing, going from man to man, checking who was merely injured and who was gone. Gray Knight hobbled over to Conroy who lay face down on the floor. With his boot, he rolled him over. Conroy flashed his pistol. Gray Knight fired his gun.

Girard yelled, "No!"

Conroy's mouth fell open, the gun dropping from his hand. The Welshman fired again. The damnable Gray Knight had ruined any chance of Girard questioning Conroy. Dead men couldn't lead Edwin to the Tailor.

Ada whimpered, her arms tightening around her brother. Edwin felt the shame. He'd given the promise he would not intervene. Gray Knight had one goal in mind, to enact revenge for his fallen comrade.

"A few tried to escape, but they didn't make it past the stairs." Gray Knight pointed to Rochelle. "No one leaves this room."

33

Lady Ada Whitworth

A LANKY WELSHMAN WITH GRAY SPINDLY HAIR AND OVERGROWN sideburns stepped over Conroy's limp body. There was authority in the way he moved and how the other men gave him deference. Ada's lungs screamed at her, her breathing far too fast and shallow. Her tongue was thick, her cheeks wet with anxious tears.

In the corner, the doctor hunched over a wounded soldier. The unharmed men blocked the physician from attending to Conroy's men. Ada needed the doctor to come to Nikolas. Her brother was shot. He wasn't fatally wounded, but Ada had watched her father succumb to a supposedly benign fever. He needed help.

With a murderous glint in the Welshman's eyes, he aimed his gun at Nikolas. Ada leaned over, covering her brother's chest. She would not give in. Her skirts were soaked in Nikolas's blood. The walls and floors were smeared with blood from both Conroy's men and the Welsh soldiers. In a flash, the danger shifted. She'd been terrified of Conroy and his partnership with the spy. But the tide had turned.

The room was eerily silent and heavy. The horrific stench was silenced by the surrounding death.

Ada flinched at the sound of the Welshman's boots stepping.

Nikolas mumbled in her arms. "Let me go, Lady Ada."

Lady Ada. There was affection in his voice. She shook her head. He squeezed her hand. *Lady Ada.* Ada had given up hope, believing Nikolas would never accept her.

The Welshman was upon them, his eyes dark and his lip curled. He was a force to reckon with. He had wide shoulders and a steady hand. He was a man undeterred by death. Blood and destruction surrounded him, and yet his focus was only on Nikolas.

Girard cleared his throat and scooted closer. "My dear ..."

"No." Ada closed her eyes. She had to save Nikolas. He had been the worst of brothers—that was a fact—but she couldn't let him die. Not like this. Not when he was beginning to let her in. She had so many questions about their childhood, about his mother. She needed more time. Desperate, she searched her mind. There had to be a reason Girard needed Nikolas alive. She opened her eyes, her hand gripping Girard's forearm. "P-p-p-please."

The duke tilted his head, an apology in his expression. His gaze flicked from her to the older Welshman. Girard's dark eyes and furrowed brow had given him a conceited aura, but now, Ada saw the duke in a new light. He was serious, not solemn and different, not dark.

"Nikolas could help you." She avoided their gaze, terrified that her tongue would betray her. Her hand gripped Girard's sleeve tighter, her knuckles white. "Conroy's dead. You'll need Nikolas if you're ever to find the Tailor."

"They're known for shooting first and asking questions later," her brother added dryly.

Girard paused, his gaze drifting to her brother. "He's proven we cannot trust him." There was a lilt at the end of his statement, an almost question.

The Welshman motioned for another soldier to join him. He nodded to Girard. "You gave me your word, Your Grace."

"I did," the duke whispered, his lips forming a taut frown. "Ada ..." He paused, his shoulders hunching.

"Please, sir." Ada turned her attention to the Welshman. Her gaze fixed steadily at his chest instead of his face. "He's my brother. He could help you."

"The only way this twit could help the country is by dying," the soldier said dryly. He cocked the gun. "Step aside, milady."

"No!" she screamed. She dropped the duke's arm and pulled on Nikolas.

Wincing, Nikolas whispered, "Walk away."

"Don't do this." Ada had spent her life wishing for sibling affection. But only now, when his death was inevitable, did he sprinkle her with bits of tenderness. This couldn't be the way it all ended. There had to be another way. Life wouldn't be this cruel.

The Welshman narrowed this gaze at her. "Are you in league with Lord Rochelle?"

"She is not." Girard stood with a snap, the shins of his trouser smeared with Nikolas's blood. His stance was wide, his arms taut. A few inches taller than the Welshman, Girard was an impressive opponent. "Ada has been trying to free herself of him."

The soldier motioned to her. "I can make her free. Forever."

"She has a solicitor who can testify of her plans." Girard leaned forward, towering over the older soldier. Ada felt a glimmer of hope. She'd never had anyone in her corner, not since the late earl had died. No one—including Nikolas—had defended her character like this. Mr. Thomas had kept her secrets, but he'd never stared down a gun.

"Didn't think you had it in you." Nikolas smirked, his lips trembling. He was slowly succumbing to shock. "So, you can solve a mystery, Your Grace?" A tremor started in his fingers, growing up his arm. "Have you figured out that *le Tailleur* isn't French yet, or am I'm still lying?"

Both Girard and the Welshman exchanged a curious look. It was the second time Nikolas had mentioned the Tailor being English.

"He's telling the truth," Ada said in a breathy whisper.

Girard's stance relaxed, his hands no longer fisted. Even the Welshman took a step back, his brow furrowed. The duke had once accused her of being an accomplice to her brother. She had never thought the day would come when she would agree with Nikolas or that he would care for her feelings. Several weeks before, she had confessed to Mr. Thomas that Nikolas becoming a fugitive would be a welcome event. She had wished him harm. Guilt pricked her. She had hoped he would get caught, and be locked in chains. And now she was begging for his life. She hadn't truly forgiven him, but she couldn't stand by and watch him die. Not when she could save him.

She tucked her chin, keeping her eyes on Nikolas's chest instead of Girard or the Welshman. "If you don't believe him, at least, let me take Nikolas's place."

"No," Girard and Nikolas said at the same time.

Ada's head snapped up. "Then provide another solution. I am not giving up."

Girard's eyes were wide, and Nikolas smirked. Her brother chuckled and propped himself up with his good arm. His pallor was turning sickly, but his charm was still at the ready. "As much as I love people fawning over me, I do believe these gentlemen have better things to do, sister mine." He glanced up at Girard. The arch of his neck and the plea in his eyes gave him a youthful, almost innocent look. For a moment, he was simply Nikolas Whitworth, not the cruel brother or the Tailor's errand boy. "Take care of her. I've made my bed, and I have just enough courage to lie in it."

"Oh come off it." Girard scowled. "It's a touch convenient that you decide to become noble when death is at your door."

Ada groaned. She gripped Nikolas's shirt. "Tell the truth for once. Can you—will you—help them find the Tailor?"

"I do not know who the spy is, only that he is a member of the *ton*." Wincing, Nikolas tried sitting against the wall. "He knows exactly who to pressure and which weaknesses to exploit."

Girard eyed the Welshman. He rubbed his neck and kneeled next to Nikolas. He waited a beat before helping Nikolas adjust against the wall. "What do you mean who to pressure?"

"He's lying." The Welshman growled.

"No." Nikolas sighed and shook his head at the duke. Ada felt a flicker of panic. Nikolas didn't want the duke's help. "I am quite acquainted with the Tailor's methods." He motioned to the room. "And yet, he still bested me."

"*We* bested you," the Welshman snapped. "Because of you, one of our own is dead."

Nikolas frowned. "The Tailor calls you the queen's personal death squad. He hates the monarchy and everyone surrounding the crown."

"Lord Pichon." Girard wiped his face and sighed. "The Tailor was after the queen's cousin."

"You cannot believe him." The Welshman stood over Girard, his aim switching between Nikolas and Girard. "You gave me your word."

"I would love nothing more than to see Rochelle rot." The duke's gaze flitted about, to the Welshman and to Nikolas—to everyone but Ada. "I am sworn to protect the queen as well. I cannot keep both promises."

The Welshman aimed the gun to the ceiling and fired a shot. Ada flinched, shaking her head. In a flash, Girard was at her side. He wrapped an arm around her, bringing her to his chest. "You're safe."

She sank into him. "P-p-p-please."

With hands on her shoulders, he pushed her back, eyes searching her face. "Ada ..." Dark circles underlined his eyes. "Your brother is a known criminal." When Ada whimpered, he squeezed her shoulders. "He's all but confessed."

"He has never been a saint, but he is not the devil." Ada spoke slowly, sucking in breaths between the words. "But he wants to find the spy just as much as you do. Can you at least delay his death a while?"

The Welshman paused, his shoulders relaxing.

"The Tailor will have your head before you ever get close." Nikolas waved a hand over his body. "Shall I offer myself as evidence?"

"You are not dead." The soldier narrowed his eyes. "And your wounds were my doing, not *le Tailleur*'s."

Girard motioned for the doctor and stood over Nikolas. "Rochelle, if you betray—"

"Thank you." Ada rushed toward the duke, wrapping her arms around his chest.

The Welshman cried out, firing another gun in the ceiling. Girard wrapped an arm around Ada, holding her close. Above her head, he said to the soldier, "I've not broken my word. I've only delayed it."

In hesitant steps, the physician came to Nikolas. The older soldier barked orders to his men. Girard's arm stiffened, keeping Ada close. His other hand cradled her jaw.

At their feet, Nikolas chuckled. "Does this mean you'll paint a prettier picture of him tomorrow?"

Ada winced, wishing Nikolas would keep his mouth shut. Girard didn't need to know about the *Thames Tales* just yet. He'd kept her brother safe. She leaned into his touch. "Thank you."

Nikolas groaned under the doctor's prodding. He tried once more. "Girard doesn't know, does he?"

The duke rolled his eyes but didn't look down. His gaze was steady, never leaving hers. Comfort enveloped her, warming her to the bone. She was safe. With Girard, she would always be safe. His thumb caressed her jaw. "Know what, Rochelle?"

Ada stiffened, glancing down at her brother. "Nikolas knows nothing."

Amusement tugged at his lips. "Rochelle, I do believe you're in my debt. I would start talking if I were you."

Nikolas beamed. "He's looked past your stutter—"

"Your stutter is the least of my worries," Girard whispered in her ear.

She left his embrace and pointed to Nikolas. "If you breathe a word, I will kill you."

Her brother shrugged, pulling his arm from the doctor's hands. "I think he'll forgive you for the *Thames* cartoons."

Ada wrung her hands. She risked a glance at the duke.

"The handwriting. It was feminine." Arching an eyebrow, he looked past her, appearing to be deep in thought. "That was you. It was always you."

She inhaled sharply and glanced at her feet. "I can explain."

"I suppose that solves quite a few of your secrets." He came closer. "Mr. Thomas's parcels?"

Ada nodded.

With his finger, he lifted her chin.

She closed her eyes. Ada couldn't look at him. The disappointment in his eyes would be too much. He'd never forgive her, not now. She'd sketched him again and again, poking fun at all that he held dear.

"Am I truly that comical as the Dark Duke?"

Ada's eyes shot open. She started to protest but froze—the Duke of Girard was smiling, his eyes crinkled.

He tilted his head. "It appears I need to reread a certain newspaper."

34

Edwin Harrison, Duke of Girard

In the back garden of his Westminster estate, Edwin checked the perimeter for the fifth time. He and the Welsh soldiers were at an uneasy truce. They would still assist with security but were eager to get answers. With Rochelle's help—if the plonker could be trusted—Edwin no longer feared the French ambassadors. Lady Catherine would be at the ball tonight with her betrothed. There was relief knowing his future was no longer tied to her. His ancestors came from French royalty, but his heart was in England. Or rather, his heart belonged to a lady with feral golden curls.

He tucked the thin box under his arm. He'd ordered new gloves for Ada weeks before—the day he saw his mother's monogram on the leather. There were four more pairs in his study but tonight, no. Tonight, Ada would have white silk to match the misshapen pearl on her necklace. She would have a pair that had never been worn before—not a cast-off like his mother's gloves. He couldn't wait to commission a new wardrobe for her. His housekeeper nearly burst into tears. The woman had mistaken his intent. He wasn't announcing an engagement. He was simply doing his gentleman duties.

The moment the ball was over, he planned to whisk Ada and her brother off to his Welsh estate. Gray Knight all but demanded they be moved closer to a Welsh foothold, and even Rochelle admitted his first communication with the Tailor had been near the Welsh and English border.

Edwin was just as eager to be home. As a child, Wales had been a comfort, but as an adult, it'd been a reminder of all that he lacked. Lady Catherine grew up in the next county over—perhaps on some level, he had avoided going home, knowing that his future with her would never have satisfied either of them.

Miller came down the walkway, his gaze on the overhead planters and lights. He ambled toward Edwin, his hands clasped behind his back. For being twice Edwin's age, he was surprisingly spry. "Has everything passed your inspection? Or rather inspections?"

"There's only so much I can ask of the Welsh soldiers at the moment." Edwin had betrayed their trust, according to the Gray Knight. But he would do it again to see the relief in Ada's eyes. She'd clung to him. He couldn't deny her. Nor did he want to.

Miller stepped to the right. He arched his eyebrow and searched behind Girard. He then stepped to his left. "You seem to be missing a certain lady."

Edward straightened his stance, the box containing gloves under his arm. He would not defend his near-constant companion. He'd refused to leave Ada's side when she packed for the ball. At her townhome, she had tried to hide her portrait and charcoal sketches—and more importantly, her cartoon clippings. He smiled at the memory of her blush. She'd covered her head in her hands, stuttering fiercely.

"You've already lost your belle?" Miller *tsk*ed, his eyes crinkling. "That does not bode well for your marital aspirations."

"Marital aspirations?" Edwin had been buried in plans for the ball and in extricating Ada from the legal mess Rochelle had placed her in. The ninny had thought an asylum was safer than Edwin's estate. It wasn't the first mistake the earl had made. Desperate men rarely made good choices—a fact he worried about. He'd given in to Ada's plea and, in his own desperation to make her happy, saved Rochelle. They still had not untied the legal paperwork for her mother. She was being evaluated daily at her London townhome. Ada had relinquished her opinion on her adopted mother, opting for Nikolas to decide her fate.

Miller chuckled next to him. "You've not heard a word I've said."

"I heard you well enough." He didn't bother scowling. Miller would never be scared of Edwin. The solicitor had known Edwin far too long.

Miller eyed him. "Your father would be proud."

"And why is that?" He ignored the lump forming in his throat. The entire Westminster estate was filling with dignitaries for the queen's international ball. His father held up his end of responsibilities, but he would never have hosted a ball. Nor would he have gone so far as to be proud. His mother—if she still held her wits—would have been more impressed.

"I believe the saying is *going out on a limb*? You went against your rigid nature that you've adopted," Miller mused, his smile crooked. "Proud, yes. He would most definitely be proud. She's a good match, Your Grace."

"Rigid nature?"

Miller held out an arm. "It's what makes all this possible. Your meticulous tendencies make you a powerful advisor."

"And a bore."

Miller shrugged as they neared the steps to the house. "But I do think congratulations are in order."

"For being the one and only person to force Rochelle into silence?" Edwin wasn't so daft. He knew Miller was hinting, once again, at Ada. He'd begun to hope for a future with her, but their lives were entangled in complications. Edwin needed to smooth the knots before promising forever.

"Is her lineage your biggest obstacle?" Miller lowered his voice. "She appears to be painfully aware of her low status."

Edwin paused mid-step. He'd once insulted her lineage. The injury, he assumed, had not yet healed. "She spoke to you?"

"Her brother will be charged for treason." Miller raised his eyebrows. "I would think that would be on anyone's mind. She was in the very room when he confessed, was she not?"

"Yes." He broke the word into two. When Edwin was in her presence, he didn't think of her brother. Or any of her supposed faults. She was a rarity, a gem. He'd been more worried about how his newly tarnished reputation would affect her. The paper believed he'd bullied her into submission. His mood was light and the future didn't feel quite so lonely when she was around. "I know the next year or two will be consumed with chasing *le Tailleur*." He frowned. The bloody criminal wasn't even French.

"I've seen you more distracted in the last few months than ever before." Miller started up the steps. The orchestra warming up echoed from inside the house. "Perhaps if you were settled, you could focus on the hunt."

"There are whispers." Edwin had never cared about the *ton* and its gossip, but with the Tailor being a member of the upper echelon of society, Edwin needed to keep an ear on the gentry. He could not encourage confidence if he was the target of rumors.

"You have a powerful tool in your pocket, Your Grace." Miller grinned and took another step. "There is a certain artist that sketches the gossip cartoon. That particular artist holds more sway than you or she realize."

"She has not sent in any new sketches ..." Edwin let the sentence fall. He could use her influence, but Edwin would be no better than Rochelle. Ada should be cherished not swung like a hammer to do his bidding. "I cannot ask that of her."

"Maybe you should just ask for her hand." Miller took the last step to the landing. He turned but instead of meeting Edwin's gaze, the solicitor searched the garden. "I knew your father when he was just a boy. I saw him fall and rise again many a time. I know—without a doubt—he would approve of Ada. He would welcome her as a lady. They would share stories of their difficulties."

Edwin faltered. "You knew he couldn't read?"

His father's weakness was the family's greatest secret. They were not ashamed of the late duke. Keeping his secret was out of respect, not embarrassment.

"How do you think he wooed the ladies?" Miller leaned forward, a glint of mischief in his eye. "Only your father could turn an obstacle into a romantic whim."

"You jest." Edwin could not believe it. His father was not a romantic.

"He begged your mother to write a letter for him." Miller chuckled, his gaze still on the garden. "It was the letter asking her father for permission to court her. She blushed while he dictated all her qualities."

The orchestra quieted, signaling the start of the ball. The last of the dignitaries would have arrived and gone through their announcements. The pull of responsibility wasn't there. His life for the past decade seemed dull. The Dark Duke of before would rush inside. And yet he found himself at Miller's side, his gaze on the garden his father had renovated.

Miller placed a hand on Edwin's shoulder, whispering, "There will be children in this garden. And your father will look down on them fondly."

35

Lady Ada Whitworth

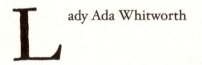

Ada sat at the vanity but her view was on the duke's Westminster garden below instead of her reflection. Girard had hired a maid to attend to her hair. The poor woman had spent the better part of the afternoon wrestling with her curls. The moment she was done, they'd begun to fall—and again, the maid would beg for another try.

Stone cherubs and overhead lights lined the garden walk. Ada wanted to be outside speaking with Girard rather than in the chair. The duke had been kind, and she knew her time was coming to an end. He was taking Nikolas to Wales where her brother believed the Tailor was playing puppeteer to the *ton*.

She'd sent a new sketch to the *Tales* last night. Mr. Thomas had come to visit in Girard's carriage. The duke had made sure Ada was stocked with plenty of wove paper and charcoal pencils.

"I'm done, my lady." The maid left with a curtsey.

There were still a few minutes left before the ball. Ada had hoped to speak with the duke privately before the attendees arrived. She had tried—and failed—to leave before the queen's event. Ada's childhood wasn't surrounded by dukes or dignitaries. Her late father wasn't even an earl until she was nearly grown.

Nikolas was next door, but he'd already shuffled to his bedroom. He was forever accompanied by three Welsh guards. They made their disgust known. Nikolas was rather harmless at the moment—and on crutches. His tongue was still sarcastic, but the tone had softened. He'd even left a letter from when their father was alive, a note from one of her childhood doctors stating Ada was of sound mind. The letter was part of Nikolas's plan. He would have sent it to Mr. Thomas, allowing the solicitor to free Ada from the asylum.

She'd folded the letter and tucked it into her pocket. She wanted to have a piece of her father with her tonight. Girard was convinced her stutter was like his father's inability to read well, just a personality tick, nothing more. Nothing less. Slowly, Ada began to believe it and slower still, she began to forgive Nikolas. They kept dancing around important topics, neither eager to tackle his mother's mental state. With Girard's help, a rotation of doctors was overseeing and evaluating the countess. Lady Rochelle had yet to show her unstable side and kept to herself, replying to her daily correspondence.

Tomorrow Ada would be leaving, but not for London. With Mr. Thomas's help, she was headed to France. She hadn't told Girard yet. She didn't know if it would affect him. For years, she dreamed of freedom, and as of tomorrow, she was of age. Nikolas was no longer a threat. Ada wanted to travel the world and meet other artists. At least, that was what she told herself at night.

There was a growing sense of peace within her. Perhaps it was from slowly accepting her stutter or maybe the healing of her fractured relationship with Nikolas. But just as the peace filled her, a sense of loss tugged at her heart.

She went to her window and, with a hand on the glass, she followed Girard's movements toward the house, his friend Miller at his side. The duke was never alone. He would not miss her. Ada swallowed hard. She'd treasured their days together. His study was busy with men coming and going, but the morning and nights were theirs alone. Their morning walks, with her arm in his, were something she would never forget. She still didn't know the names of all the flowers in his garden, but her trunk was bursting with dozens of colorful paintings. After dinner, in quiet companionship, he would read the papers—and smirk at her cartoons. Her tongue had loosened, the stutter almost gone in his presence. She'd spoken more with Girard in the last few days than she'd conversed with Lady Rochelle in years. Their time together had brought back the tender feelings from her childhood, those of comfort and warmth.

But Girard took his responsibilities seriously, both from the crown and his lineage. He was a duke and would rise to the privilege of his birth. As much as it hurt, his consistency was what Ada admired in him. Lady Rochelle and Nikolas were mysteries. Even now, Ada didn't quite understand her brother. But with Girard, she never had to guess if he would stand in her presence or greet her with a smile. Without hesitation, he would offer his arm.

Ada wasn't naive enough to think he'd do the same tonight. She was welcomed at his Westminster estate because it was the safest home in the country. That, and her brother was on house arrest in the bedroom next to hers. Girard was kind, honest, and a warm friend. She would never forget him. A lump formed in her throat. By jove, she would miss him.

The orchestra had quieted downstairs. The ball was starting. Ada searched her bed for her gloves where her maid normally laid out her outfit. None were there. There were dozens of nobles in the grand ballroom just below her. She could not descend without gloves. Her tongue thickened, her heart racing. She could not embarrass the duke, not tonight. He'd already risked his name by allowing Nikolas in his home.

A knock sounded on the door. *Blast.* She didn't have time for Nikolas and his jokes. Only her brother would think it funny to hide her gloves. Another knock. She swung the door open. "If you took—"

Girard stood on the threshold, his hand in the air from knocking. His suit was tailored to perfection, his shoulders broad and his frame steady. He filled the doorframe. Her tongue loosened. She had nothing to fear, not with Girard at her side.

He pulled a slender box from under his arm. "Apologies. I'd meant to bring this to you an hour ago."

Ada stood there dumbly. "What is it?" The last time she opened a box like this, her father had commissioned a bonnet for her. That was years ago.

"I was rather hoping you'd open it." His eyes crinkled.

Her pulse hummed at the sound of his voice. She clasped the box and untied the ribbon with a quick pull. He took the ribbon from her hand, allowing her to open the box with both of hers. Inside lay two silk gloves, white as snow.

"They're new, Lady Ada." His words were a caress.

Lady Ada echoed in her mind. She felt the beginnings of grief. She'd not yet left Girard's side, and she was already mourning the loss. He stepped inside and took the box, setting it gently on the bed. Other than Nikolas and her father, no other man had ever been in her bedroom. He held her hand and slipped a glove over her fingers. Her skin prickled.

"You are quite adorable when you blush." His lips curled into a mischievous smile. "Oh, and deeper still. Have I embarrassed you?"

Ada couldn't answer. She could barely breathe. Girard had no idea the impact of his touch. And there again, she felt the loss. His world would keep turning. He was off to save the country from a spy while she would be painting silly pictures. She blinked and looked away.

"Have I offended you?" He lifted her chin, his eyes heavy with worry. "I did not mean to overstep—"

"No," she managed, her throat thick. "I'm going ..." She took a breath. He squeezed her hand and patiently waited. "I'm going to miss this."

"London?" He arched an eyebrow.

Ada's heart sank. He couldn't be this daft. She'd known the gap between them. He was a duke, and she—she wasn't even the daughter of an earl. But she had pride to spare. She would not admit her hopeless whim.

"Have you ever been to Wales?" Girard offered his arm. Her heart twisted at his plans to leave. He'd spoken of taking Nikolas to his estate up north.

"Wales?" She would play the part and pretend that tonight would last forever. Tomorrow would come soon enough. They reached the corridor. "No, I've never been. Perhaps one day."

He went rigid, a hand on the rail. "Oh." His voice dropped.

"Oh?" Ada was lost.

"I thought." He cleared his throat. He pulled at his cravat, a nervous habit. "I apologize. I had just thought ..."

"Thought what?" She placed a hand on his. If he kept at it, he'd be disheveled before the night began. "Are you nervous?"

He ran a hand through his hair. "I thought you were coming."

"Coming?" With a hand on his cravat, Ada froze. *I thought you were coming.* "To Wales?"

"I've ..." He caressed her cheek. They were but inches from each other. "I've not made myself very clear, have I?"

"To Wales," she repeated. Her mind blanked. He could not be asking her to join him. "To be with Nikolas?"

He cupped her jaw. "To be with me."

"T-t-t-to ..." She blinked. A tear ran down her cheek. He couldn't mean what he said. Didn't he know that she could never be a duchess? She pointed to her mouth and shook her head. She'd accepted that her stutter was a part of her just as her golden curls were, but a duchess, that was too much. She turned to leave.

He wrapped his arms around her, whispering, "I don't give a fig about your stutter. So long as you don't leave me."

Don't leave me. She covered her mouth. This was a dream. This couldn't be truly happening.

He circled her. "I promise to protect you. To love you."

Ada opened her mouth, but the words wouldn't come. Tears of frustration spilled down her cheek. She'd not even dared to dream of this moment. And her tongue was ruining it. She waited for him to turn, to throw his hands in the air and walk away. He smiled and brought his forehead to hers. He held her hand and said, "Squeeze my hand if you love me."

Ada squeezed his hand, a rush of warmth filling her. Her skin hummed at his nearness. He didn't need her words, only her. Stutter or not, she was loved.

He lifted her chin with his finger. "That is all I need to know." He kissed her forehead and squeezed her hand twice. "I suppose I should have asked your brother for permission."

Ada shot him a look. She might love her brother, but she would have the final say in her future, thank you very much.

Girard laughed. "I don't know which is more becoming, your blush or your scowl."

She swatted his shoulder. He slipped a hand to the back of her neck and kissed her softly. Warmth filled her. She leaned into his embrace. He kissed her nose, her jaw.

With his hand in her hair, she whispered, "I love you."

He stood back and smiled. The Dark Duke was replaced. There was joy in his crooked smile and a mischievous glint in his eyes. "Marry me."

Her mouth fell open. *Marry me.* With a trembling voice, she spoke to his chest. "I'll make a terrible duchess."

"You can't be worse than the Dark Duke." He grinned and offered his arm. They came to the staircase and walked arm in arm down the steps.

"Yes," she blurted. She touched her cheek, feeling the blush. "My answer is yes."

He beamed at her. "What would the *Thames Tales* think of the dreadful duke marrying his golden goddess?"

Grinning, she shook her head. "My unruly curls are more Medusa than goddess."

"I beg to differ, Ada."

They descended as she fought tears—of joy, not frustration. They turned the last bend and a hush fell upon the crowd. A crush of silk and suits covered the enormous ballroom. Her heart raced. At the last step, she could hear the whispers. *That's Rochelle's sister. The duke keeps her under lock and key.* Girard stiffened next to her.

She was the lowly orphan, and he the duke. He had no need to threaten her. She needed him, not the other way around. "They think you're blackmailing me?"

"I tried that." He smirked. "It didn't work."

Ada smiled. He'd accused her of many things. The most powerful people were staring at her. In the very center was the Queen of England. And yet Girard did not shrink from Ada. He knew she stuttered, and yet he stood beside her. She could do the same. With Girard at her side, she could do anything.

Ada leaned her head against his shoulder. He smiled down at her. Her heart raced. She squeezed his hand and stared straight ahead—above the crowd's gaze. She could be brave. She inhaled slowly and said, "I have an announcement." She didn't know what she was going to say, she only wanted to prove he wasn't the bully the *ton* believed. "The d-d-d-d ..." Her voice shook.

Ada blinked, her heart sinking. She thought she could be brave enough, strong enough. But here she stood, and even with her hand in Girard's, her mouth wouldn't obey. She swallowed the rising panic. She could never be the duchess he needed.

Girard squeezed her hand. She made the mistake of looking his way. Her throat closed. Her tongue was thick. She opened her mouth. The words wouldn't come. He would finally see, finally know, that she would never be whole, that the world would always question her. She stepped into the rail, the letter crinkling in her pocket. Her thoughts turned to her father. He'd tried to convince Ada that she was endearing, stutter and all. That she brought beauty into the world. He'd devoted endless effort into her talents.

She placed a hand in her pocket, her fingers wrapping around the paper. Her tongue may rebel against her, but Ada would not back down. Without her stutter, would she have dedicated her hands to art? Peace settled on her shoulders. Ada wouldn't change her history—or her stutter.

Girard wrapped an arm around her and leaned in. "Trust me."

Her heart skipped.

With his gaze on her, he shouted, "I've asked Lady Ada Whitworth to marry me."

Her pulse raced. With a mischievous grin, he leaned in. He gently tipped her chin and kissed her. The panic fell from her shoulders, the tightness in her throat disappearing. She kissed him back, smiling against his lips. He wrapped an arm around her, steady and true.

Miller shouted from somewhere in the crowd, "Congratulations, Your Grace."

Gasps from women and whispers of their vulgarity erupted.

Girard chuckled. "I believe we'll be forced to marry, my dear."

"Not until I give approval," a woman said.

They broke apart. In front of the staircase stood Queen Victoria, her crown perched on a glorious stack of brunette curls. Girard would not abandon her. She glanced up at him. The Duke of Girard was home—she was safe. And loved.

Girard bowed. "Your Majesty—"

The queen held out her hand, silencing the crowd. "May I present the future Duchess of Girard?"

Girard mouthed *thank you* to the queen. She nodded solemnly to the duke and handed Ada a piece of paper. It was an advertisement for the royal exhibition—her father *and* Sir Lyell were featured. The late Earl of Rochelle would finally be recognized.

Ada clasped the paper to her chest, wishing her father could witness the moment.

Queen Victoria winked at Ada, whispering, "I do believe your job is harder than mine."

"To be true." Girard beamed down at Ada. "Although, Your Majesty, if she'd asked for the keys to the kingdom, I would have gladly handed them over."

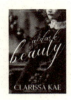

ALSO BY CLARISSA KAE

Of Ink And Sea

Pieces To Mend

Taming Christmas

Once And Future Wife Series

Once And Future Wife

Disorder In The Veins (Winter 2021)

Victorian Fairy Tales

A Dark Beauty, Beauty & the Beast

Cinders Like Glass , Cinderella

A Light So Fleeting, Rapunzel

ABOUT THE AUTHOR

Clarissa Kae is a preeminent voice whose professional career began as a freelance editor in 2007. She's the former president of her local California Writers Club after spending several years as the Critique Director.

Since her first novel, she's explored different writing genres and created a loyal group of fans who eagerly await her upcoming release. With numerous awards to her name, Clarissa continues to honor the role of storyteller.

Aside from the writing community, she and her daughters founded Kind Girls Make Strong Women to help undervalued nonprofit organizations—from reuniting children with families to giving Junior Olympic athletes their shot at success.

She lives in the agricultural belly of California with her family and farm of horses, chickens, dogs and kittens aplenty.

www.clarissakae.com

facebook.com/AuthorClarissaKae
instagram.com/clarissa__kae